Coming Home
for
Christmas

Coming Home  for Christmas

Jenny Hale

bookouture

Published by Bookouture

An imprint of StoryFire Ltd.
23 Sussex Road, Ickenham, UB10 8PN
United Kingdom

www.bookouture.com

ISBN: 978-1-909490-11-6

For Justin, who believed in me before anyone else.

ACKNOWLEDGEMENTS

My deepest gratitude goes out to my friends and family who listened to countless hours of talking along this journey.

Many thanks to my editor, Kate Ahl, who never ceases to inspire me.

And finally, a big, huge thank you to Oliver Rhodes for his wisdom and endless patience.

Chapter One

With an aggressive nudge, I moved a box down the hallway with my foot. The mortification that I had worked so hard to keep at bay was bubbling up, despite my attempt to squelch it. As a kid, I can honestly say that I never pictured this in my vision of Allie's life. Where, along the line, did I lose the busy job, the supportive husband, and two kids? I didn't even have a cat. Don't all single people have a cat?

"You here?" I heard my mother say when I dumped an armful of hanging clothes onto my purple and white checked high school bedspread. It had slightly yellowed with age.

"Yeah." The front door swung shut, rattling the adjacent wall. It had always rattled that wall. No one knew why; perhaps it was because the whole house was the size of a deck of cards, and if we blew just the right way, we could knock it down. It had been a good house, though—full of happy memories.

I looked up from my unpacking to find my mother and Megan, my sister, filling my doorway as if they were sealing me inside. I took in a deep breath and let it out slowly just to make sure that I could still breathe.

Megan pushed past Mom and plopped down onto my bed, sending clothes to the floor. "Wanna get a cup of coffee?"

I piled my hair up on top of my head with my fingers. Truthfully, a cup of coffee did sound nice, but I'd rather pout just a bit longer. It had been eleven years since I had even contemplated moving back home, and now, at the age of thirty-two, it was actually happening. I let my hair loose and scratched my scalp.

Something about moving home as an adult made the space feel even smaller than it had while growing up. I hoped that I wasn't imposing on Mom too much. She'd never tell me, though, if it were too much for her. She'd just straighten the mass of shoes at the front door or stay up a little later to finish the extra laundry so that I could have a free washing machine when I needed it. That's how she is. She'd endure anything for family because having us home, she always says, means more to her than all of the inconveniences. I love her for that.

Moving back was only temporary, until I could find a job—I had three applications out there, and was just waiting to hear back. Even still, it took some getting used to. Thankful as I was that she'd offered to have me, I didn't feel like an adult, living back with my mother. I felt as if I'd have to start handing her the keys to my car every night before bed.

"Coffee? Yes or no?"

"It sounds good, but I have some unpacking to do."

"Oh, please. You have tons of time for that. What the heck else are you going to do around here besides unpack? Mom still doesn't even have cable, you know."

"I do so!" Mom piped up from the doorway. She slugged Megan's arm affectionately.

From that angle, Mom was standing just as she had so many times when I was young, and a pang of nostalgia pinched my chest.

Have you finished your homework? There's a boy at the door. Do you want dinner? Don't be too late tonight; I need to know where you are before I go to sleep. All of these moments flashed before me like photos in a flipbook. My mother's face was so much older now, so weathered; her familiar smile making new creases where her smooth skin used to be. In a way, it was good to be home. I was glad to see her. I rolled my head around on my shoulders to release the tension.

"Hey, Debbie Downer, let's go." Megan yanked me out the door, past my mother, and into the hallway where we both stumbled over yet another dozen or so boxes.

We squeezed ourselves into my sister's newest triumph, her prized BMW—an indication of the success she'd had in real estate over the years. I had told Megan many times how proud of her I was for her accomplishments, and I was, truly, but it didn't stop the inadequacy that I felt when I saw the tangible evidence of her achievements.

"Careful," she warned as I tugged on the door handle to shut myself in. I couldn't help an eye-roll—don't think she caught it, though.

✳ ✳ ✳

Two patrons entered through the shop door next to where we sat. Cold air blew around my torso, and a chill crawled up to my shoulders. I regretted taking off my coat and hanging it on the back of my chair when we came in. The door swung closed, although no circulating warmth seemed to return.

"I have another idea for employment," Megan said from behind her coffee cup. She hesitated, because I had already told her I didn't want any handouts. I had accepted one of her handouts when I'd taken the nanny job. Okay, her last offer had given me a wonderful job for eleven years, and a chance to use what I'd learned in college, but I wanted to get my own work this time; we'd already talked about it. Whatever she had to say, it didn't matter, because I was back out there. I had things in the works.

"You're quiet," she said, breaking me from my thoughts. "And you're *never* quiet."

Even though I wanted nothing to do with the idea of my sister finding me another job, the suspense of not knowing was killing me. I could at least hear her out. "Tell me whatcha got," I offered.

"Look at this," she pulled a rolled magazine excitedly from her bag and slid it across the table. The main feature was a glossy picture of the Ashford estate, an early twentieth century manor. "They're one of my clients, and they need a house manager until it sells." Megan tapped the photo.

"Intriguing." I took a drink of my coffee, and it sent a shiver through my limbs. It was really cold outside. "Why would I be good at that?"

"You are personable and organized; you'd be a shoe-in!" Megan swung her legs from under the table and scooted her chair adjacent to mine, like she'd done when we were kids when she wanted to tell me a secret. She'd always lean in as if the proximity would make our conversation more significant. Tufts of auburn curls bounced softly around her face, and I suppressed the urge to scoop them up into a ponytail. "I think they're willing to pay... *well*," she whispered dramatically.

"And why should I consider this job over the others?"

"Because you could still apply for the other jobs, but you'd make a ton of money while you're waiting. And I know how you love history. This house is *ancient*."

"So, what happened to their old house manager?"

"He left. Lots of family drama, I hear, since *he* is the one who owns the house." She uncapped her cinnamon lip-balm and dragged it across her lips. "Robert Marley, the heir to the house—irritatingly unfriendly—wants to sell the mansion. His family's all up in arms about it."

I peered at the magnificent structure on the page. The Ashford estate was the stuff of storybooks with its sprawling brick façade and a staircase that looked like an enormous smile. It seemed way out of my league.

"I don't know, Megan. I don't want you to give me another job." Even though I said the words, the idea was eating away at me.

Megan exhaled in that motherly way that always made me feel very small. Her limbs were still, other than her finger nails drumming the table. Then, she stopped tapping abruptly and said, "What if I had nothing to do with it?"

"What do you mean?"

"You could flip for it. Tails, you send in an application. No harm done."

That was how Megan and I had decided everything growing up. It started when my grandmother made up her mind that we should collect coins. Every holiday, from the time I was four, Gram would thrust new coins into our hands; some in velvet boxes, others in cellophane. She would've been horrified if she'd found out that each coin had been mercilessly torn from its package and fingered by both Megan and me as we determined who got the next flipping coin.

It's how my sister had gotten the biggest bedroom when I was nine and she was twelve, and how I had gotten to keep our fish, Oscar, in my room in the sixth grade. Now, it seems that it's how I would be deciding between normal, everyday employment opportunities or living in the clouds and applying to run a multimillion-dollar mansion.

But I didn't want Megan's help this time, or her ideas. She was the firstborn. She was the successful one. She was on her own and living nicely. I was... a glorified babysitter, living with my mother. It sounded even worse spelled out in my head. It was time that I proved myself, made something of my life.

"I won't get involved," she pressed. "I'm just the messenger," she said. When I shot a frosty glare toward her for even putting me in this position, she shrugged in the "why not" gesture and nodded toward my purse. "I know you still carry it around for luck," she said with a smirk.

As if I hadn't been humiliated enough by my recent move home, the fact that I did, indeed, have Gram's coin in my purse—only because I had no way of packing it, and it was easier just to zip it in my wallet for the time being—made my cheeks sting.

I blew air through my lips and pulled out my wallet, retrieving the coin.

Gram had given it to me in 1983, four years after it was originally minted. She'd actually given it to Megan, but I had taken a liking to it and swore that I won every time I flipped it. Megan let me have it because she didn't like the way Ms. Anthony glared at the edge of the coin. It creeped her out, she'd said. But I always wondered if she just knew how much I wanted it, and that's why she really gave it to me.

Megan pulled in a sharp breath, her eyes as big as saucers. I don't think she really believed that I had it, and I was too aggravated to explain myself.

The thought of being able to work in such an historic and fantastic home kept rolling around in my head. Even if it wasn't permanent, it would be amazing.

"Management is great on a resume," Megan said.

I rested the silver Susan B. Anthony dollar coin on the top of my thumb. Its surface felt as cold as the weather outside. The late November air was just enough above freezing to cause the snow to fall in wet droplets that clung to the window, sliding down it like thin, transparent ribbons. Getting an interview for this would be like winning the lottery.

With my free hand, I pushed a loose strand of hair behind my ear, and suddenly, a fizzle of excitement swam through me. "Tails I apply for the job." I sent the coin into the air. It flipped over and over before bouncing onto the paisley-patterned carpet. A depiction of an eagle over the surface of the moon shone up at me. Tails.

Chapter Two

A man by the name of Gerard stood outside the Ashford estate in an all white coverall uniform. He looked like some sort of painter, but I thought he probably wasn't. Maybe the grounds keeper? I'd never seen a grounds keeper, so how would I know? I followed him inside the breadth of space that was the entranceway, and all of the irritation I felt regarding my sister's help melted away.

The scent of lavender wafted around me as I took in the massive foyer. Crystal and brass light fixtures dripped down from the ceiling like a frozen fountain. Underneath them, a table the size of a ship anchored the open area, a five-foot bloom of wildflowers erupting from its center.

I'd never been in a home that needed a staff to run it before. Wouldn't it be weird to live in such a place, with strangers lurking around?

The wooden floors leading to the office gleamed with a thick, translucent wax. The shine was so vibrant that I couldn't tell if they were wet or not, so I walked carefully just in case. How many people had trodden down the hallway that I was walking at this moment?

When I reached the office door it was open, so I walked in. Books, new and old, lined the walls of the room from floor to ceiling. Two windows balanced the space and allowed a magnificent view of the front lawn. Perched in the center sat an enormous claw-foot desk, casting a lengthy shadow in my direction.

A man with dark hair and a strong jaw-line was on the other side of the desk, his eyebrows pulled together in concentration, the office phone pressed against his ear. He looked up only long enough to shoo me toward one of the chairs on the other side. I sat down and pressed my hands down onto my lap before they started to tremble.

As he spoke or argued—I couldn't tell—I tried not to stare at him, but his looks were striking. He seemed like the kind of guy who probably had never been through a fast food drive-thru or hit old baseballs at Battlefield Park. He looked like the type who knew the local jeweler by name and had private airlines on speed dial. With all my mental strength, I pulled my eyes from him and looked out the window.

"Good morning," he said in a commanding voice as if he were speaking to a crowd of people. "Gerard, that will be all," he nearly barked in Gerard's direction. I glanced over at Gerard. He turned to leave, seemingly unfazed by the man's sharp tone.

My gaze snapped back over to the man. He didn't seem much older than me, but I could feel his years of life experience run laps around mine. He stood and extended a hand in my direction. "Robert Marley. You must be Megan's sister."

Ugh. *I have a name!* "I'm Allison," I stuttered. "Allie, actually." I leaned over nearly on my tiptoes to reach across the massive desk between us and shook his hand. We were close enough that I caught his scent—a subtle mix of spice and laundry soap. I found myself holding his hand a little too long, not wanting to let go. He pulled his hand from mine slowly, motioning for me to sit as he lowered himself back down across from me, his eyes appraising. His gaze moved around my face carefully, putting every nerve in my body on full alert.

"If I could, I'd like to just go over the requirements of this position." His head was down now, and he was fiddling with some paperwork. I was glad for that because when he looked at me, I felt like my heart would beat right out of my chest.

"Your job will be to manage the daily goings-on with the house as well as with the sale of the house—lawn maintenance, cleaning crew, viewing appointments, and those responsibilities concerning my grandmother, Pippa Marley."

I willed myself to pay attention to his words, but all I really wanted to do was take in the sight of him—the starched collar of his shirt, the tiny lines he created between his eyes when he was reading.

He looked up. I wasn't sure what to do, so I smiled.

"She lives in the east wing of the house," he continued. His eyes met mine. "We have staff devoted to her care, so you would manage them as well."

There was something about the way that he looked at me that sent my stomach fluttering. I'd never been this nervous in my life.

"Do you feel comfortable with that?"

"Um, yes. Fine."

"Excellent. Can you start tomorrow?"

Had I missed something? "So, I have the job?"

"Yes."

"No interview or anything?" Had I looked so convincing, so intelligent, that he didn't even need to have more?

"You *are* Megan Richfield's sister, correct?"

"Yes."

"Then, no. No formal interview."

While I love my sister more than anyone in the world, that answer had made my skin crawl as if a thousand spiders had been unleashed on it.

"How's tomorrow then?"

I filled my lungs with air and let it out to steady my nerves. "Fine." He stood, and I could tell that he wanted me to follow. He was walking me out. That's it? I'm about to make every decision regarding this house for the foreseeable future, and that's all he has to say?

"I'll give you an itinerary, and we can communicate via email." It was as if he were watching for some sort of reaction, studying me as I digested this information. I smiled up at him once more, unsure of what exactly to do. I could see a hint of softness behind his eyes despite his generally brisk demeanor.

"You can use the computer in my office. I've arranged for the staff to have the yellow room in the staff quarters made up for you. You will be able to come and go as you please." Just as I thought he'd finished, and we'd emerged again into the entranceway, he cleared his throat and added, "And you'll be organizing the family meeting this Christmas."

What the heck is that? I stopped and faced him. "Family meeting?"

"The house has been in the family for... a while. My sister Sloane and my brother Kip want to visit once more before we sell. We always spend Christmas with Pippa anyway, so we're having one last meeting of our family at Ashford over the holiday."

"Okay. Well, I suppose I'll see you then," I struggled for something interesting to say.

"No, it will just be my siblings at the meeting. Sloane will have her two children, Paul and Sammy, and then there's my younger brother, Kip. That's it. I'll give you the specifics later."

"So, you're not coming?" He wasn't coming to his own family's Christmas celebration? What a Scrooge!

He paused for a second, looking at me, evidence of contemplation in his eyes. What *was* he thinking about? "Can't get away from the office. LaGuardia is horrendous during the holidays anyway, so I'd rather not bother."

"Okay."

He guided me to the large front door through which I had entered only a few minutes earlier. In the moment of silence that followed, Robert looked at me as if he were about to say something, but he said nothing.

He inhaled sharply, and on an exhale of breath he said, "Well, that's that. When you come tomorrow, Gerard will have your keys to the house, your sister can keep you abreast of any showings, and your itinerary will be waiting in my office. Gerard will show you where to go."

"You won't be here tomorrow?" I heard myself say. Why did I just ask that? Of course he wasn't going to be here. That's why he'd hired me!

A hint of amusement surfaced behind his eyes, and felt my legs getting wobbly. "Nope," he said, "The house will be all yours."

I struggled again for anything else to add. See you soon? No. Chat soon? Nope. Thanks? Not appropriate. Awkward...

"Miss Richfield, it was nice to meet you."

"Likewise," I said, willing my tongue to get the word out in spite of my dry mouth. I walked into the bitter cold of winter as I stepped onto the enormous landing that preceded the grand staircase. "Bye." That was all I could get out before the door shut behind me.

✳ ✳ ✳

It was my first day at Ashford. I was hopeful that the day would go well. So far, everyone on the staff had been pleasant, although no one stopped what they were doing to say hello, which was good because I was afraid to speak for fear that I may say something awkward. But I'd gotten a smile or two. I needed time to absorb my surroundings, get my bearings.

It seemed almost as though they already knew who I was. Either that, or they were used to having strangers lurking around the premises. I wasn't sure. At home this morning, I had wanted to make certain that I looked like I belonged here, because every fiber of my being felt out of place in this fantastic estate. I'd shined my shoes, pressed my clothes, and spent an extra thirty minutes on my hair. I looked the part, but still didn't quite *feel* the part.

I placed my fingers on the keys of Robert Marley's computer, already feeling invasive for tapping the little buttons that had supported his fingertips, and it came to life. The itinerary sputtered from the printer across the room. Nervously, I plucked the page from the machine and began to read his message:

...Be on the lookout for Tom. He'll be stopping by each day promptly at nine to bring Pippa's groceries.

Pippa's groceries? Wasn't that his grandmother? Why did he call her by her first name? It sounded so... My cell phone rang in my pocket. It was Megan.

"Hello?"

"How's it going?" She sounded extra chipper this morning. She must have had her daily coffee without me. I wrinkled my nose at the thought.

"As well as can be expected. I've only been here about twenty minutes." I toyed with the brass drawer pulls of the desk and ran my hands along the grains on its surface.

"Well, get your work hat on, because I have a showing for you already! Someone called in this morning and left a voicemail. I've set up the walkthrough for two o'clock."

So that's why Megan was so cheerful. She stood to make a mint on the sale of Ashford. Meanwhile, I would make nothing, *and* I'd be unemployed. With a gold Marley-embossed pen that felt heavier than a small elephant, I jotted the details onto a pad of paper that was placed neatly on the desk, and then got off the line so that I could call Mr. Marley. He hadn't left me any further instructions after today.

I dialed his number. Ringing… Voicemail.

"Mr. Marley, it's Allie. Megan called with news that someone would like to view the house. Um. I'll just try and get you by email. So… check your email. Thanks." I hate leaving messages.

"Call me if you need me. Bye." I ended the call and blew out the rest of the air that I'd been holding in my lungs the entire message.

Just to be nosy, I sat down at the desk and pulled out the desk drawer. Nothing interesting. Pens, sticky notes, a stapler. Next to the computer, I tilted a photo toward me of Robert holding some sort of framed award.

With a click of the mouse, the Marley computer lit back up. I opened the email screen and hit the icon to compose a message to Robert. This guy was not one for conversation, so I kept it brief: "Megan has someone to look at the house at two o'clock. How should I proceed?"

Almost instantly, I received a response. Is he Charlie from Charlie's Angels? I wondered. I gnawed on my thumbnail. I guess that

would make me John Bosley. Hm. I'd much rather be Jill Munroe.
I read the response:

> *Pick up the in-house phone at the base of the intercom system
> and dial eighty-eight. It's located near the home security panel,
> behind the butler's pantry, off the kitchen. This will summon the
> household staff to the kitchen where you can prepare them for the
> showing. I've already informed them of their duties should you
> require their services. I'll send you an itinerary at eight o'clock
> every morning. Good luck.*

I typed him a return email: "Thank you so much for the information. Hope all is well in New York."

I waited.

No response. This guy was a piece of work.

✳ ✳ ✳

The expansive hallways opened out like the type of mazes through
which those laboratory rats are made to maneuver. I kind of felt
like one of them: doing all of this work for a little cheese at the end.
Eventually, I located the kitchen and ran into Tom.

"Hello!" He offered a weathered but pleasant expression and an
outstretched hand. "Tom," he said, clasping mine. "Nice to meet
you. I bring Ms. Marley her groceries since she has some trouble
getting out to us."

He let go of my hand and began unpacking the most gorgeous
provisions I'd ever seen. Organic, glossy fruit and vegetables, loads
of fresh bread, meat so pink that I thought it may jump out of the
package and head back for the farm; it all bulged haphazardly from

reusable tote bags. I peeked around in one for some chips or something I could snack on, but they contained nothing prepackaged.
My stomach announced its emptiness.

"Hungry?" a voice came from behind me. I turned around to
find a petite woman clothed in a black uniform dress and white
apron. Couldn't the Marleys be original? I wondered if she cringed
every time she put that outfit on. Patting my shoulder, she said,
"I'm Anna. I can cook you something." With a delicate finger, she
coaxed a runaway piece of hair back up into the bun that sat at the
back of her head.

"Nice to meet you, Anna. Thanks for the offer, but I actually
need to find the control-panel-thing. I have to get everyone together. Maybe after our meeting I can eat something."

Anna showed me to the back of the butler's pantry where a panel
of buttons rivaling NASA's Mission Control extended the length of
the wall. My fingers dangled at my sides, unsure of what to touch.
As soon as I located the phone, I picked it up, dialed eighty-eight,
and hung it back on the cradle as Anna instructed. Then, we walked
back to the middle of the kitchen to wait as staff members began to
assemble from all parts of the house like magic. Tom quietly exited,
and a few of the Ashford employees greeted him on his way out.

Once it seemed like almost everyone had assembled, I began my
first speech to the staff. "Good morning!" I called out in my best
speaking voice. There must have been thirty people in front of me.
As I opened my mouth to speak again, I noticed the staff members
exchanging glances.

Anna leaned toward me, her face unworried, and whispered into
my ear, "You need to wait for Ms. Marley to arrive." She winked and
patted my arm. Why didn't Robert tell me that? Jerk.

A few minutes went by, and then as if on cue, the crowd parted, and a fragile woman, with wisps of hair so silver they looked almost blue, came rolling in on a motorized scooter. She looked as if she were headed for church, with pearls dangling from her ears and around her neck, a ruffled shirt with opal colored buttons and a dark blue pencil skirt. The wheels of her scooter stopped just short of where I stood. She looked up at me, a displeased expression on her face. Unsure of what to do, I smiled uncomfortably. From the sight of her, I thought I may be forced to curtsey. She shot me a look that I interpreted to mean *get on with it.*

I explained to the staff that we'd have to get the house ready for a showing at two o'clock and then dismissed them. Short and sweet. I didn't want to drag anything out with Pippa Marley's eyes burning into me the whole time. She obviously had more important things to be doing. Although, at nearly a hundred years old, I couldn't imagine what.

The staff erupted into a quiet frenzy as they completed their assigned duties. Anna went to work cooking something, and Ms. Marley carefully dismounted her scooter, settling on the window seat in the kitchen. Anna glanced over at her, but she never addressed her.

I felt inclined to greet Ms. Marley despite her less than warm reception, so I walked over and stood next to the seat opposite hers. She seemed so frail sitting there, as if she could break if she moved the wrong way, but her eyes exuded wisdom and the sort of strength only gained through many, many years of life. Without offering my hand—partly because I was too nervous to hold it steady and because it was becoming increasingly sweaty—I said, "My name is Allison Richfield. Allie. Mr. Marley hired me to manage the house in his absence."

Ms. Marley clicked her tongue and waved a dismissive hand. "Absence," she huffed. Then she clenched her lined lips together in a tight little scowl.

I peered through the wavy glass window at her view. A massive field of green, lightened in color by the winter weather, stretched out before us. Gray clouds blanketed the sky, completely obscuring the sun. Sparkling amid the muted color above, white lights were being draped on the trees. I hoped whoever was hanging them would finish before the visitors came at two because only half of the trees were lit.

"Do you like living here?" The thought, meant for merely my own contemplation, had accidentally come out.

Ms. Marley's head snapped up in my direction. "Are you implying that I do not?" Her eyes bored into mine as if I had some sort of insider knowledge about her that I wasn't sharing.

"No! Absolutely not!" My cheeks burned, and I couldn't stop blinking my eyes. I jammed my hands into my pockets to keep them from visibly shaking. "I'm implying that you must." I took a deep breath and let my head pivot back out to the yard where one of the staff had started to add greenery to the light fixtures surrounding the patio. "It's beautiful here. Surreal that a home so lovely is way out here in this part of Virginia."

"Mm." Ms. Marley seemed to be chewing on some thought. The gray clouds shifted in the sky, blowing along the edge of the window's view. I watched them for some time before she said, "I've loved it and hated it." Then, without warning, she looked up at me and smiled. The smile dissolved, however, as quickly as it had emerged.

"I think I'd love it," I decided aloud.

With force behind her eyes, she said, "When I was your age, I loved it too." Then she looked back out the window.

I sat down beside her on the window seat. I didn't ask first, suddenly reconsidering my choice, but Ms. Marley didn't seem to be bothered by my decision. She even shifted a bit to the other side to ensure that I had enough room. What had made her so bitter? Sure, I had Megan's rundown of how she didn't want to sell the house, but there was a hardness to Ms. Marley that told me there might be something more. We sat together, watching the lights being strung in the trees, until Anna came over and tapped me on the shoulder.

"I've made brunch." Then she turned to face Ms. Marley, her fingers intertwined and unstill behind her back. "Your grapefruit and toast await you in your room, Ms. Marley," she said, but Pippa didn't even glance Anna's way. She got off of the seat, marched over to her scooter, and began to make her way back to her room. As I watched her go, I decided that I kind of liked her. Something about the way her eyes looked made me feel like there might be a part of her tucked away that no one had seen for a long time.

Anna brought a tray and set it down on a silver stand that rested next to the window seat. The aroma whipped me back to Sunday mornings at Gram's when Megan and I would visit with Mom. Gram provided the only cooked breakfast we ate all week. Mom worked so much that usually we poured ourselves a bowl of cereal in the morning or we grabbed a piece of toast.

Anna had prepared scrambled eggs, ham, sautéed mushrooms and tomatoes, and toast with jam and butter. I took my first bite and had to remind myself to eat slowly so as not to make a spectacle. It wasn't until that moment that I realized how hungry I was.

On bite number three, my cell phone buzzed. Setting down my fork, I checked the screen. It was Robert, so I answered.

"Allison?"

Who else would it be? "Yes?"

"I failed to mention in our interview that you'll need to check email every hour between eight o'clock and five o'clock each day. This way I can keep in touch. I'm sorry I didn't mention that. I'm still getting used to having someone doing my work for me."

"That's fine."

"Did you find everything satisfactory—your room, the staff?"

"Yes. I just met your grandmother."

"Ah. And how was she? Good spirits?"

How do I answer that? Would I call her behavior good-spirited? "Uh, I couldn't say..." I didn't want to alarm him or anything, so I quickly added, "We just talked about the house."

The air between us was uncomfortable and quiet.

"I hope she didn't burden you with her incessant griping about moving. Pippa can't take care of that house by herself anymore. It's just too big."

"No one in your family wants to live here? It's so beautiful." If Megan were here, she'd have been mouthing the words *Shut up!*

"No. No one wants to live there. That's why we're selling it."

"I just think it's an amazing home."

"Thank you. It has... many memories." I could hear him soften ever so slightly. Then, all of a sudden, the edge to his voice returned, and he said, "I'm glad to hear that your transition was smooth. Let me know if you have any concerns."

"Thank you."

"Well, good-bye."

Before I could say good-bye, he was gone.

Chapter Three

Was this guy for real? I had checked my email four times so far, every hour on the hour, just as Robert had said. There were no new emails any of the times I checked. Why was he having me walk all the way to the office to pull up email every hour if he wasn't sending me anything? I secretly wanted him to email, not to give me more work to do, but so that I could learn more about Ashford and the family who owned it.

I've always been a hopeless gossip. Though I never gossip myself, I just really enjoy hearing it. I love piecing together stories and theorizing about what makes people tick; what causes their actions. The Marley family and its giant house were certainly interesting. And the two Marleys that I'd met so far were enough to keep me going for days. I'm sure whatever created those two personalities could fill volumes.

The grandfather clock in the entranceway chimed twice—two lengthy gongs. Megan had just called and said she was on her way. I took a few free moments to roam around Ashford. Sprigs of evergreen and red berries peppered the interior. Along the entire length of the banisters, fresh garlands dripped in thick bunches. Every fireplace blazed with a bright orange glow and popping embers. Outside, white lights dotted the trees like fireflies. If I hadn't been working there, I'd have thought I was on the set of a Christmas movie. A Christmas movie with an old, bitter woman who lurked just off set.

Pippa's scooter was rattling down the hallway. As she came into view, I watched her until she brought the contraption to a stop directly in front of me. Her stance was clearly rigid today. "My driver is taking me to town for some Christmas shopping. I won't be in the way during the showing."

I nodded as professionally as I knew how. Without any further explanation, she turned and rolled toward the open front door where a very bulky driver was waiting—his suit bulging around his arms—to help her out of her scooter, down the cascading staircase, and into a sedan.

The front door wide open, they descended the stairs, the driver steadying her with one arm while lifting the scooter with the other. He folded down the device and popped it into the trunk just before I closed the door, blocking out the bitter winter air that had been gusting inside.

By the time Megan rounded the corner, Pippa was driving away. Curiosity got the better of me, and I leaned closer toward the frigid glass of the window to get a glimpse of Ashford's visitors. Behind Megan's car, a midnight blue Range Rover followed. Both cars came to a halt in the center of the great half circle of a drive. Megan's look of contemplation was evident through the windshield as the Range Rover drew closer. I, too, wondered who it could be. My sister and the potential buyers exited her vehicle and walked up the staircase toward the front door.

The couple admired the fresh Christmas swags that adorned the exterior of the house. Behind them, the door to the Range Rover opened and a single man got out. He stepped around to the other side and pulled out two large duffel bags, his eyes on the group of people climbing the stairs. A pair of skis, or maybe a snowboard, was secured to the top of his car. He left it, thank goodness. Megan was still talking to the potential buyers about the exterior of the house. *Get them in here,* I thought. *They're probably freezing!*

As the man from the Range Rover approached, I had a better look at him. He was about my age, wearing a green fleece pull-over, a stocking cap, and sunglasses—the kind you'd see someone wear on the slopes in People magazine's two-page spread on celebrities in Aspen. I wondered what he wanted. Robert still had not produced any real itinerary other than the introductory note he'd sent, so I wasn't sure of anyone else who may be stopping by. Unless Pippa was taking skiing lessons, I doubted he was at the right house.

The doorbell rang, echoing throughout the entryway. I promptly opened the heavy front door to greet Megan and her clients. We exchanged pleasantries, and Megan began telling them about the house, so I let her pass by me as she entered. Her voice was more crisp than usual, more formal, and she looked like she had a rod up her back. But she was good at this, it was clear.

Rubbing my hands together for warmth, I waited in the open doorway to greet the stranger. He bounded up the steps two at a time, toward me, a friendly expression on his face.

"Hey, there!" he waved. As he leaped up onto the final step, he slid off his cap to reveal a mess of curly blond hair. "You must be our new house manager. I'm Kip."

Kip.

"Hello, Kip." I shook his hand. His gloved grip was firm. "Robert told me that you were coming. Are you here for the family meeting? I'm so sorry, but I haven't gotten any more information than that. I know I'm supposed to be organizing something…" I caught myself talking animatedly with my hands, so I quickly stilled them by my sides.

"Family meeting? What the heck is that?"

My thoughts exactly. "Mr. Marley said…"

"Forget what Robert says. *Family meeting* translates to: those Marleys who have a heart are coming together to have Christmas here at our house one last time before Robert sells it. So, the only thing you have to organize is the daily stock of alcohol, because we're gonna need it. Is Sloane here yet?" He breezed past me and shut the door with his foot.

"Wait!" I said as quietly as possible, shuffling behind him, my arms now folded around me to keep from shivering to death. "There's a showing going on right now."

He turned around. "Now? Is that who was in the other car? A potential buyer? God, I hope they don't like it." He gripped the back of his neck and squeezed it like he was relieving some sort of pressure, and his expression wasn't still, as if he were contemplating something.

"How could they not love it?" I smiled despite myself, taking in the spectacular architecture that surrounded us.

"Let's just hope they don't." His face was serious. A loud smacking sound echoed through the space as he dropped his duffle bags in the middle of the floor and headed toward the kitchen. I followed him, grabbing—lugging, rather—his bags, trying not to scratch the freshly waxed floors.

Lobbing his gloves onto the counter, he opened a kitchen cabinet and pulled out a pint glass. "Wine or beer?" he asked, his hand disappearing into the cabinet for the second time.

"Oh, I can't drink while I'm working," I said, as I dumped his bags behind the massive counter and rubbed my now-aching bicep.

"Who says?" He pulled out another pint glass, apparently making the decision for me, and then began rummaging in the refrigerator.

"Well, no one, but I'm working. People don't usually drink while they're on the job."

He washed his hands at the sink, flicked the water into the basin, and chopped a few lemon slices on a small cutting board, setting them aside. "Maybe not in this country, but in other countries they do."

He poured two beers. The label was unfamiliar. "Pretend you're in Europe." He handed me a pint. It had a lemon round floating on the top.

I held the glass, but didn't drink it. Kip took a gulp of his. "Ahh," he said, licking his lips once. It was the same sound that a seven-year-old makes after guzzling a cup of Kool-Aid. I waited for him to wipe his mouth on his sleeve, but he didn't. Looking at him, I thought I could probably tell what he looked like as a kid, imagining his young face with a fruity mustache. He had a boyish quality to him, but he was very rugged as well. I wasn't nervous around him anymore, which was weird because, if I had been in a bar, I'd have been a bundle of jitters around someone that good-looking.

"You *can* drink, you know," he said.

I took a diminutive sip.

"That didn't count." He scoffed. "I've just driven eight hours after skiing for the entire weekend. No one is here besides you, me, and the random people touring my house. I want to have a drink and relax with someone. It's Christmas, for Christ's sake."

"It isn't Christmas *yet*." I took another sip to appease him.

"Where's Pippa?" Kip gulped more beer until the last of the foam slipped down his glass into his mouth. He opened a cabinet, revealing a neatly lined trash can. The lemon from his empty up-turned glass slid into the trash just before he got into the refrigerator again and pulled out another beer. Plop, another lemon slice. Fizz, more beer.

"She's Christmas shopping. Why do you call your grandmother Pippa?"

"Isn't that her name?" He had finished half of beer number two and had set it down to strip off his fleece. I took another sip as he draped it on a nearby chair.

"But she's your grandmother. Why don't you call her Grandma or something?"

His eyes were all glittery in the afternoon light. "She didn't let us." He cocked his head to the side. "Have you *met* Pippa?"

I suppressed an urge to laugh.

Kip walked around the counter and lightly touched the small of my back. It took me a bit by surprise, so I covered my shock with a larger gulp of my beverage. He ushered me into the sitting room and gestured for me to take a seat on the settee next to the fire. I hoped that Megan had shown this room already.

"What would Mr. Marley say if he saw me sitting on the sofa having a beer?" I raised the question as I sat down.

Kip rolled his eyes. "Who cares?"

"I do. He's my employer."

I watched as Kip rested his drink on the mahogany coffee table and looked around in vain for a coaster.

"You're not doing anything wrong," he said.

"I'm not doing *anything*. Period."

"Touché," he grinned at me, looking me up and down. "You're entertaining me. Believe me, Robert knows that I need entertaining," he said, his expression like a seven-year-old again.

I couldn't help but smile at him. How could these two brothers have been raised in the same household? My thoughts were interrupted by the sound of footsteps. Jumping up and leaving Kip in the sitting room, I walked briskly over to the entranceway. Megan showed her clients out of the front door.

Putting her hand to her ear in the I'll-call-you gesture, she shot a glance over toward the sitting room and raised her eyebrows.

She received a harsh stare-down in return, and I shook my head, then turned back toward Kip and the beer that was most certainly making a ring on Pippa's table.

❊ ❊ ❊

Kip and I had talked for almost forty-five minutes before I noticed that it was nearing three o'clock. As politely as I could, I attempted to leave the room by mentioning my duties. Kip rolled his eyes—the common response, it seemed, to any mention of his elder brother. I excused myself and went into the office.

No emails. Ugh. So, I decided to send one to Robert.

"Dear Mr. Marley…"

I deleted it.

Do I need to write *Dear?* Okay, try again.

"Mr. Marley, the showing went well, but it seemed quick. Kip is here. How should I plan for the family meeting?" I would have loved to put the word *meeting* in quotes. It wasn't any of my business, I told myself, and hit send.

A few moments later, I had a reply. So, I guessed email was Robert's communication tool of choice. That figured.

I read the reply: *Kip is there? Already? I don't think Sloane will be there for a few days. Please don't allow him to occupy all of your time. He can be demanding. (He's the third child and used to getting what he wants.) Find him some crayons and a coloring book to keep him busy.*

I responded: "He's not so bad." Send.

Response: *Really.*

(I noted the period.)

"He's nice." Send.

Response: *I'm sure he is.*

What was that supposed to mean? I left him hanging on that point and returned, "What do I need to do to plan for the family meeting?"

I pushed myself back and forth in the desk chair, the rollers sliding silently on the hardwoods. Robert's message came across a few minutes later:

Pippa's fingers give her trouble, Sloane doesn't have time, and Kip… well, he just won't, so you will need to wrap everyone's presents for Christmas Eve. I know that isn't the job of the house manager per se, but I couldn't think of a staff member who would be better suited.

You will need to ensure that Anna has what she needs for Christmas dinner. (She knows what to make.) And, most importantly, make sure that Kip is in attendance. He has a mind of his own.

We may or may not have a small open house, but I'll send information regarding that in a while if the family decides to have one this

year. In a few weeks, you will need to organize the delivery of the
Christmas trees for the house. I'll forward more info on that later.

I will FedEx you payment for the staff and for Pippa's caretakers,
and you can give them Christmas Day off. This means that you will
be the only person working on Christmas Day. I hope that's all right.

I had to work on Christmas Day? I supposed it only meant that
Mom and Megan would have to wait for our gift exchange. I was
sure they would understand. But I had never had Christmas away
from my family before, and I felt a pang of sadness.

Nonetheless, I replied, "No problem. I'll go and make sure Kip
is comfortable."

Response: *You do that.*

I cut my eyes at the screen. Was that hostility I noted? It was so hard
to tell in an email. The response didn't settle well with me, though.

Chapter Four

There was a creak in the floorboards, so I looked up and saw Kip standing in the doorway. I quickly exited out of the screen.

"How long have you been standing there?" I asked.

"Not long," he said. "Want to get a bite to eat?"

"It's only," I looked at my watch, "three thirty."

The alcohol had turned Kip's cheeks the color of pomegranates. "It's late, and I haven't had lunch yet. Anna can whip up something for us." He walked toward me, so I moved around to the other side of the desk to meet him half way. "What did Robert have to say?" he asked, visibly relaxed.

"He told me to keep you on a short leash."

"Really?" Kip laughed. His hands were casually tucked away in the pockets of his jeans, and he swayed backward on his heels a bit. "What else did he say?"

"That I should get you some crayons and a coloring book to keep you busy."

"That's not how I keep busy," he was shaking his head, a flirty little grin on his face. Closing the distance between us, he stopped just before we were beyond each other's personal space. This guy seemed a little too big for his britches.

Taking a step back, I attempted to discourage his baiting. This was obvious flirting, and I was working. How could I get him to refocus? Abruptly changing the subject, I asked, "Do you read?"

"What?" Kip seemed taken off guard, as expected.

"That's how *I* keep busy. Do you read?"

The skin between his eyes furrowed. "Uh, no. I don't read unless I have to. Or unless it has something to do with sports. I'm extremely competitive, and sometimes I'll resort to reading if it's the only way to find out a score."

Our conversation was interrupted by the sound of a small motor heading our way. We both turned toward the door to find Pippa rolling through it.

"Kip!" she nearly shrieked, climbing off of the scooter. I hadn't seen that much gusto in Pippa since I'd arrived. She glanced my way briefly, but her focus was on Kip. "When did you get home, darling?" He leaned forward as she air kissed him on both cheeks.

"Around two." He grabbed her hands gently and held them out at her side, looking her up and down before letting go. "You look well," he said. There was a tenderness in his eyes. It changed his face from the flirty one I'd seen previously. Suddenly, I felt like an intruder, and I had a strong desire to leave them alone.

"I know. Now, quit flittering around," she waved her fingers in the air, "And help me get my shopping bags." Pippa clambered back up onto the scooter and motored out of the door, Kip following behind. I was left alone again in the office and actually a little relieved.

❋ ❋ ❋

At five o'clock, I hadn't seen Kip since he'd left with Pippa. I leaned over the desk and checked email for the last time. I actually had a message. It read: *Your itinerary will be waiting at eight a.m.* I was just about to shut it down when a second message popped up: *Have a nice evening.*

I responded, "You too," and hit send. I don't know what came over me—maybe it was seeing Kip with Pippa, maybe it was the way this house seemed to need a family—but I wanted Robert to come home for Christmas. I typed, "Just getting a head count. Are you sure you aren't coming for Christmas?" and hit send. My hands were damp, as I waited for a response. The computer screen glowed in the dusk light that had filled the room as I slid down into the desk chair and stared at the monitor. An oak clock above the doorway clucked out the minutes as I sat. Nothing.

At five twenty, I shut down the computer and headed to the yellow room to put on some comfortable clothes. It had been an eventful day. I hoped that Anna would bring me some dinner in my room because I didn't really want to see anyone else.

❋ ❋ ❋

Anna had brought by a plate of dinner, and the empty dishes sat in the hallway beside my door as she had instructed. Just as I was climbing into bed, my cell phone vibrated on the bedside table. Megan was probably calling to tell me to pack my bags because the house had been sold.

I quickly answered it. "Hello?"

There was a shuffling sound and then, "Allison." This was definitely not Megan's voice.

"Mr. Marley?" My dinner settled like a load of bricks in my stomach as I registered who was on the line.

"Please, call me Robert."

"Okay. And you can call me Allie."

"Are you busy, Allie?" Robert asked.

"Um," my mouth was suddenly so dry I could barely form words. "No." And my heart was pumping overtime.

"I just wanted you to know that I won't be coming to Ashford this Christmas because I have to work, despite what Kip may have told you."

All of a sudden, I couldn't remember how I had asked the question about him coming for Christmas. Did I ask it professionally? I know what I was thinking in my head, I just hoped that I hadn't asked it that way.

"Kip didn't tell me anything. I was just…" Oh! Thank God! I remembered my email. "I was just getting a head count."

My whole body seized in surprise as I heard an unsuspected knock at the door. "Can you hold on one second?" I said into the emptiness that was radiating from my phone. All I could hear was my own pulse thumping in my ears.

"Sure." Robert was quiet.

With my hand placed over the receiver of the phone—as if that really does anything—I opened the door. Kip stood in the doorway with two bowls of ice cream. "I heard that you had dinner in your room, but you didn't order dessert." Then he grimaced, noticing that I was on the phone, and locked an imaginary lock on his lips, tossing the invisible key over his shoulder and nearly spilling ice cream all over the hardwoods as he walked past me into my room.

Ugh. I didn't want dessert with Kip, and I didn't even want to plow through another conversation with Robert right now. I just needed a hot shower and an early night.

With one finger held up to keep Kip at bay, I put the phone back to my ear. "Would it be possible for me to call you back? Kip's here."

"Is that so?" his voice had changed. It was inquisitive in a way, and almost wary. "No need to bother. I'll send you the itinerary at eight. Good night."

"Okay, then… Good night." The line went dead.

I put the phone back on the table and turned to Kip, who was holding what was beginning to look like ice cream soup in two bowls. "Thank you for bringing me dessert, but I'd rather not have any." I smiled my most chipper smile.

"I wanted to say sorry for leaving you today after Pippa came in. I think she likes my visits, and I feel like I should spend time with her when I'm here. The three of us are all she has left."

"She doesn't have anyone nearby? Your parents or anyone?" I was instantly sorry for asking. The answer may be a long one, and I really just wanted to go to bed. I also must stop butting into my employer's family. What was wrong with me?

"They were killed when I was four years old. Pippa raised us." He set one bowl on the table next to my phone and took a dripping bite of the other ice cream before walking over toward me. He passed me and sat down on my bed.

"That's horrible." I felt a cold draft against my back, as I leaned against the extra-large windowsill. I drug my fingers from side to side along its surface, feeling the thick lacquer under my nails.

"Anyway!" Kip popped up off the bed. "Enough of that gloomy stuff. Want to come downstairs and hang out? We could have a drink, play some pool…"

Did he have no shame, trying his pick-up lines with the help? Shaking my head, I declined before he could finish. "Thank you for the offer, Kip, but I'm beat. I think I just want to turn in for the night."

Kip waited briefly, his face set in a hopeful expression, perhaps to see if I'd change my mind. Then he shrugged and said, "Okay, have it your way." The door groaned as he opened it, and he turned around to face me. "If you change your mind, my room's over in the east wing, two doors down from Pippa's."

"Thank you. I'll keep that in mind," I said and practically pushed him out of the door.

❋ ❋ ❋

I awoke at seven a.m. to my phone chirping at one-minute intervals. A stream of sunlight momentarily blinded me when I rolled over to grab it. One missed call. Megan had called at nine sixteen p.m. I decided she was probably awake and dialed her number.

The phone rang once, and she greeted me with, "So, you weren't out all night with Kip Marley or anything, were you?"

"Absolutely not," I said, sitting up in my bed. Dropping my feet over the side, I stood up. The cold of the floor's surface seeped through my socks. A chill ran up my bare legs, and I resolved to wear pajamas with bottoms from that point on.

"Well, it's a no go. The Ashford estate was at the top of my client's price range, and he opted for another home a little further from the city."

"Did you make the sale on that one?"

"Yeeees!" she squealed, and I had to pull my phone from my ear to save my eardrum. "I can't wait to get presents for everyone. Get excited! Yours will be a good one!" Her voice was sing-songy now.

"Congratulations. Oh! I forgot. I have to work here on Christmas Eve and Christmas Day. When do you want to get together to do presents?"

"You have to work? Even Wal-Mart closes early on Christmas Eve."

"I know. I'm so close to you and Mom, and I can't get home! Mr. Marley has a nice little list for me to do." I noted the time. "Speaking of which… I have to go. I have to get ready for the day; he's sending me my itinerary at eight, and I'd like to give Mom a call."

"Mr. Marley runs a tight ship."

"Yeah." I sighed. "Call me later."

We said our good-byes, and I quickly dialed Mom's number. She answered on the first ring.

"Hey, Mom. Just wanted to see how you were."

"Good! How's the new job?"

I paced over to the table opposite the bed and grabbed the earrings that I'd set down there. With the phone on my shoulder, I put one of them on. "It's nice! I'm enjoying it so far," I said, switching ears so that I could put on the other earring. "I just wanted to call to tell you that I won't be home for Christmas…"

It was the first time I'd ever missed a Christmas at home, and I knew Mom would be disappointed. I told her about work and Robert's plans for me and listened to her tell me in her most optimistic voice how it would all be fine. We'd just postpone our family Christmas until I could get there. Even if I had semi-bad news, it was good to talk to her, and felt reassuring to hear her voice.

After I'd finished the call, I pulled my hair back, washed my face, did my makeup and slipped on some work-appropriate clothes. Then, I headed downstairs to the office to see what Robert had waiting for me.

I checked email. No messages. Annoying. I walked over to the computer, logged on, and sent my itinerary to the printer. First on the agenda: Supervise cleaning staff. Find out any maintenance concerns, inspect rooms for quality, and check on Pippa; make sure everything has been taken care of regarding her room. Pulling it from the printer, I folded the itinerary into the size of a credit card, slid it into my pocket, and headed over to the east wing. I figured I'd check on Pippa first to get that out of the way.

Following the heady aroma of recently ground coffee, I meandered into the kitchen to find Anna making a fresh pot. Thank God. She prepared a cup for me with just the right amount of cream and sugar and pushed it across the counter.

"How long have you worked here?" I asked, making conversation.

Her eyes on the food she was preparing, she said, "Since the kids were little."

"Really?" I took a sip. "What were Robert and Kip like then?"

A wistful look came over her as she pulled a utensil from a drawer and began to mix a lump of batter, pressing the substantial clay bowl into her bosom. "I got this job when I had nothing at all." She shook her head. "It was my last hope for any kind of life, and, in some way, I think the Marleys actually *saved* my life." She set the bowl down and walked around the island, wiping her hands on a kitchen towel.

"How did they save your life?"

She sat down next to me on a barstool. "I couldn't have children of my own, and my last relationship had ended on that note. My ex-husband had been the breadwinner, and when he left, I had very little. No job, no chance of children…" Anna sat, her long legs delicately crossed. "Then I saw this pale, lanky little six-year-old running through the hallways with a wooden sword and shield. I took one look at him and just knew that this was where I belonged."

"Robert?" I asked.

"Yes. Robert was the reason for my employment with the Marley family, and now he will most likely be the reason for my *un*employ-ment." She smiled weakly. Standing back up, she said, "You had better check on Pippa. Wasn't that where you were headed?"

I didn't want to leave. I wanted to hear more about her, about Robert, but I took my cup of coffee with me and left her, heading for the east wing.

Pippa's door was closed, so I gave it a few quiet taps with the back of my hand. As I listened to footsteps creeping closer to the door, I sipped my coffee, letting the caffeine spread through me. The door opened, and I was taken aback to see Kip grinning at me, a muddle of curls on the top of his head. It was clear by the squinting of his eyes that he was trying to focus through his obvious fog.

"Morning." He rubbed the gold scruff on his chin, and it made a scratching sound.

I looked past him into the room. The bed was a chaotic jumble of khaki and dark green blankets, wrinkled and draped from one end to the other. Clothes in piles littered the floor. He'd only been there a day. Not even that.

"I'm sorry," I looked back at Kip, "I thought this was Ms. Mar-ley's room."

"Two more doors that way," he reached out his arm and pointed past me into the hallway, his face leaning precariously close to mine. I backed away, stumbling slightly.

"Sorry again. Go back to sleep. I was just checking on your grandmother." I leaned toward him, causing him to step back in response, and closed his door, most likely leaving him still standing on the other side. Then I hurried down the hallway to Pippa's room and knocked.

The door opened, and Pippa stared blankly at me. She was already dressed—shoes, pearls, everything—and she was holding a book in her hand, her finger wedged between the pages. "May I help you?" She was much more pleasant since Kip had come home.

"Robert gave me an itinerary for the day. He told me to check that the staff has cleaned your room to your satisfaction." My hands began to shake despite her agreeable disposition, so I cupped them around my mug.

"The staff has done the same job today that they have done for... I don't know, fifteen years? Is that how long we've had this particular staff?" She looked off into the air, possibly contemplating her own question. Her eyes where bright and shiny, like they were too alive for her face.

"I'm not sure how long they've been with you. Do you need anything?"

"I'd like you to smuggle me in a cup of that coffee that you have. It smells divine." Pippa leaned a fraction closer to me and whispered, "They don't let me have the caffeine, but for God's sake, I'm ninety-two years old. Does it really matter?"

"I'll see what I can do." From the look of it, Pippa was in a *much* better mood today.

I walked down to the kitchen gulping my coffee, so that I could enter with an empty cup. The perfectly clean spigot and knobs glistened beneath my hands as I set the cup in the sink and turned on the water. "I'd actually like another cup of that, I think," I said to

Anna. She grinned and retrieved another mug. Then she poured the coffee, but she added only a little cream and sugar this time.

Anna caught my gaze. "Well, if Pippa's going to drink it, I'm certainly not going to put very much sugar in it. The caffeine's bad enough." She carried on stirring and handed me the cup with a wink. Note to self: Don't try and hide anything from Anna. Apparently, she can read minds.

I gingerly carried the steaming cup back down the east wing. Pippa's door was open, so I let myself in. She was sitting by the window reading her book. She offered a hint of a smile, as I handed her the cup. "Anna knew it was for me, didn't she?" she asked, after her first sip.

"How did she know? I just asked for a second cup."

"I ask for coffee every morning. She only lets me have it on the odd day. Maybe she felt sorry for me today."

"Why would Anna feel sorry for you?"

"Because, dear girl, it's December thirteenth, the anniversary of my son's death."

My breath caught. "Oh! I'm so sorry. I had no idea..." My hand covered my mouth, as I said the words.

"How could you have known?" She took another sip of her coffee and closed her eyes. "This is lovely. Thank you." She set it down on a small, round table near the window.

"How was your son...?" I tried to get the phrasing right. "How did you lose your son?" There I go again. It's an illness, really, the nosiness. But I felt terrible for Pippa. And I wanted to hear the story.

Pippa picked up her mug once more and hoisted herself up off her chair. She ambled across the room, then motioned for me to go through the door as she followed. The door closed on her scooter and she grabbed my elbow. We walked together to the end of the east wing.

Chapter Five

At the very end of the hallway, we entered a sort of family room. There were modern couches, chairs... and an extremely large television anchored on the wall at one end, thin and sleek and out of place in the traditionally decorated room. Pippa sat down on the sofa and patted the cushion next to her. I complied.

She took a dainty sip from her mug, holding it with both hands. "I only had one child," she began with little fanfare, "Samuel was the most amazing baby. Never cried." She took in a long breath and then exhaled. "He was truly lovely." She smiled in my direction, and her smile reached her eyes. "Henry and I didn't think we could have children. Then, when I was twenty-nine, long past the thought of having babies, I found out that I was pregnant. A gift from God above."

I watched her, almost afraid to blink. Pippa took another draw of her coffee and shifted her frail body slightly. "His life was so short." She shook her head, the corners of her mouth turning down. "It was December thirteenth, 1982. Samuel and his wife, Carolyn, were off to a Christmas party. I was watching the children at the house, in this very room..." She looked around for a long while.

"Kip was doing a puzzle." Her finger extended in the direction of the corner behind us. "We had a small games table over there at that time, and Sloane and Robert were drawing—pencil sketches, I believe." Her vision was occupied, as if she were watching the scene unfold in front of her. She brushed a disobedient strand of her silver hair from her forehead, pushing it back toward the neatly pinned bundle at the back of her neck.

"There are several moments in time when I can remember the exact minute—like a dividing line, splitting my life into distinct parts. That evening was one of those moments. On one side of the dividing line was my normal, happy life. On the other, an unthinkable life, one that I never expected to experience but one that was thrust upon me in full force.

"The phone rang. I answered it with the most euphoric feeling. I remember that. Up to that point, I had been utterly content. The kids looked over to see who it was. I remember shaking my head, confused, because I didn't recognize the voice on the other end. The kids went back to their activities as I listened to the stranger. That stranger was a police officer. He had called to inform me that Samuel and Carolyn never made it to the party. Their car was hit head-on, as they drove down the winding road leading out of the village toward the city, ripping them away from their family."

"I'm so sorry." A slight wetness pricked my eyes. I wanted to say something consoling, but I was at a loss for words.

Pippa's petite chest expanded, as she took another deep breath. She had wrapped her hands tightly around the mug again, holding them in that position as if warming them. "Kip was young. Only four. He was sad but resilient. In time, he made his peace with the loss of his parents. Sloane took it very hard. She was—and still is—

the spitting image of her mother, you know. Carolyn's death caused a chasm within Sloane that has never been filled. She doesn't talk about it at all, and she avoids most emotional circumstances even now. Probably why she's divorced." Pippa digressed.

"How was Robert?" I regretted my frustration with his terse behavior since we'd met.

Pippa's eyes focused on something above us, maybe the crown molding framing the lofty ceiling. "Before his parents' death, he was the most sensitive, caring child."

Her face livened with the memory of him. I hadn't seen Pippa smile at all yesterday and yet, today, on the anniversary of her only child's death, she smiled incessantly.

"After their death, he drew into himself. He was nine, you see, the eldest of the three. He took it quite hard. And now…" Her expression fell. It was obvious that Robert's current behavior concerned her. "He's nearly unbearable."

"Unbearable? Really?" I knew that he was not the most enjoyable person to talk to, and he struggled with conversation, but he didn't seem *that* bad.

"He's pulling my home right out from under me, selling it for his own profit, and putting me up in some warehouse for the elderly that will most undoubtedly be cold and smell of its decaying inhabitants." Her scowl had returned.

"I'm so sorry. Isn't there anything you can do to make him keep the house?"

Pippa set her mug on the end table next to her and stood up. Smoothing her skirt, she looked down at me. "Apparently not." She began to walk toward the door. "Do you mind helping me back to my room? I don't need anything else." Her exasperation had returned.

She waited by the door until I joined her. Then, while holding my elbow for support, we walked to her room, the swishing of her skirt and the thudding of our shoes the only sounds between us.

After depositing Pippa at her bedroom door, I checked my watch. Eight fifty-two. I had to check email and then receive Tom McCray from Miller's Grocery. On my way to the office, I thought about how, after Pippa's story, I wanted so badly to unload on Robert, send him an email with my thoughts on the sale of her home. What a callous thing to do.

But the more I thought about Robert, the more confused I became. He really didn't seem as despicable as Pippa had made him out to be. Then again, I had only known him a short time. Could I even use the word *known*?

I entered the office and walked over to the computer, logging on and checking email right on time. One message. Amazing.

I opened it, and it read: *Please notify me of any maintenance concerns estimated over five hundred dollars. I will need to adjust billing and payment.*

I still had to check with maintenance and the cleaning staff to see if there were any issues. My time had been consumed with Pippa, although I didn't mind. When she opened up, her stories were fascinating.

I replied, "No maintenance concerns as of yet. I'll keep you posted on any that pop up."

I hit send and moments later received a reply: *Thank you. How are you this morning?*

My eyes widened at the sight of his question. What prompted this moment of good etiquette? I responded, "I'm well. Thank you." What was it with this family? Everyone seemed to be overly chatty on the saddest day in family history. Weird.

I felt the impulsiveness swelling inside me. I fought the urge, but I just couldn't keep it contained. My fingers moved slowly across the keys, "Are you okay today?" Send. It was done. It couldn't be retrieved from cyberspace. A now-familiar cold, wet sensation spread over the palms of my hands, and I wiped them on my trousers.

Reply: *Yes.*

I chewed on my lip. He obviously wasn't elaborating. I typed back, "I hope so." I waited a few minutes and got no response. Typical. The screen went dark, as I logged out and headed toward the kitchen to see Tom.

When I got there, Tom was already busily unloading groceries while Anna packed them away in the proper locations. He shot up a quick hand to say hello and continued to unpack. "Were you able to deliver everything on the list?" I asked.

"Yes, ma'am." Tom said, his face creasing as he spoke.

"Great, thank you. Is there anything you'll need from me?"

Tom stopped briefly to answer. He brushed off his hands. "When you've worked out with Anna what you'll need for tomorrow, email the list over. Usually, Robert sends it around four in the afternoon."

"I already have it on my list for today. You'll have it by four." I stepped toward the door to allow Tom to finish his delivery. With a quick wave, I hustled down the hallway to begin checking rooms for quality and maintenance concerns.

❊ ❊ ❊

By lunch, I had met with the cleaning staff, determined there were no maintenance concerns, checked all unoccupied rooms personally, submitted the maintenance report to Gerard, monitored the grounds staff and ordered materials for them, as well as received a full report from Pippa's medical team. (Big exhale.) I was starving, but I had one more thing to do before lunch: I had to check email again.

There had been no messages since my little inquiry into Robert's emotional state. He wasn't going to spill any beans, that was for sure. The one thing about me that everyone who knows me can substantiate is that literally everything that I think eventually comes out of my mouth. So, I guess that's why I wished that Robert would open up a little. He seemed so stiff in his responses. Granted, he may be holding back because he didn't know me from Adam, but, from what I'd heard from Pippa, he was just impassive in general. It was strange though; for some unknown reason, I felt like even though he was holding back, he was letting me in a little bit. It didn't make any sense; it was just a feeling. Just like the feeling I got holding his hand a little too long when I'd met him. His warmth spreading to my palm. It was only a moment, but it felt like I'd had a little glimpse of him.

I decided to email Robert, since once again I had nothing waiting for me. I typed: "Ms. Marley's medical team has completed her daily status chart, and I've entered the data electronically. I've attached it for you. I've also attached the billing details from them."

The screen glared at me. I decided to make it a personal goal to get this guy to talk. I couldn't define why, I just felt so sad for him and his family, I guess. Hoping to elicit some reaction, I finished with, "Will you get to see Ms. Marley soon, since you won't be here for Christmas?"

I waited a few seconds and then got a reply: *Thank you for these. And, no, I will not see Pippa soon.*

My fingers hung above the keyboard, aching with reckless energy. Then they started clicking away. "I'm sure she would be delighted if she could have the whole family here on Christmas." Send.

Response: *I doubt that.*

Unable to stop myself, I typed, "Why?" None of my business, obviously, and I already knew why.

Response: *We don't understand each other. Please don't waste your entire lunch fretting over our family. We're all fine.*

I wanted to tell him that the rest of the family seemed fine; it was *he* who seemed to have the issues. But I couldn't possibly type that, could I? I looked up from the screen to see Kip blocking my view to the hallway with a smirk on his face. My eyes darted to my watch. Twelve twenty-three. "Just get up?"

Kip's smile widened. "Not too long ago. How are you this morning… afternoon?"

"Fine, thanks."

"You looked really intense just then. What was Robert saying? Did he give you a list of things to do?" He shook his head. "I swear he makes things up. He would pace around this house constantly busy with something, and I always wondered what he was doing."

"I was just asking Mr. Marley if he was okay today, since it's such a sad day."

"Oh, I didn't know that you knew what today was." He walked into the room, his face more somber. "Did he respond?"

"Barely."

"What did he say?"

I recapped our conversation, or lack thereof, for Kip. "How did *you* know what today was?" he asked, approaching the desk. When Kip asked me a question, it was as if what I had to say was the most important thing in the world. His head was turned just slightly to the side, the skin between his eyes creased, his entire body so calm and unruffled. His unassuming nature was quite attractive, and I could see why the girls were always chasing him, as Megan had divulged that day at the coffee shop.

"Ms. Marley told me when I went to check on her." I logged off the computer and walked over to him just as my stomach growled. "I have to eat something. Have you had lunch?" I asked.

Kip's head shook back and forth and his grin returned. "Not yet. Let's go out. You need to get out of this house anyway."

"It's not like I'm being held captive."

Kip guided me toward the door, his hand on the small of my back again in the same way that he had gotten me to sit on the couch the other day. It was a little too personal, but I let it slide. We slipped on our coats and headed outside.

Walking toward his Range Rover, I pulled my coat together to keep warm. Kip opened the passenger door for me before going around the front of the car and sliding into the driver's seat. "I just have to be back by one thirty, so that I can finish the itinerary items," I said, climbing in, closing my door.

The side of Kip's mouth turned up, as he started the engine. "Yeah, sure thing," he said, with a note of sarcasm, as he sped away from Ashford.

Chapter Six

I peered out of the window of the car. Rolling fields swept past me in a rush as we sped toward town. Kip continued to look straight ahead when he asked, "What's it like to be... in a normal family?"

What an odd question. "What do you mean?"

His eyes ping-ponged from the road to me—back and forth. "To grow up with two parents in a regular house? What does that feel like?"

"Well, I didn't grow up with two parents, only one, and I don't know any other life, so it's difficult to put into words. I guess it was nice. What's so bad about your upbringing?" The sun peeked out between the trees, dropping fragments of light and dark onto Kip's chest.

"Nothing's bad, really." He steered around a sharp curve. Gripping the steering wheel with both hands, he said, "I just always wondered what it was like to grow up in a house with normal siblings. I guess I'm saying that I'm aware that our family isn't typical."

I pondered the idea of normalcy some more. "Well, my family was like any other family, really. We had our squabbles and annoyances, but we were family, so we persevered through whatever issues we had." I looked past him out of the window. Kip was obviously speeding, but I didn't mind.

"You said you didn't grow up with both parents." Kip clarified.

"My dad left when I was little. Mom never told us why, but my sister thinks he was having an affair." I felt like I should be somewhat emotional about this fact, but the truth was, I really didn't remember him, so I was indifferent to the situation, really.

There had always been, though, this tiny scratching at the back of my mind, knowing that he willfully chose to abandon Megan and me. Sadness wasn't the right word to describe what I felt about his absence; it was more like disappointment because he had never given me a chance. I think it's this single idea that makes it nearly unbearable for me to see people give up on each other. Life's just too short for that nonsense.

"Tell me about *your* family," I asked impulsively.

"What do you want to know?" Kip asked.

"What are they like?"

Kip took some time to formulate a response as the pine trees gave way to rolling hills of green. Then he said, "Well, Pippa's great. She was the best mother and grandmother I could ask for. She did a good job raising us." He maneuvered the car around another sharp bend in the road. "She wasn't as fond of Robert, though."

"Why not?"

"She and Robert are a lot alike. They're both pretty stubborn. When Mom and Dad died, they started to butt heads and never really recovered. They both hold in their anger, you know?"

The funny thing was, I did know. I could tell that almost immediately. "They couldn't come to terms with things?"

"No. It's really strange because Pippa seemed to deal with the rest of us pretty well. She and Robert just never let it go." The car came to rest in front of a tiny restaurant just off the country road. Just like our car ride, the conversation came to an end. Once we had exited the car, the pause had been just long enough that I couldn't get it back, so I abandoned the questions that I had and followed him to the door.

Upon entering, Kip was greeted by name immediately. He allowed me to go through and followed behind. There were only a handful of tables in the dining room—all with white linen cloths draped over them and lit candles extending out from a heap of fresh Christmas greenery. Two of them were occupied, leaving one open table.

A man wearing all white approached us. "Allie, this is Doug Asher." Kip clapped him on the back. "He's the chef here."

Mr. Asher offered his hand in greeting. "What will we be having this afternoon, Mr. Marley?" Mr. Asher asked with a look of genuine pleasure radiating from his features.

Kip turned to me. "Do you like fish?" I nodded. "Doug's sea bass is amazing." He turned back to Mr. Asher. "We'll both have the grilled Mediterranean sea bass fillet." It did not go unnoticed that he ordered our entrées without the aid of a menu. There was something very alluring about the Marley way of life, and I couldn't help but be drawn in by it. It was an odd sensation to go through the day as I normally would but have absolutely nothing seem real. Did people really live like this?

Discretely, Kip whispered something to Mr. Asher and the chef executed a minor bow before motioning for us to take a seat. Before I could get my hand on the back of the chair, Kip pulled it out for me and then went around to his side of the table. It was unexpected to see him display such manners. I would have thought that propriety of this form wouldn't even have occurred to him. It was a pleasant surprise.

The interior of the establishment finally came into view once I sat down. The walls were clad in deeply stained wood with modern art in bright colors spilling out from every wall. The lights were dim even in the daytime, and a fire was alight in a wood-burning fireplace at the end of the undersized dining area. A bar with highly glossed surfaces nestled at the other end was dotted with a few men in business suits. White lights and holly hung from the sparkling stemware dangling above the bar.

Kip took notice of my observations. "It's nice, isn't it?" I nodded, my eyes still scanning the interior. "Usually you have to make reservations, but it's more of a dinner spot, so I figured I'd give it a shot for lunch. After all, it's already nearly one, so most people are back to work."

Back to work. I needed to eat quickly so that I could get back in time to check email, and I still needed to meet with Anna.

"What are you thinking about?"

"You said work, and it got me thinking. I need to be able to check my email and meet with Anna. Robert's expecting me to perform my duties."

Kip's face contorted into a look of irritation, as it usually did when matters concerned his brother. "Does it matter if you perform them?"

"Yes. Despite what you think, this is a job for me. I make the only money I have doing this. If I lose my job, I have no money."

A sudden look of understanding washed over his face. "Sorry. I was looking at it from my brother's perspective, not yours. I won't let him fire you."

"Thank you, but I also need to do as he asks. He is my employer after all. Even if he is your annoying brother."

"Okay, I'll be on my best behavior from now on. I'll take responsibility for this afternoon. Let me contact Robert personally and inform him that it was my fault you aren't on time. He'll believe me, don't worry." Under the table, Kip retrieved his phone and began texting discretely. "Done," he said as he slid his phone back into his pocket.

A woman, who had been behind the bar, came over, balancing a plate of cheese and bread and two glasses of iced tea. "Complements of the chef," she beamed, gingerly setting them in front of us. "Both the cheese and bread were made here by Doug," the barwoman-waitress added before leaving us for her perch at the bar.

I nibbled on our appetizer and took a few sips of tea.

"So, how did you end up being our house manager?" Kip asked between bites of bread.

"I flipped for it."

"You what?"

"I flipped a coin." I started from the beginning, telling Kip about the years that I had been Nathan's nanny, and how I got news of the job opening from Megan.

"What if it had been heads?" he asked. "What would you have done then?"

"I guess I would have stayed home with my mom and looked for another job." Now, I couldn't imagine doing that. For one thing, I'd submitted three different applications, and I had yet to receive a call regarding any of them. For another, I was finding my time at Ashford very much to my liking. There was something comfortable about it, even though it was unlike any home I'd ever known. "What about you? Do you always live at Ashford or do you have an apartment somewhere or something?"

"I live at Ashford, but I travel a lot and stay mostly in hotels."

"Isn't that lonely?"

"Sometimes, but it's better than staying home and listening to Robert and Pippa bicker."

"Where will you live after Ashford is sold?"

He took a swig of tea and then held the glass up as if looking for something in the liquid. "Maybe I'll travel… Not sure."

"Nobody wants to buy Robert out? Keep Ashford?"

Kip shook his head. "We all got a rather large inheritance when our parents died. Sloane sank some of hers into a home that's now being sold, the profits split in half because of her divorce. I don't know what she's done with the rest. Robert used his to invest in some properties. He, just like the Marleys before him, is a real estate investor. And me, I've kind of been living on mine. I use it as an escape from our crazy family. We don't have enough to buy him out."

So that's what Robert does. He's an investor. Kip was clearly waiting for me to continue the conversation, so I said literally what I was thinking. "I didn't know what Robert did for a living until now."

"He's made the money back a few times over already, I'm sure."

There was something in his eyes, and I wondered what Kip was thinking. Then he looked directly at me, changing the subject, and said, "I wasn't planning on staying all the way until Christmas because I can hardly endure the drama, but I'm considering changing my mind." An odd look inched its way across his face.

"Why are you thinking about staying now?"

"Because the house has something that interests me."

"Which is?"

"You." He took another sip of his drink, his gaze on me.

I blinked over and over. My eyes couldn't stop twitching. I didn't know how to respond to this. In my mind, it was Kip's friendliness that had brought us to lunch today. Had I led him on in some way? I didn't think so.

"Say something." He was beginning to look wounded by my lack of response. Was he used to having women fawn over him at the slightest hint of interest?

"I don't know what to say..."

Kip composed his face, and then a smile stretched from one side to the other. "Let's flip a coin."

"What?"

Our meal came, and the woman behind the bar refilled our glasses. My temples were starting to throb.

"Heads, you go on three dates with me—real ones. Tails, I leave you alone and try to be a good boy at the house."

Chewing on my bottom lip, I contemplated these options. I hadn't had enough time to even think through any possible feelings—or non-feelings—for Kip. But, then again, it was only three dates. Why not? I reached into my purse and pulled out my Susan B. Anthony coin and set it down on the table.

"You actually carry around a coin for flipping purposes?" Kip asked, visibly amused.

"I've had it since I was a kid. And I was moving, so I had it in my purse..." Why bother explaining now? I pushed it across the table and picked up my fork, stabbing a bite of sea bass and placing it in my mouth—it was absolutely delicious. "You flip."

Kip picked up the coin and turned it over in his hand. "Heads, right?" he more directed than asked. Then he flipped it into the air, caught it, and pressed it onto the back of his other hand. Slowly, he uncovered the coin, revealing its face.

Heads.

His eyes met mine. "Three dates it is," he said, grinning, but it wasn't his usual, playful grin. It was an inquiring smile, a request for acceptance. He reached out to pass me my coin, and his fingers lingered on mine slightly longer than they should have. I had not until that moment seen him this vulnerable, this unsure. Maybe there was more to Kip Marley than his trust fund after all.

❆ ❆ ❆

We didn't arrive back at the house until nearly two o'clock. "You go and see Anna, and I'm going to check on Pippa," he said. "I'll find you later to discuss our first date." He was outwardly glowing with jubilant energy.

Dating hadn't been at the forefront of my recent past. I had been so busy as little Nathan's nanny that I was a little out of practice. Kip Marley was not the worst person in the world to be dating, and he did seem to genuinely like me. I pulled out my phone and texted Megan: *Going on date with Kip Mrly. Fil u n latr.* Then I went to find Anna.

As Anna and I were making the order for Miller's Grocery, Kip came up behind me and put a hand on my shoulder. "I just spoke with Robert. He said to check email when you can." He leaned closer to my ear. "After that, see Pippa, and while you're over there, pop down to my room for a minute." Anna watched the exchange with an interested eye. "See you in a few." He threw up his hand on his way out.

I smiled uneasily at Anna. She returned the smile, showing no opinion on her face, and we continued with our list, but I knew what she must be thinking. She knew Kip, and she knew, I'm sure, what he was like with women—not "the help" kind of women, but *women.* Kip didn't usually whisper in the ear of his employees.

I could feel the sting rising up my neck from embarrassment. What was I doing, allowing him to ask me out on dates, mixing business with pleasure? Because, like I always do, I relied on fate—the flip of a coin. I should've thought it through; I should have stopped it before it started because now, good or bad, I was stuck with the outcome.

I took the grocery order to the office and set it on the desk. Punching in the website of Miller's Grocery, I completed the order form and sent the order, then I checked the waiting message:

Gerard mentioned that the septic system has backed up. He tried to find you, but was unable to locate you at the time. Kip informed me that he held you hostage for lunch. Gerard needs you to schedule someone to come and alleviate the problem since it is beyond his capabilities.

For the second time today, I felt the prickle of embarrassment. I returned, "I'm so sorry that I wasn't here. I didn't finish with the morning itinerary items until well into my lunchtime, and Kip offered to take me out. I won't let it happen again." I hit send.

In his usual fashion, Robert responded quickly: *Where did he take you?*

"I can't remember the name, but there was a chef named Doug. It was small." I sent my reply.

Robert returned: *Bonacci's. He's pulling out the big guns. How was it?*

I couldn't pinpoint exactly why, but I felt very uncomfortable having this conversation with Robert. I replied reluctantly, "It was really nice. I had the sea bass."

Response: *Did Kip get Doug to send out any appetizers? Spending the extra twenty minutes to have appetizers is a real indication of his interest.*

"The chef sent out his homemade cheese and bread," I sent.

Response: *Not too bad. I think he's smitten. Lucky you.*

How should I respond to that? Thank you? Great? I stared at the computer screen, unsure of what to say when a second message popped up: *Let me give you one piece of information about Kip, and I'll refrain from interfering any further. He can be charming; I've seen it many times before. But he has a very short attention span.*

I sent back, "I'll keep that in mind," my face feeling hot under my skin. What must Robert think of me? I wasn't the type of person who would date someone related to my employer. So why had I ever agreed to flipping that coin?

Without even a beat between thoughts, my mind went straight to Robert and the amusement he'd been hiding that day—his eyes dancing with something behind them, the corners of his mouth turning up just enough to know the smile was there behind his features, waiting. I longed to see it again. With a few clicks, I logged out and headed to the east wing to check on Pippa.

Chapter Seven

My shoes clacked along the floor's surface in the broad, echo-ing hallway on my way toward the east wing. A piece of woodwork caught my eye, and I stopped to examine it. Etched in its surface were a mass of markings, like the teeth of a colossal comb, showing children's heights throughout the years. What tiny heads leaned against this door frame to be measured? I ran my hand over the names. Adelaide. Hester. Philomena. Charles.

My fingers came to rest on another name. Robert. I slid my hand along the wood, feeling the texture of the letters. Further down, I noticed Kip's name and his sister Sloane's. I found Kip's various height markings and did the same for Robert. Would the new buyer sand and paint over this bit of history?

"That one there is mine," Pippa's voice came from behind me as she reached her unsteady hand around me, touching the name Philomena. "I don't know why my father wrote my whole name. I was never called that." Her eyes slid up and down the piece of wood.

"I was just coming to see you. Do you need anything?"

"I was taking a walk." She continued to look at the list of names before us. "I ran into Kip. He tells me you two spent a little time together." Pippa was cordial as she finally pulled her gaze up to my face.

"He took me to lunch. At Bonacci's."

Her eyebrows raised in response. "And how did you find Bonacci's? Was it to your liking?"

"Yes, it was nice, thank you." I couldn't detect the motive in her question.

"I shall suggest that Kip rein in his extravagance," she said, more as though she were thinking out loud, than addressing herself to me particularly; her eyes focused somewhere in the distance behind me.

"What do you mean?" I asked.

"Well dear, a hundred dollars a plate seems a little much for a Tuesday afternoon lunch with an employee."

Before I could respond, Pippa grabbed my elbow for support, her feet still planted in front of the names before her. Her eyes roamed the names again. The whole time, I was contemplating two things: First, the reality that I had eaten one hundred dollars' worth of food for lunch. One hundred dollars! I did a quick calculation. Mom would have had to work four hours to pay for what I had just eaten, yet Kip had thought nothing of spending it at the drop of a hat. And second, that Pippa seemed to be insinuating that there was more going on between me and Kip than just business. Both of these facts were surprisingly troubling.

"It's so depressing that these names in the hallway may be destroyed, painted over by a new owner," I said, trying to change the subject.

"That's the least of it, dear," she said, looking straight ahead as she spoke. Then, without any prompting from me, she began to tell me another story.

As Pippa spoke, her hands were completely unoccupied except for the one holding my arm. Her limbs were still, her facial expressions neutral. I wondered if she had always been like that or, if at ninety-two years old, she just couldn't afford exerting the energy. Nonetheless, when she spoke, I listened.

"Ashford is my maiden name," she began, reaching out her delicate hand and letting her fingers trail the woodwork, each name running under her fingers. "The house was built for my mother, Philomena Ashford. I have her name. My father, Herbert, was a wealthy heir to an oil fortune in Texas. He sold the company and moved to Virginia to build his dream home. He used his money to invest in properties in the area, and he found that he had a knack for it.

"I was raised along with my four siblings in this house. I married my husband Henry Marley in this house, and we had Samuel here. Samuel married Carolyn here, and their children were raised within these walls. Since its creation, this house has been in the sole possession of our family, and now Robert wants to give it away, sell its history, and render its years of labor pains for our family meaningless." Pippa's eyes were glassy with emotion.

"I just don't understand why he would sell it off. Can't he find some use for it? It doesn't seem like he needs the money." I was thinking out loud.

"Because for some God-forsaken reason that I cannot explain, he doesn't care." Pippa shook her head, and we worked our way down the hallway.

A voice broke through our discussion. "Pippa, are you going to hog her all day, or can I have some time with our newest employee?" Kip was leaning against his doorway as we neared his room.

"What could *you* possibly need?" Pippa asked him, an amused expression playing around her eyes.

"Don't be nosy," he teased.

Pippa released my arm and began to toddle toward her room. "I'll leave you two to sort out your business, and Kip, we'll have a chat about your lunch…" she said without looking back.

"Your grandmother says that you need to—and I quote—rein in your extravagance."

"In what way?"

"Kip, you didn't tell me that our lunch wasn't exactly… cheap."

"So? You're worth it," he turned the corner of his mouth up again in that arrogant but likable way.

"Stop trying to flatter me." I gave him my most serious look. "Really, you just met me. Where will we go from here if you're spending that much money on our first lunch out?" I raised my index finger into the air to quiet whatever was about to come out of his mouth. "And! I don't have the kind of money that you do, so it doesn't take that much to impress me."

"What if I'm not trying to impress you? What if I just think you're worth that much?"

"That's a load of crap." I flinched at the straightforward way that the words came out but quickly recovered. Oh well, it was out there now. I might as well just say the rest of it. "You're so used to sweet-talking to get your way that you're not even making sense. How can you even know if I'm *worth it*? You don't know me at all. So don't give me that." The whole time I was talking, Kip was shaking his head back and forth, looking seven years old again.

"That's not true. I'm not trying to flatter you," his voice was slightly louder than normal. "You don't seem fazed by me," He closed the already small gap between us. "What I mean is, you don't seem fazed by money in general and, from what I can tell, you don't care about *my* money." His expression turned sober, removing any shred of little boy I had seen previously. "You seem so genuine. And smart... I've never dated someone who actually reads! Books! I think that someone like you—someone who is caring and unaffected by my flirting—is worth a hundred dollar meal."

My mouth opened to retort, but nothing came out.

The intensity melted on Kip's face, and his features became softer. "So, where should we go for our first date?" he asked, that smirk returning.

I struggled to maintain my poise. I should really put a stop to all of this, but he was reeling me right in. "Like I said, it doesn't take much to impress me."

"Well, were you impressed by my speech just now?" His chest was puffed up in pseudo arrogance.

"You were a little dramatic, don't you think?" I grinned, playing along.

"You liked it," he teased.

All of a sudden, I had an idea: "It's easy for you to spend a hundred dollars. Let's see what you've got when you can't rely on your money." Kip cocked his head and watched me with a perplexed expression. "For our first date, you can't spend more than twenty bucks. I want to see how much of your time and creativity I'm worth." I backed away from his door. "I have to go now. I have a house to manage." Then, I went straight to my room for some solitude to settle my nerves.

❋ ❋ ❋

When the day's tasks were finished, it was about six o'clock, so I checked email once more before I turned in. There were no messages, and, for some reason, I wished that Robert had emailed. I never thought for a moment that I would become this invested in the Marley family. Nothing had gone according to plan since I'd arrived, so I decided to continue the trend.

Impulsively, I composed a quick email to Robert. "Kip wants to take me out on a date." I hit send. I had no explanation for it, but I wanted Robert's approval. I probably should ask him for consent in terms of my employment, but it wasn't that. I wanted *him* to be okay with it.

He responded immediately with: *Do you want to go?*

I typed, "Not sure. I told him that if he really wanted to impress me, he couldn't spend more than twenty dollars. I want to see how creative he can be." Send.

Response: *That should be interesting.*

I asked, "Do you think he's up to the task?" Send.

Response: *Uncertain. He'll be out of his comfort zone.*

"Where would you take a date if you only had twenty dollars?" I hit send, and my fingers began to tremble. I was crossing the business-personal line. I imagined him studying my face the way he had that day in his office, looking for answers in my eyes. His brows pulling together as he looked at me. The clean, spicy smell of him. What was I doing? This had started as a conversation about Kip and me. I was leading it in entirely the wrong direction.

Blank screen.

Come on! Robert, open up! "Cat got your tongue?" Send. Oh my God, he was probably fuming.

After a moment's pause, I had a response: *I'm finding that you are many things, but one that you are not is patient. Give me a minute to contemplate, please. I'd like to think it through.*

Floored by his comeback, I had to close my gaping mouth. I hadn't seen such regular banter emerge from Robert in an email before. With a smile that would not straighten out no matter how hard I tried, the urge to push further began itching me from the inside. Should I? Yep. "Why don't you ponder the idea and give me a call when you have something. I'm going up to bed." Send.

I wiped my damp hands on my shirt and logged off the computer.

❄ ❄ ❄

Now more comfortably dressed in some sweats, I was in the kitchen making a quick bowl of mixed fruit before bed when I heard the moan of the front door. Who could that be? As I walked toward the entryway, I saw a brunette waif of a woman clad from head to toe in Giorgio Armani, dragging her matching luggage through the open doorway, two small children in tow.

"May I help you?" I asked, figuring it must be Sloane Marley.

The two children maneuvered around her and ran past me into the formal sitting room, giggling and squealing the whole way. Should-be-Sloane dropped her bags and held out a deliberate hand. "I'm Sloane Marley. You must be the new house manager." She was noticeably trying to refrain from looking me up and down as I stood before her in my sweatsuit.

I glanced down at myself. "I was just changed for bed. Forgive my appearance. Please, let me help you get your bags," I reached for the largest one.

As we heaved her luggage into the kitchen, Gerard quickly whisked the largest one away as Sloane asked, "So, who's here so far for Christmas?"

"Kip is here and Ms. Marley, of course."

"When's Robert supposed to get here?" she asked, slightly out of breath. With a designer heel-clad foot, she shoved her smaller bag close to one of the larger ones. Obviously preoccupied, her gaze wheeled around the kitchen as she asked, "Where's Anna? Is she off yet? I'm dying for a bite to eat."

"I can call her for you. And Robert said he isn't coming."

"No worries. I'll call her. Robert's not coming? Oh, give me a break. He's so melodramatic. I can't believe he's sulking like that."

"Sulking?" I couldn't resist.

"He and Pippa had it out over the sale of the house. I know she wants to keep it, but it's huge." Sloane's immediate openness was surprising. Snapping me out of my thoughts, Sloane continued, "With Pippa's health failing, Ashford was left to the three of us. Robert has been putting a ton of his own money into the upkeep of the house *and* Pippa's round-the-clock care. She's ninety-two years old. She doesn't have to live here to be happy even if she thinks she does."

"Can't you guys just wait until she's... gone?" I asked in a hushed voice, afraid she may be lurking somewhere in the shadows. Honestly, it probably wouldn't be that long, I thought.

"Robert didn't want to lose money paying for staff and upkeep for the next, maybe, ten years. Pippa's a firecracker. She'll probably live to be over a hundred. He can sell it now and then invest the proceeds."

My cell phone buzzed in my pocket, and the suggestion for Robert to call me came rushing into my mind. Thinking quickly, I grabbed my fruit and said, "Sloane, I have to get this—probably more work to do. Do you mind if I leave you and make my way to my room?"

She waved a well-manicured hand at me. "No, no! Please! I'll see you in the morning."

I thanked her and hustled down the hallway until I was out of earshot before I answered the phone.

"Hi." Robert's voice was less tense tonight.

"Hi," I said back to him. I wasn't quite sure how to proceed. We were out of the realm of business etiquette.

"Busy?" he asked.

"I'm about to eat a bowl of fruit. Do you mind?"

"Be my guest. Chomp away." He was so relaxed.

I wondered if he still hid his grin even when no one was looking. The idea of it amused me, and I had to stifle a huff of air that escaped with a giggle. "So, I take it that you've planned your twenty-dollar date." My heart was thudding in my chest.

"Yes." I could hear his presence, his shifting and swallowing.

"And?"

"Well..."

"Wait!" I cut him off. "I'm walking down the hallway to my room. Let me get inside before you get into it." As I headed toward my room, my head was swimming with the knowledge that Robert was getting personal. What would he tell me? I was giddy with anticipation.

Wobbling against the doorknob with my elbow—the fruit in one hand and the phone in the other—I pushed open the door and shuffled through it, closing it behind me with my knee. Like a schoolgirl, I plopped on top of my bed, poised to hear Robert's date. "Okay, go."

"Well," he cleared his throat and then took a breath. I could tell by his change in breathing that he'd become a little nervous. "So, here it goes. I would take my date to a little brook that flows down the hill behind Ashford. At just the right time every evening during the warm months, a family of ducks stops by, and at dusk you can watch the sun disappear behind the house. That would cost nothing. We'd go inside, and I would play "La Vie en Rose" by Louis Armstrong on the old record player that we have in the sitting room. The cost of that is also free, but I'd have to borrow the record from Anna because it belongs to her."

Who was this person talking to me now? It was as if I had never spoken to this man before. He seemed so different than the person who was causing such grief within his family. More interesting was the fact that, so far, everything he was telling me about this so-called date involved Ashford. So, why did he want to sell it? It was baffling.

"Okay, so if I cover all the five senses, what does that leave? Sight, sound…" I imagined him counting on his fingers. "Taste. After dinner, which I suppose I'd have to make myself with twenty dollars worth of ingredients, I'd take her back outside. We'd take a walk. What does that leave? Smell. I would point out the white rose bush growing alongside the brook. I might even pick one for her if I felt so inclined. Cost: free." He was getting into this. Robert was so calm and sweet—unlike the closed-off person with whom I'd been conversing the last few days.

"And then, touch." There was a slight pause. "I would spread a picnic blanket for us to watch the sun as it sets. Then I'd let my date decide what she wants to do for touch."

Wow. I didn't quite know how to take Robert at this moment. He seemed so sensitive. I exhaled, suddenly realizing that I had been holding my breath. "Nice."

After Robert's explanation of his twenty-dollar date, it was difficult to define the parameters for conversation. A loaded silence filled the line between us. Then Robert began to speak first. "I'll be interested to see what Kip thinks up. You'll have to let me know how it goes."

"I will." What was happening? Why was I encouraging this sort of discussion with Robert when I had just agreed to three dates with Kip? This flirty provocation wasn't in my nature. The line was uncomfortably quiet, so I attempted to fill the absence of conversation. "Sloane's here."

"Oh?"

"She said that you're being melodramatic." I thought I could at least offer that, since he'd been so candid about the date.

"What?" he asked, his voice now dubious.

"She said that you need to stop pouting—no, sulking—and come to Ashford for Christmas."

"Did she?"

"Yep."

"Well." And the door to Robert's thoughts slammed shut. He was short again. With that one word, he made it clear that he was not going to offer any further insight into his decision to stay away.

I figured I'd let him off of the hook since he had been so open about the date. "I need to go to bed. I'll be waiting for the itinerary at eight."

"Have a good night. Do let me know how it goes with Kip."

"You too. Have a good night."

We said our goodbyes, and I put my phone on the table. Just as I was climbing under the covers, the phone rang again. Scrambling to answer it, I hoped that it was Robert changing his mind about Christmas. It was Megan. She had another showing. Next Thursday at ten a.m. But that's not why she was calling. She wanted to know about Kip, and I remembered my text. So, with a pounding sensation growing in my head, I gave her the bare details. After I hung up, I climbed into bed and thought about how tomorrow, I'd like to walk down to that brook and take a look at it.

Chapter Eight

I was downstairs at approximately seven thirty, so I decided to venture to the kitchen to see if Anna had made any breakfast. Sloane was sitting on a stool at the island, sipping a cup of tea from a traditional cup and saucer when I arrived. Her appearance was plainer today. "Good morning," she said, before taking a sip and then blowing on the liquid's surface.

"Good morning." I helped myself to a glass and a mug. Anna breezed in and out as she collected the necessities for cooking breakfast. I poured some juice from a crystal decanter for later, made a cup of coffee, and gestured toward a stool next to Sloane. "Do you mind?"

"Be my guest," she politely shifted in her seat, allowing me more personal space on my stool. I climbed up beside her. Anna had now stationed herself on the other side of the island and was cutting vegetables. Perhaps she was making omelets. I was hopeful that she would.

We sipped our drinks for a moment in silence, until I caught Anna's attention. "Anna, do you, by chance, have the old record called 'La Vie en Rose'?"

It was as if I'd just stood on my chair and thrown my mug onto the tile floor, watching it shatter into a million pieces. Both women's heads whirled up, with looks of complete confusion on their faces. *What* had I just asked?

"Why do you want it?" Anna asked, still wearing an apprehensive expression.

"Robert said you had it. I just wanted to listen to it."

Sloane searched my face before she asked, "Robert told you about that song?"

I was afraid to answer. "In a general sense. He just mentioned that song, and that Anna was the one who had it." I felt more uneasy the more I spoke.

"And *Robert* told you this?" Sloane asked, more clarifying than asking.

"Yes." I didn't want to say any more.

Then Sloane's expression changed from trepidation to a look of awe. Her eyes scanned me up and down, and she asked, "How much do you talk to Robert? …to know such a personal bit of trivia?"

"I don't really talk to him much. And I don't know the story behind this particular song. He just said that…" What do I say? That he'd play it on our imaginary twenty-dollar date? "He just said that I might like it. That's all."

"He said *you* might like it," she repeated.

Yes? "Yes." There was no going back now. "Is there a story behind that song?"

Anna continued to chop faster and looked only at her vegetables, but Sloane set down her cup and saucer and leaned in closer. "That was our parents' favorite song," Sloane began. "They danced to it all the time when we were little. Kip doesn't remember as much, but Robert and I know all of the words." Anna looked up at Sloane through her eyelashes, but continued to chop.

"I wonder why... he'd think that I'd like that song then." I said aloud after sipping my coffee. The warmth from the cup sent a shiver through my shoulders.

"Well, that's what really shocked me," Sloane said. "He once told me that the only song of any meaning to him was that song. So, when I got married, he played it for me, and when I had my babies he played it. And, he told me that the next time he played it, he hoped it would be for his own someone special."

In my head, I went into rationalization mode. It was only a fictitious date. Maybe that's why he had picked that song. It most certainly couldn't have anything to do with me.

Anna had stopped chopping. "I have it on my iPod. I'll get it for you." She hurried out of the room. Sloane resumed sipping her tea, not taking her eyes off me. I wasn't sure what to say, if anything.

When Anna returned, she had her iPod with the song already selected and paused. With a curious expression, she handed it over to me.

"Do you mind if I borrow this for a little while?" Anna shook her head. "I'm just going to take a little stroll outside. I'll be back in the house by eight." Walking out of the room, I could feel both sets of eyes bearing down on me from behind.

After I'd put on my coat and scarf, I let myself out of the back of the house. My hands were a little jittery, and I wasn't sure if it was because of the coffee or the events that had just transpired. I placed the headphones on my head and walked the lengthy piece of property toward the edge of the hill behind the house. The ground was steep beneath my feet as I made my way down the incline to a small patch of woods. Ambling through them, I came upon the brook that I was almost positive was Robert's. It snaked the entire length of the property. A mass of spiny stems jutted out near the brook, and I thought that it must be the rose bush he'd mentioned. Of course, there were no roses in December.

It was cold and foggy, but I sat down on the wet ground and hit play on the iPod. I watched the water bubble in front of me as I listened to the words to Robert's song with new meaning. After the song was finished, I found it difficult to get it out of my head.

❊ ❊ ❊

I arrived back at the office at exactly eight a.m., and the itinerary was already waiting for me. No messages.

Opening a new screen, I sent a message to Robert: "Come home for Christmas."

Response: *I'll be in Spain.*

"Really? Why?" Send.

Response: *Business.*

I went out on a limb. "You love this house. Why won't you come home to your family for Christmas?"

Response: *I don't love that house. It's a financial waste. And, I'll see my family another time. I have to go to Spain.*

"You don't love this house? Then how come on your imaginary date, you decided to stay at Ashford? You spent the whole date here. You even borrowed a record from Anna who is at this house. Explain that." Send.

Response: *I'd rather not.*

Take a chance for once, Robert! Open up! I didn't know how far I could push him. He was still, my employer, even if we did have a bizarre working relationship. I replied, "Suit yourself." Send.

I looked up and Kip was walking into the room. "You're always in here emailing Robert. At least I know where to find you."

"You're up early," I said.

Kip walked around the desk. "Sloane made me get up." His expression was playful. He moved nearer to me, invading my personal space. His face was too close to mine. "It's good to see you," he beamed down at me.

"It's good to see you awake before noon," I said. "Have you thought about our date?"

He gently reached out and held my elbow. "I'm still thinking. These things can't be rushed."

I backed up slightly. "You've got nothing," I kidded.

Kip stepped forward, filling the space between us again. "Give me time. I want it to be perfect, and you won't let me spend any money."

"You have money. You have twenty dollars." I stepped back again.

Kip allowed me my space this time. "Wanna meet me for lunch today? It'll be free. We can eat in the kitchen." His warm smile was easy to like. I enjoyed being around him. It was entertaining, to say the least.

"Sure."

Kip backed his way to the door. "Can't wait," he said and left the room.

I stood in the empty office just looking around. Already, I felt so close to this family. I noticed that I had a message waiting, so I opened it. It read: *Believe me; nothing about this situation suits me.*

I closed the message and quickly stepped away from the computer screen, feeling as if Robert had been spying on me. Before walking out, I shot one more look at the computer just to be sure he couldn't see me.

❀ ❀ ❀

In the butler's pantry I dialed eighty-eight on the intercom-thing. The staff arrived in the kitchen as did Pippa, Sloane, and Kip. I took in that moment. Already, I recognized so many faces. Breaking up this group seemed unimaginable. "We have a showing scheduled for next Thursday at ten a.m. Staff, please don't start any large tasks until after the showing. Let's get the house ready. Marley family, you will need to be prepared to vacate different areas as they are being shown on that day." I clasped my hands together. "That's all! Thanks and have a great rest of the day." I walked out of the room and said a prayer that the house wouldn't sell.

Pippa tottered out behind me, so I seized the moment and turned around to face her. "Ms. Marley," I began, a little anxious. "May I ask you a personal question?"

She grabbed my arm and turned me in the other direction. "Let's go to the sitting room, shall we?"

I took Pippa into the sitting room and helped her lower herself down on the large settee. She looked at me expectantly, her frail body as still as a statue. I bit my lip. Then I blurted before I could change my mind, "Tell me more about you and Robert. Why are you two so... unfriendly?"

With her hands elegantly resting in her lap, she took a deep breath and exhaled before answering. "We are very much alike, Robert and I. I think we are so alike that we can't understand each other, if that makes any sense at all. He was short changed, you see." She paused as if finding the words. "Carolyn, his mother, was gentle and loving, and she also had a way of telling you just what she was thinking—very straightforward.

"She always asked direct questions and expected no-nonsense answers. She loved Samuel more than anything, and they radiated happiness when they were together." I had only a moment to digest this information before she continued. "Robert was robbed of that relationship and left with only mine and his, and it proved to be less than perfect. Both of us managed our grief with anger, and we fought like the dickens. When one fights with another long enough, the fury consumes the relationship. It's unfortunate." Her eyes were distant.

"Robert told Allie to listen to 'La Vie en Rose'," Sloane's voice cut through the air as she entered the sitting room.

Pippa glanced in my direction before her eyes rested on Sloane. "Is that a fact?" Her head then pivoted back to me, and she scanned me from head to toe as if just now actually noticing me.

I shrugged, feeling the embarrassment swell within my body. "He just said that I might like it." I was really stretching the truth. He never actually said that *I* would like it. He did say, however that he'd play it on his twenty-dollar date, which may or may not have been with me. I watched their glances, loaded with insinuation. Faking a look at my watch, I lied, "Oh! I really need to get going. I have some things to do before the showing next Thursday."

I dismissed myself from the room and headed to the office to check email. When I got there, I was a little disappointed to see that I had no messages. I typed, "You have a showing at ten o'clock Thursday," and hit send.

Robert responded: *Great. Let me know how it goes.*

"Sure." Send.

I wanted to ask him why he'd chosen "La Vie en Rose" for his twenty-dollar date. I wanted to ask if the date was with me or a fictitious person. I opened an empty message screen, and I started to type, but I couldn't do it. The delete key depressed beneath my finger until all of my typing had been erased. Then I walked out of the room, the song in question still swimming around in my head.

Chapter Nine

The showing was over, and I needed to email Robert to let him know. I still hadn't asked him about the song; I had lost my nerve. He had shown in the past that he wasn't keen on answering personal questions, and this one was about as personal as it could get, so he probably wouldn't answer it anyway. I sent him the septic bill.

There was a message waiting on the computer. It read: *How did the showing go?*

I responded, "I'm not sure. I didn't get to talk to Megan. I'm almost certain she'll call me shortly." I hit send, and in seconds, my phone started ringing. Wow, Megan was right on the mark. I answered.

"I thought we could talk instead of email. It may be a little easier," Robert's voice came through my phone, and instantly, I became all twitchy and short of breath.

"Sure," was all I could say.

"How has the day been going? All go well for the showing?"

"Yes." I swallowed nervously. I wanted so badly to cut to the chase and get to the questions that I wanted answered, but I was too nervous to do it.

"Everything else going all right?"

"Yes. I was just about to take my lunch break. I'm eating at twelve with Kip." I added, "In the kitchen," just to make sure it didn't sound too romantic.

"I hope that's not his twenty-dollar date." I could sense Robert's humor even without seeing him. If I closed my eyes, I could almost remember the scent of him, almost smell it.

"No. But speaking of the twenty-dollar date…" My pulse began pounding as I continued, "Tell me about 'La Vie en Rose'." There. I did it. I felt like I was about to pass out, but I did it.

The other end of the line was quiet, and I sat on pins and needles, hoping that I hadn't ruined the conversation. "What about it?" he said finally.

"Tell me the history of it," I said.

"What do you mean?"

"Look, I mentioned that song to Anna and Sloane last week, and they acted really weird." I couldn't bear to tell him the whole story. Okay, here it goes—the most important question. "I hadn't heard it before. I told them that you thought I would like it. *Do* you think *I* would like it?"

"I don't know… You might like it, yes."

Did that mean what I think it did? "When Sloane told Ms. Marley that you talked to me about the song, she stared at me really strangely." A burst of laughter on the other end sent me jumping out of my skin. "What's so funny?"

"You'd have to know the whole story…" Which I was nearly sure that I did.

"So, are you going to tell it to me?"

He was still chuckling. A flutter of happiness swam through me at the sound of it. "It's a story for another time, perhaps.

I just find the mental picture of those two amusing. I probably gave them enough to talk about until after the holiday." He laughed again.

I decided that maybe I should ask my next question while he was obviously in a good mood. One last shot for Pippa. "Robert," I began in a more serious tone.

His voice became gentle. "Yes?"

"Why are you selling this house?" I chewed on the inside of my lip as I waited for his answer.

"I've told you why." He was humorless now.

"You haven't told me the real reason that you're selling." Then I let him have it. "Ms. Marley told me the story about your parents, and I know how you and Ms. Marley don't get along. But, Robert, this is your house. It's been in your family for generations. Why would you want to get rid of it?"

He cleared his throat. I could hear his sigh in the quiet of the line. *Please answer me, Robert.*

"The only thing that connects me to that house is tragedy. My parents died when I was young, and I grieved there. Pippa raised me, and we didn't get along the entire time, and I was angry there. Now, it's nothing but a shell of lives that are gone and used up. Kip is a disaster—no offense. He has no direction and lives on his inheritance. And he's never there. Sloane is getting divorced and trying to raise two children alone. And not at Ashford. And Pippa… Pippa's wasting away in there by herself. They don't need that house, and I don't want it. I don't want that house," he repeated.

"Ms. Marley sees it differently, you know."

"Of course. How could she not see it differently?"

"I see it differently too." I went out on a limb. Who was I to have an opinion on matters of this house? I was just the sister of the real estate agent for God's sake.

"Tell me how you see it, Allie." He was not nearly as tense-sounding as I had anticipated after this discussion.

"I've seen the staff and worked with them. Anna has always been a soothing force in the house since you were little. Your name—along with others in your family—is carved into the woodwork in the hallway, etched into the history of this house. The rooms have witnessed your family's growth for generations. The staff would be split up, the walls painted over, and Pippa would be left to live in some hospital-like setting somewhere."

He countered, "I have nothing more to put into that house."

"What about a family of your own? Don't you want that?"

"I'd rather you not worry about these matters." He sounded irritated.

Kip popped his head into the study. "Hey," he whispered loudly, "Anna has our lunch ready." His eyes were on me expectantly.

I mouthed, "Okay" and gave him a pleasant look even though my insides were turning over. Robert still hadn't responded. "Robert, I have to go. My lunch is ready."

"So it is." And he was back to himself.

❊ ❊ ❊

After taking a few moments to collect myself after that call, I met Kip in the kitchen. My stomach felt uneasy, and I didn't know how to resolve the situation. With all my inner strength, I tried to push it out of my head and enjoy my lunch.

The table in the kitchen was aglow with candlelight from the center of the table. "Candles for lunch? You shouldn't have," I kidded.

His eyes sparkled, and I could see a resemblance to Pippa as he leaned around the table and pulled out my chair. "I've thought of my date for us," he beamed.

"The *twenty-dollar* date?" I reminded him.

"Yeah, and don't forget that we flipped for three dates. This is only the first of three."

"I haven't forgotten," I said. I hadn't forgotten because I kept playing it out in my head. Why had I agreed to go on dates with Kip Marley? I should not have been involved with a member of the family for whom I was working, no matter how flirty he was. But I *had* agreed. Because it was nice to be pursued, even if he was a playboy. "So, tell me about this twenty-dollar date."

Anna came over with two loaded plates and set them in front of us. When I thanked her, I swear she looked as if she were assessing us. I couldn't tell if I was being paranoid or observant. Maybe I shouldn't eat lunch with him in front of her anymore.

"It's a secret," Kip interrupted my thoughts.

I pulled my eyes from Anna and looked at Kip. "What's a secret?" I asked.

"Our date."

"Oh yes! Sorry, I was thinking about work." I wiggled my fingers in the air, as if pushing the thoughts away from the space between us. "Done now. Won't do it again. Let's talk about our secret date. When is it?"

"Tonight."

"You look very proud of yourself," I said, cutting my chicken into bite-sized pieces.

Kip raised his eyebrows. "I am," his head bobbing up and down.

"What time should I be ready?"

He pursed his lips in thought. "How about seven?"

"Sure. I'll be ready at seven then." I stabbed at my vegetables until I could think of something to add. "So, what have you been up to today?"

"Really, just planning the date and hanging out. I played darts down in the game room for a while, and I went to visit Pippa."

I glanced over at Anna who was wiping the counters down. She didn't look up; her lips pursed. Inside I cringed again at what she must think of me right now. I wanted to rush over to her and explain that this was not like me at all. I didn't normally do this sort of thing. But I knew how it looked. I was crossing a line, getting involved personally with one of the Marleys.

"Did you tell Ms. Marley about our dates?" I asked. I didn't want to even ask the question out loud, but I was genuinely curious after Sloane and Pippa's short discussion of my connection to Robert's song.

"I did." He looked up from his food.

"What did she say? Was she okay with it?"

"She told me not to play around and only to date you if I was serious about you." He took another bite. "I think it's because you're an employee."

Or because your brother might be interested. "You're probably right." I looked down at my food and felt my cheeks getting hot with the thought. Might Robert really be interested? I felt an inexplicable connection to him, but was it all in my own head? No matter, even while he was miles away from me, I pulled toward him like North pulls to South.

❃ ❃ ❃

After lunch, I checked email, and I actually had a message. I couldn't hide my excitement as I opened it. But when I started to read the words, my heart dropped into my stomach.

The message read:

Allie, you have full control of the house. I am leaving this evening for Spain to view a property earlier than originally planned. If there is an offer on the house, please email me and I will respond accordingly. Otherwise, there will be no need to email me until you hear differently. Refer to past itineraries for general maintenance and staff management. Any questions can be directed to the staff or other family members. Thanks.

Thanks? That's all? *Thanks?* Where in Spain was he going? When would he come back? I could feel a disturbing and unexpected sense of worry spread throughout my body. I stared at the screen just hoping to get another message, but there was nothing. He was gone. Off-line.

I wandered the house for a while. No one was checking on me anyway. For a part of the day, I went to my room and took a nap. I felt low, knowing that I wouldn't be corresponding with Robert in the near future, or maybe ever. Then I was kind of angry, and I couldn't explain why. The creaks and groans of the house were the only sounds surrounding me as I sat in my room until it was time to get ready for my date. With resolve, I got myself together, and I went to see Kip.

Going through the grand entranceway at the front of the house, I approached him from behind. He moved from one foot to the other, seemingly a little nervous as he stood there, unaware that my eyes were on him. Wearing an unfussy sweater and a pair of jeans, he heard my footsteps and turned around. His scent wafted toward me—he smelled a little like the fresh cedar that our neighbor used to stack up in the strip of grass between our houses growing up. I was glad to see that his clothes were casual because I too had jeans on. With a warm expression, he put his arm around my waist. I stiffened a little in response, but I made a conscious effort to relax. After all, this was a date. No matter how I had been feeling about Robert lately, he wasn't here, and Kip was. And he was giving it a good effort so far.

He led me to the sitting room where he had a fire going and a lavish spread of food set up on the floor just in front of the hearth.

"I'm nearly sure this didn't cost twenty dollars," I said, pointing to the grapes, cheeses, little sandwiches, and freshly roasted nuts, all neatly arranged. I was willing to bet that Kip hadn't prepared it, after seeing the state of his bedroom.

"I stole it from Anna."

"I don't think stealing is part of the deal. All of this costs money."

"It didn't come out of *my* twenty bucks," he grinned down at me.

I let it slide. He was trying, after all.

A basket of card games sat next to the spread. Boxes of Old Maid and Go Fish peeked out from the basket. "Those are Sammy and Paul's." He looked at me with a slight note of insecurity on his face. "*They're* free, right?" I accepted his statement with a nod of my head, and Kip leaned in close to my ear, "Plus, I have to admit that they're kind of fun to play." The hair on my right arm stood up as his breath fell along the base of my neck.

I sat down on the floor in front of the array of finger foods. Kip uncorked a bottle of wine and poured two glasses. He placed them next to the food.

"Where'd this wine come from?" I taunted him.

He exhaled in mock annoyance. "The cellar."

I shook my head back and forth. Then he sat down beside me, his legs stretched out straight on the floor and crossed at the ankle, leaning back on his hands. The air smelled of burning embers, and my face felt warm from the glow of the fire.

"This is our appetizer," he explained, suddenly sitting up. I thought again that he looked a little nervous. He handed me a glass of wine.

"Thank you," I reached out for the glass and took a rather large swallow to settle my nerves.

"Our dinner's coming."

I nibbled on the snacks while Kip reached into the games basket to retrieve our first game. His face was turned down toward the basket, and I could see the familiar redness on his jaw line from shaving. The thought that he'd spruced up just for me made me smile. He pulled out a baggie with slips of paper folded inside it. "I made this game for us so that we could get to know each other better. You have to answer truthfully," he explained.

I took a sip of wine, and it went down easily, the warmth of it slipping through my body. Kip reached into the bag and pulled out a slip of paper. "You first," he said softly.

I opened the paper and read aloud the statement. "Tell me three habits that the perfect person must have or not have." I thought about this. "Number one: He has to floss his teeth."

"Done," Kip said.

I continued, "Number two: He can't chew with his mouth open." I huffed out a chuckle through my nose as he pointed to his closed lips while he chewed his sandwich. "And three: He can't bite his nails." With one hand in the air, Kip showed off his perfectly trimmed fingernails.

Setting down his glass, Kip reached into the bag and pulled out a slip of paper. "Tell me one thing you hate and one thing you like," he read. "I…" There was no pause for thought. He shrugged and then explained, "I made these, so I already have all of the answers."

With a grin on his face, he continued, "I hate having to be somewhere at a specific time, and I like the way your head turns to the side a little when you listen to people talk."

My head straightened from its cocked position, and I shot him a playful look. I reached in and pulled out another slip, and, just as I was about to read it, the familiar sound of bells rang through the house. Kip hopped up. "That will be dinner," he said as he bounded toward the front door.

He returned moments later, with a gourmet-looking pizza box balanced on one arm. "This was my twenty dollars." That crooked grin returned to his face as he set it down near us. "I'll divvy the pizza. You go ahead and read your next question."

I smoothed the next piece of paper between my fingers. "If you could go anywhere in the world, where would you go and why?" I looked at the words until they became distorted in front of me. Where would I go? "I don't know," I answered honestly.

"You don't know? Come on. Isn't there some place you've never seen before that you'd like to see? Or isn't there anyone out there who you'd like to visit?" A thought hung in the air, dangling in front of me, but I wasn't allowing it to register. Against my will, it came to me anyway. I was *not* going to say Spain. "Australia, I suppose. That might be fun." I took a bite of my pizza, chewed, and swallowed.

Kip pulled out the next slip of paper. "Tell one thing you like about the other person." His eyes studied me. "Physically, it would be your legs, but really, I like your personality." The corner of his mouth turned up in that seductive way of his as he said, "If I'd have said just that I liked your personality, you might have thought that I didn't think you were attractive. So, I threw the legs in to make sure that you knew that I think you're… pretty amazing all around."

I could feel my skin prickle as Robert came to mind. Did Robert think I was pretty amazing all around? An unexpected anxiousness crept up within me all of a sudden. What was I doing? "Thank you," I said, my thoughts still elsewhere. Robert was in Spain, so he must not think I'm amazing-anything or he'd have come home. And here was Kip, trying his very best on our date. Focus. Kip. Not Robert.

He reached over and held my chin, pulling my face up toward his as smoothly as if he'd done it a million times before. "I do think you're amazing," he said, leaning closer to me. My limbs began to feel weightless and unsteady. His lips pressed lightly against mine, and I could feel his soft, unfamiliar skin against my face. I closed my eyes and lost myself in the moment.

Chapter Ten

The house looked as if someone had flipped a Christmas switch. The Dunford Nurseries' employees were unloading trees by eight a.m. They carried in two enormous Spruce trees, one for the entranceway and one for the sitting room. The staff busily unpacked lights and ornaments. And—relatively unusual for December in Virginia—snow sheeted down in a symphony of white outside.

Sloane and her kids were making a gingerbread house with Anna. "Good morning," I said, joining them. Paul, who had just had his fourth birthday, he was sure to tell me, was attempting and failing to hold up the sides of the house, while Sammy, the one-year-old, was eating nearly all of the gumdrops. Anna refilled them as needed. I reached over and held up one of the rectangles of gingerbread as Paul squeezed icing on the edge as well as my four fingers.

Kip rounded the corner and came over to us, standing behind me. I twisted up to see him. "Did Sloane get you up this morning?" Sloane shook her head. "It's…" I released the gingerbread and turned my icing-covered fingers over to view my watch. "Eight fifteen."

Kip took my hand and started to nibble the icing off my fingers. "Good morning. And no, Sloane didn't wake me up. I wanted to get up."

"Oh really," I said skeptically, reclaiming my hand and wiping it with a towel.

"Yes. Really. And the Christmas tree guys were being loud." He leaned in and snatched a tiny kiss near my ear. Anna was looking. Judging me, I could tell. I pulled away quickly, but Sloane caught sight of it and clamped her eyes onto Kip for an instant as she leaned in to help Paul. I shouldn't have let him kiss me last night, I thought. It had moved the relationship to a different level—one with which I wasn't entirely comfortable.

"Moe, Mummy?" Sammy asked for yet another round of gumdrops.

"No, sweetie. It's too early in the morning. Let's use what's left to decorate the house."

Kip settled next to Sammy while I got up and made my usual cup of coffee. Paul reached over the decorative treats to grab another bag of icing. I took the steaming cup back to the table, the cool winter draft wrapping around my ankles.

"Uncle Kip, can you cut the tip for me?" he asked. Kip dutifully prepared the bag of icing while slipping gumdrops to Sammy under the table. "Who is that lady?" Paul asked Kip as he took the icing from his uncle.

Kip followed Paul's line of vision over to me. "That's my friend Allie. She's really nice." I could see Paul digesting this information. Kip continued, "I like her a lot," he said, reaching across the table and tickling Paul on his sides. Paul squealed with delight and knocked half of his house over.

"Uh oh," remarked Sammy as he grabbed the rolling gumdrops and popped them into his mouth.

"Careful!" Sloane frantically grabbed the pieces of house that had fallen while eyeing Kip and me. She gently helped the kids pile up the pieces until they resembled a house again. Her eyes darted from the house to me and then to Kip in that order, her lips slightly pursed.

"So!" Kip turned to me. "What do you want to do today?" If he noticed Sloane's expression, he was obviously ignoring it.

"I have to work."

"When do you get your little itinerary from Robert?"

I suppressed a cringing feeling. "Robert's in Spain, so he isn't sending anything."

"What?" Sloane looked up from the pile of gingerbread.

"He's doing some business in Spain, apparently," I said.

"That's a load of bull," Sloane spit. "Kip, can you help the kids while I chat with Allie?" She asked, practically dragging me out of the kitchen by the arm.

Once we were out of earshot, Sloane whispered anxiously, "*What is going on?*"

"What do you mean?"

Her eyes swung up to the sky in frustration. "One minute you're telling me that Robert is offering to play you his favorite song in all of the world—and let's just say that Robert does not possess an overabundance of favorite anything—and the next, you have Kip planting kisses all over you. *What is going on?*"

Oh, God. How do I explain? I decided to just give it to her straight. "Robert is my employer. He simply suggested that I might like that song. There is nothing going on there. But Kip has been flirting with me since he arrived." I discretely leaned backward to catch a peek at him through the doorway. He was helping Paul add the roof.

Sloane studied the space above my head, contemplating some thought. "Allie, Kip flirts with everyone, and *any* mention by Robert of that song is a major thing. He does *not* throw that kind of information around in common conversation. It means more to him than you think it does."

"Let me explain the context." I gave the details of the twenty-dollar date and told Sloane how I made Robert come up with one as well. "I asked him later if he thought I'd like the song. You know, to clarify if the date had been for me. He just said that he did think I might like the song. He didn't bother to elaborate, and I'm still not very clear if he meant anything by it at all. That was it—he thinks I *might* like the song."

"I'm sure you've figured out that he's a man of few words. He meant that song for you, Allie. I think he's interested." Sloane headed back into the kitchen.

Clearly, Robert wasn't interested if he'd chosen to go to Spain instead of coming home for Christmas.

Kip was sitting between the boys, eating gumdrops and wiping icing on his shirt. Paul was laughing and spreading more icing on Kip's hands. Noticing our entrance, Kip stood up, licking his fingers. Just then, Anna walked in, gave us a little look, and began organizing cabinets for Tom McCray's arrival.

"We should probably get out of Anna's way," Kip suggested to me only. Sloane continued to watch us. "And," he whispered in my ear, "I have an idea for something to do today."

❆ ❆ ❆

By late afternoon, the snow had collected in billowing drifts on the grounds. Most of the house staff had been given time off because of the accumulation, and I had little to do. So, I turned up at one of the many back doors to the house wearing, as Kip had instructed, a thick coat, scarf, hat, and gloves. I opened the door, and Kip trudged up from outside wearing the ski gear that he'd worn when he'd first arrived at Ashford. He was dragging what looked to be a wooden children's sled. After catching sight of me in the open doorway, he lumbered through the ever-deepening snow to meet me.

The sled slid haphazardly toward my feet as Kip came to a stop in front of where I was standing. His cheeks were pink from the wind, and his sunglasses had snowflakes collecting on them. "Here…" he motioned toward the sled.

Anxiety knitted in my stomach. "You don't really want me to get on that thing," I said as I looked up at him, blinking the falling snow from my lashes. It was coming down now in gigantic wet flakes, falling like icy feathers to the ground.

Kip turned around and waved his arm through the air, "You have never been down a hill as fun as this one. I used to ski it as a child."

He pulled me toward him with a gloved hand. "Come on, I'll ride with you." Then he began to guide us through the back lawn toward the top of the hill leading down to Robert's brook.

"Isn't there water at the bottom of this hill?" I asked apprehensively.

"Sure, but we won't slide into it. We'll slow down just before the embankment of trees. I've done this before, Allie. You're in good hands," he teased.

Kip placed the sled at the top of the hill, his thick gloves black as night against the snow, and motioned for me to get on. I obeyed and scooted to the front of it. He stepped around the back of the seat, straddling me, resting his feet atop the blades. Using his hands to push off the ground beneath us, he sent the sled down the hill toward the brook below. He grabbed onto me, holding onto my waist firmly with both arms.

The air was momentarily knocked out of my lungs as we plunged forward. The wind stung my face and Kip's arms pressed into my body. Against my will, a scream exploded from deep within my chest as we plummeted toward the base of the hill.

After what seemed like hours, not minutes, the sled came to rest at the bottom, dumping us into the snow in a chaotic heap of arms and legs. I scrambled to arrange myself with my trembling, gloved hands as Kip disentangled himself from my limbs.

"Was that not the best hill you've ever slid down?"

My breath billowed out from my mouth as I attempted to form words. "That was a little much," I panted. Kip grinned and began to brush the snow off of his clothes. I walked a few feet and put my hands on my knees, letting my head fall forward to regain my breath. After I felt like I could stand without passing out, I started to look around. We were beside the brook. It was completely frozen. The rose bush held lines of snow on its bare branches. A few brown leaves peeked out from beneath the blanket of white covering the trees.

"It's not much to look at right now, is it?" Kip had joined me.

"It's really pretty," I remarked. "Do you come down here a lot?"

Kip pouted and shook his head. "I've never given it much thought, actually. I can't tell you the last time I've been down here."

"Did you play down here as a kid or anything?"

"No, not really. Robert used to come down here and read a lot when he was a kid."

The brook looked barren, but I imagined what it would be like in the summer. I let this thought warm me as the snow fell on its icy surface.

❅ ❅ ❅

I was frozen to the bone by the time we made it back into the house. Kip suggested that we have some of Anna's hot chocolate. He explained how she made it herself with dried milk, cocoa, raw sugar, and her own homemade marshmallows. Apparently, it was to die for.

While Anna prepared our beverages, I stopped by my room to freshen up and dispose of my winter garb. As I was unwrapping my wet clothes from my body, I noticed that my phone had a missed call. A tingling sensation swam through the palms of my hands as I picked it up. I held my breath, and I hit the button to see who had called. Then my shoulders fell. It was Megan. I dialed her number.

"Where have you been?" She was clearly annoyed.

"I was outside sledding with Kip."

"What?"

I knew that would get her.

"So, dish up. What's going on with you two?"

How to explain? "I'm really not sure."

"Do you like him?" Megan asked, no longer irritated, but with an unmasked giddiness.

"What is this? Seventh grade?" I couldn't help but smile.

"You know what I mean."

I thought about this question: *Do you like him?* I didn't really know the answer to that. "I don't know if I *like* him or not. He's a nice guy." I struggled for an explanation.

"You either do or you don't." Everything with Megan was always clear-cut. She never had any gray areas. My whole life was a gray area.

"I'll let you know when I make up my mind. How about that? So, why did you call me? Any reason in particular?"

"Yeah. I have an offer on the house."

Chapter Eleven

I sat in front of the computer, my hands trembling with the thought of what I was about to type. The keys clicked slowly beneath my fingers as I composed my message: "Robert, there has been an offer made on the house. Please advise." Send. I waited, hoping that Robert was by the computer.

After twenty minutes with no response, I went to the kitchen to meet Kip. Paul and Sammy were seated in the kitchen slurping their chocolate milk and nibbling cookies while Anna concocted our beverages, making small talk with Kip. Had those kids left the table at all today? Sloane came into the room with a worried look on her face.

"Is everything okay?" I asked.

Her eyelashes were wet, and the rims of her eyes were dark red. "I may not be able to stay for Christmas here at Ashford. Jackson, my ex-husband…" Her eyes blinked rapidly, and she swallowed hard. "His lawyer called and told me that we have to meet in South Carolina to finalize who gets what in this God-awful divorce, and I have nothing to do with the kids during all of this…" Despite her efforts, the tears came anyway.

I walked over to her and rubbed her back up and down, unsure of how to comfort her. "I could watch the kids for you while you're gone. How many days would it take?"

"I couldn't ask you to do that. You don't have any kids of your own, and you can't imagine what round-the-clock work they are." She cleared her throat and discretely wiped under one eye. Her hands were shaky, and the sight of that made me want to help her in any way I could.

"I *can* imagine! I was a nanny for eleven years. I have a degree in early childhood education. I know exactly what to do."

Sloane's eyes bulged with this news. "Really? It would only be a short time. I could fly out and be back in a matter of days. Would you mind?"

"Not at all." I looked over to Paul and Sammy who were now asking Anna for seconds.

Sloane broke into plan-mode. "This is an old house, and the baby monitors don't get good reception in here, so you'd have to move rooms, if that's okay—to be nearer to the boys. There's an available room next to Sammy's room—and Paul will be across the hall—over in the east wing." I noticed Kip perk up.

"That would be no problem." I really didn't have that much stuff, so I could move quite easily.

"I'd like to leave tomorrow morning very early if I can get a flight, so you may want to move tonight. That way you can hear Sammy if he gets up in the night. He sometimes does that when he's staying somewhere that isn't his house."

"I see."

She went on spouting times and routines for the boys. Her mind was visibly racing—I could see it on her face. Anna brought Kip his hot chocolate as he settled next to me at the table. I tried to scoot my chair a little further from his since Anna was watching. Who knows what she was thinking of me at that moment. No sense making it worse.

"Oh! And Paul doesn't nap, but Sammy does. He naps around twelve fifteen and usually sleeps a few hours. Wake him if he isn't up by three." Anna had put a pad and pencil in front of Sloane, and she was madly scribbling the details while I sipped my hot chocolate. It *was* delicious.

"Where are you going, Mommy?" Paul chimed in.

Sloane turned to Paul, and instantly I could see her cheeks redden in splotches that extended down her neck. "Mommy has to have a meeting with Daddy to see what stuff is his and what stuff is mine."

"You don't know that? I always know what toys are mine and what toys are Sammy's," he said proudly.

Her face contorted into a forced smile. "Well, some of the things we've shared so long that now I can't remember whose they are."

Paul's face was stoic when he learned this bit of information. "Yeah, that would be hard. What if you can't decide who it belongs to?"

I broke into the conversation. "They could always flip for it." I could see the interest written on Paul's face. "That's what I do. Want to see something cool? I'll be right back," I said as I excused myself.

I returned momentarily, holding out my Susan B. Anthony flipping coin.

"What's that?" Paul was obviously impressed.

"It's my flipping coin. When I can't decide something, I flip for it." I turned the coin in his direction so that he could see the profile of Susan B. Anthony. "This side is heads." I turned it over to the side with the eagle. "And this side is tails."

"Mommy should use *that* coin. Can you give it to her while she's with Daddy?" Sloane attempted to discourage her son from this request, but he was very persistent.

This coin had been in my possession since I'd received it in 1983, and I was oddly attached to it. I didn't even anticipate Paul's response—I was just trying to take his mind off of the subject with something shiny—and now I was forced to part with my coin for a few days. I'd have to let Sloane have it, or I'd seem really weird. So, I handed it over to her, watching it disappear under her fingers.

Sloane graciously attempted to give it back, but for Paul's sake, I insisted that she have it.

"Keep it safe. I've had it nearly my whole life."

Her eyebrows shot up in surprise.

"She isn't kidding," Kip piped up.

"Thank you," she said and put the coin in her pocket. I said a quick prayer that she'd take it seriously and take care of it.

❅ ❅ ❅

I went down to check on Pippa before finishing my day. She was still dressed with her heels, stockings, and jewelry on as if she had plans for the evening. "Are you doing all right this evening?" I asked her.

She was sitting by the window again, a book in her lap, looking through the antique panes into the blackness that was the front lawn. She turned in my direction. "Fine, dear," she said softly and then turned back to the window.

I pulled a chair over to hers and sat down, peering outside with her in an attempt to see what she may be viewing. A velvet black sky absorbed all that was below it. I couldn't see a thing. "There has been an offer on the house," I blurted.

Pippa spun around in her chair to face me. "And?"

"I don't know. I emailed Robert like he asked me to, but he didn't respond."

Her eyes constricted into angry slits. "Typical."

"What do you think he's doing about it?" I was genuinely curious.

"If the price is right, I'm sure he'll accept the offer." Pippa rubbed the knuckles of one hand with the thumb of the other. She seemed to notice her outward expression of anxiety and quickly stilled her fingers, resting them on her book. "He'll weigh the cost of the up-keep over time with the profit and come up with an answer that way. I'm not a mathematician, and I don't claim to know much about investments like the men in my family. Robert will, I'm sure of it, make the correct decision where money is concerned. But in matters of our family, he'll fail one hundred percent." She looked back out the window.

"How did you inherit this house?" I attempted to change the subject. "You said you had siblings. Did they live here?"

Pippa's reflection in the window was mirrorlike against the black of night. She was still seething over the offer on the house, I suspected. After a few quiet seconds, she began to speak. "I was living here with my parents when we got word that Herbert, my brother, had been killed in the Second World War. Charles was the only other son in our family so, naturally, he inherited the house."

Pippa shifted in her seat and crossed her legs at the ankles. She continued, "I had a particular fondness for the house, and Charles could see that. He signed the house over to me after finding himself a property through his investment firm. I am now the sole survivor of my immediate family and the eldest living heir to the house."

I sat tense, as she told the story. "Then how does Robert have control of it?" I asked, completely enthralled in the history she was telling me.

"About five years ago, after my husband Henry died, my health began to waver. My body was failing me, and I didn't want the house to leave the family. I signed the estate over to my grandchildren, not ever expecting any of them to want to sell it. Neither Sloane nor Kip know how to manage their wealth, and Robert bullied them into selling, dangling its profit in front of their noses." She shook her head. "Henry would never have imagined the kind of man that Robert has become."

It took me some time to absorb all of this information. I couldn't say I really knew Robert, but I *felt* who he was, even though it made no sense at all. I decided to just say the words and see how she responded. "I've seen a gentle side of him."

Pippa settled her gaze on my face. As the words came out of her mouth, they were through clenched teeth. "You cannot claim to know him."

"I can't, you're right. I've only known him a short while, but I've seen glimpses of him that seem… sweet."

She had turned back to the darkness of the window. I received no response to this comment, so I decided to gently end our conversation. "If you need anything, I'd be happy to help. Otherwise, I'm going to get my things from the yellow room and move in down the hall. I'm watching the boys while Sloane deals with her divorce." Without looking in my direction, Pippa dismissed me with a flick of the wrist.

"Good night," I offered and left the room.

I began to second-guess my opinion of Robert as I walked the vast hallways to the yellow room. Was I imagining his likability? Pippa's response was indisputably venomous with regard to him. My mind kept returning to his twenty-dollar date. That didn't sound like a man with no heart to me. The way I felt when he held my hand that day—when he seemed to hold on as long as I did... That certainly didn't feel like an unlikeable person.

Finally, I reached the yellow room where my bags sat bulging at the seams at the foot of the bed. I had packed them earlier in the day, and now they glared at me—a reminder that my stay here was temporary. The handles slid out with a tug, and I wheeled my bags out of the doorway, down the hall toward my new room.

As I reached the east wing, I found the empty room next to Sammy's. I went inside and dumped my bags on the open floor, climbing over them to enter the room. Walking past the unsettlingly high double bed, I fixed my eyes on the oak bureau on the opposite wall. Old photographs and new ones in silver frames were perched on its surface. I noticed that one photo had Kip, Sloane, and Robert. I picked up the frame and studied the man in front of me. He had a crop of dark hair, and he was thinner than I remembered. His green eyes were bright as he smiled for the camera. It looked as though he were looking straight at me—his eyes meeting mine just like they had that day we met.

After mentally reintroducing myself to his image, I followed it around the room. There was a picture of him holding up a fish, pictures skiing, and photos of him with Sloane's children. A wave of emotion—a slightly panicked feeling—came over me as if I had known him and lost him. I pushed it back down into the pit of my stomach where it came from and set one of the photos that I was holding back onto the bureau.

My cell phone buzzed, rattling me. "Hello?" I answered.

"Hi."

A cold sensation consumed my limbs as I heard Robert's voice. I had to make an effort to breathe. "Hi. ...did you get the email about the offer on the house?"

"Yes." He sat there. Deliberating?

"And?"

"I'm planning on selling."

"*What?*" I blurted out despite my attempt to be professional.

"The potential buyer has nearly settled on a price. We're just negotiating a final offer."

My eyes fell back on the photo of Robert and his siblings. How could this man who looked so loving and genuine be so cold-hearted? Pippa and her dark view of the window came rushing into my mind. "I can't believe you're selling it," I spoke to the man in the frame, shaking my head back and forth and thinking about poor Pippa.

"It's not up to you, Allie," he murmured on the other end, breaking me from my thoughts.

"You're crazy to sell this house," I resolved. "It's your heritage, your birthright. I think everyone can see that but you."

Then his voice came smoothly through the receiver, "After Christmas, you can feel free to clear your things. You don't have to assist with packing the house. I'll see to it that you are paid through the end of December, but you don't have to stay after the holiday."

Whatever, Robert. "Will you come home for Christmas?" I asked, giving it one last shot, ignoring his previous comment about my leaving. It had been almost a reflex; I'd been unloading all of my thoughts on the house, and the question had just slipped out. Anyway, the least he could do was spend a final holiday at Ashford and see his family. And me.

"Why should I come?" His voice had become mellifluous, and I wondered if he meant more by the question than what was on the surface of it. I paused, considering how to answer.

There was a knock at the door, tearing my mind from the conversation. Kip peeked his head through the cracked door. "Hello, neighbor!" he pronounced. Then, noticing that I was on the phone, he shrunk back with forced silence. Did Kip have some kind of Robert radar? How did he manage, over and over, to barge in on my most important conversations?

"Am I interrupting something?" Robert asked.

"Kip just popped his head into my room." I turned to Kip. "Do you mind if I finish this call? I'll come find you in a sec."

"Sure thing," he chirped and winked at me, closing the door behind him.

"I should probably go," Robert snapped.

"You don't have to," I nearly pleaded.

"There's nothing more to say. I'll be in touch," he said, ending the call. I sat on the edge of the bed in complete bewilderment as I clutched my phone so tightly that my knuckles were white.

After a few minutes of contemplation, I got up off the bed and went down to Kip's room. I knocked once and opened the door. "Kip," I called into the room, my eyes coming to a rest on his bed, where he lay with his hands folded behind his head, the television on in front of him. "You've tidied up the place," I said, looking around.

A smirk inched across his face as he got up off the bed, punched the button on the remote, and walked over to me. He placed his hands on my hips, causing me to squirm with unease, making it suddenly quite clear to me that Kip wasn't the person I really wanted to see.

"Do you like Indie music?" he asked, tilting his head back to look at my face.

"Indie music?" I asked. I may have heard the term, but I was nearly sure that I hadn't listened to this genre before.

"Yeah. Indie. Independent, small label."

I remembered watching these types of bands in the bars back in college, and I really enjoyed them. "Oh, I guess I *do* like Indie music. Why?"

"There's this band that's playing on Saturday, and I'd like to take you to see them for date number two. Would you be interested? … Maybe get a bite to eat first or something?"

"Sure! That sounds like fun."

"Great! I'll get you the details closer to Saturday."

"Okay," I said and pulled out of his hold. As I backed through the door, I lied, "I have to get some late work done. I'll check back in with you in a little while." Despite my best efforts to ignore my thoughts, I was still processing my conversation with Robert, and I needed time to get my head around the idea that in a few weeks' time I'd be unemployed again.

Kip followed me. "I'll walk you. Where are you headed?"

"The office."

Kip paced beside me until we got there, where I quickly sat down at the desk and pretended to delve into work. I shuffled through some papers, trying to look busy. I really just wanted to be alone with my thoughts, but I wasn't being very successful at shaking Kip.

He seemed to finally sense my need for solitude and took a step back through the doorway into the hall.

As he was leaving, I asked, "Where's this band playing on Saturday anyway?"

"Paris." He replied frankly and headed down the hallway.

Chapter Twelve

I slid my chair back, making a scraping sound, and, for an instant, I worried about the floors. Bursting out of the office after Kip, I asked, "Paris? Like, France?" My voice was coming out a little shriller than I'd wanted. "I can't go to France!"

Kip turned around. "Why not?"

"I don't have a passport."

"What happened to it?" Kip's brows pulled together, and he looked like a kid again.

"I've never had a passport," I explained.

"How can you leave the country without a passport?" He looked completely confused. It must be nice to have so much money that you can't even fathom the idea of spending your entire life in one place.

"I've never left the country. I've only been to probably..." I began counting on my fingers, "four of our own states."

"You're kidding me!" Kip was looking at me like I was one of those leaping lemurs at the National Zoo. You know, kind of cute, but kind of strange at the same time. "Well, I have some connections, and I could maybe get you a passport by the end of the week." His face contorted slightly as he contemplated this plan.

"Kip, there's work to do here. I'm watching Paul and Sammy. I can't just go to another country. I thought the date would be for a few *hours*, not a few *days*."

"Come on! Don't tell me that you wouldn't love to go," he attempted to persuade me. "You can't say that you'd rather be closed up in Robert's room listening out for Sammy and Paul."

A prickling sensation crawled up my neck with the mention of Robert's name. All of a sudden, I couldn't quite get the air that I needed. I was sleeping in Robert's bed. "*Robert's* room?" I asked, just to be sure that I'd heard him correctly.

"Yeah," Kip began walking toward the kitchen again, and I followed. "Good thing he's not coming home for Christmas," he said, "because he'd have to share the room with you." He grinned in my direction.

"I'm sure that there are enough rooms in this house that Robert could find somewhere else to sleep."

"You won't have to worry about it. Robert wouldn't come home if his life depended on it."

Or his family, I thought. I tried to smile, but it came out more like a grimace. I was glad that Kip wasn't paying attention. He'd spotted Anna and was already making conversation with her.

I turned around and walked back to the office. Sitting down at the desk, I put my head down on my arms. I needed time to process. Truth: Robert was selling the house. Truth: I would be out of a job after December. Truth: Robert would not come home for Christmas. Truth: I needed to stop thinking about him.

The last thought rolled around in my head. I needed to stop thinking about him. I needed to stop thinking about Robert. Kip really seemed interested in me. I needed to stop thinking about

Robert. I really did. *Stop! Stop thinking about him.* I considered the idea that I had probably created a fictional Robert anyway. I didn't really know him. Other than with the explanation of the twenty-dollar date, he'd not been very nice. He was short most of the time on the phone—all business—and probably didn't think a thing about me.

I got up and went back to my room. Robert's room. I sat down on the floor and unzipped my suitcases. With a plop, I dropped a pile of clothes in front of the closet and opened the doors. I stood there, unsure of what to do next. Facing me from inside the closet were shirts, sweaters, fleece jackets, dinner jackets, ties, and perfectly pressed trousers hanging from matching, shiny wooden hangers. Robert's clothes. I resisted the urge to rifle through them and instead gently pushed everything to one side, filling the void with my own things. I did the same with his shoes at the bottom.

After I got everything unpacked, I made room in the corner of the closet for my suitcases and shut the door. Everything fit, despite the fact that Robert was using two thirds of the closet.

I was glad to see that the room had an attached bathroom. I went in and drew the water in the tub. I undressed, climbed in, and submerged my entire body in the warmth of it. For a long time, I sat there, my eyes closed, my mind completely empty. Water rushed over my cupped hands as I pulled them up toward me to splash my face. Droplets trailed down my chin onto the surface of the bath. Then I tipped my head back, plunging my hair into the water. I was starting to feel better.

There was a knock at the door. Really? I climbed out of the tub, dried off with a deliciously fluffy towel, and wrapped my robe around myself. With damp feet, I padded toward the door and opened it to find Kip standing on the other side. He seemed startled by my appearance. He had that serious look on his face that he had at lunch when we flipped for our dates.

"We never got to finish our conversation," he walked toward me causing me to back up into the room. The bed hit the back of my legs, triggering them to bend against it, and I sat down. Kip sat beside me.

"I'm not going with you to France," I said, turning toward him, but he put a finger on my lips.

"I don't care," he whispered as he leaned in and pressed his lips against mine. The feeling was still so unfamiliar, the light scratch of the stubble on his face, the softness of his lips. Thoughts were racing through my head: What was I doing? I should stop him. Maybe I was over-thinking it. Maybe I should just let go and live in this perfect moment that was in front of me. I didn't allow myself to picture Robert like I wanted to. I needed to center my attention on Kip; he deserved that. He held my face in his gentle hands, and I responded by putting my arms around his neck.

I finally pulled back for a moment to speak. "What will we do for our second date, then?"

"This," he said, nibbling my neck.

Through tiny gasps of air as his lips met mine over and over, I responded, "Okay," and pushed Kip back on the bed where I curled up beside him, his lips still all over mine.

He was just what I needed to keep Robert from creeping into my mind. We lounged around on my bed until I could barely keep my eyes open. "I'll be back," he said through more kisses as he lifted himself off of the bed. "Don't move." He walked out of the room, closing the door behind him.

I channeled what little energy remained in my body and scuffled into the bathroom. Quickly, I lined my toothbrush with toothpaste and began to scrub while inspecting my reflection in the mirror, making sure to brush every single inch of my teeth. Wildly combing with one hand and brushing my teeth with the other, I attempted to make myself as presentable as possible, given the circumstances. Then I spit and rinsed my mouth out with water.

A tiny yelp escaped my lips as Kip put his hands around my waist. "I said, don't move," he said, spinning me around. He took my toothbrush between two fingers and tossed it onto the edge of the sink. Then, hooking his pointer finger in the belt of my robe, he pulled me back into the bedroom.

He had changed into some flannel pajama bottoms and a t-shirt. I was still in my robe and not quite sure how or if I was going to change into my own bedclothes. I wondered what had come over him tonight as he resumed kissing me and pulling me closer to him.

❋ ❋ ❋

I woke to light streaming in through the window next to the bed. Kip was asleep beside me. I was still tightly wrapped in my robe, thank God. Then my eyes moved back to Kip. He looked like a child again as he slept quietly next to me. He must have sensed my gaze because he opened his eyes, instantly grabbing for my waist.

"Morning," he mumbled, burrowing his lips through my hair to my neck. "I enjoyed date number two even more than the first one."

I pulled the duvet up, surrounding us with fluffs of white fabric. While studying his face, I wondered how many women had had this experience. How many times had Kip slept over with someone? Surely, I wasn't the first. "What prompted this?" I asked, gesturing to the two of us.

"What do you mean?" He was squinting slightly as if attempting to sharpen his focus.

"You've never been this forward before." Had I provoked him in some way? With the light of day shining in on my conscience, I felt a wave of anxiety. Why did I let Kip sleep over? What was I thinking? "I just wondered what made you decide to come see me last night."

"Well," he began slowly as if he were deciding something, "I had a drink with Sloane last night before she turned in for the evening. I wanted to wish her luck with the divorce proceedings." Immediately, my sense of hearing sharpened, and I listened to see if I could hear either of the kids. Nothing. Kip continued, "She asked me what I thought about you, and I told her."

He turned so that he was facing me directly. "She told me about Robert and what had... gone on between you two, with the song and everything." His hands found my waist again, and he pulled me closer. "I immediately came to find you."

I felt the trepidation scrambling around in my head. This was all wrong. Flipping coins for dates with Kip, letting him sleep in my room, allowing him to have these feelings. It was like a train with no brakes, and I found myself feeling a slight urge to jump off it. What if Robert had come home to this? What if he'd seen this? But then I thought, if Robert had cared at all, he'd have tried to come home. And he hadn't, had he?

※ ※ ※

Sammy was babbling in his crib just as I came out of the bathroom where I had dressed for the day. Kip was still in my bed. I poked him through the duvet. "I'm going to get the kids."

Pippa rolled by on her scooter at the same time that I opened the bedroom door. She slowed to bid me good morning, a look of shock enveloping her face as she peered past me into my room. Kip waved to her from under the duvet. Pippa's eyes narrowed, and she sped off defiantly.

I bit my lip on my way to Sammy's room as she retreated to the other end of the house. I knew what it looked like. Nothing had happened, but of course she couldn't have known that. What must she think of me?

Sammy was standing in his crib with a tattered cloth diaper in one hand and his pacifier in the other. Upon my advance toward him, he gingerly set both items down on the mattress and raised his arms to me. "Mummy?" he asked as I picked him up.

"Mommy's gone to see Daddy," I explained.

"Mk. Dink you!"

"Would you like some milk? Is that what you're asking for?" I giggled, picking him up and making my way to the kitchen. "Let's go see Anna. She'll get you some milk." Sammy seemed comfortable with that and hugged my neck all the way to the kitchen.

I set him in his high chair and tentatively walked over to Anna. I was nearly sure she was aware that Kip stayed over last night, so I was very cautious. She looked up at me, and I swear I saw slight irritation in her eyes. "Can I just leave Sammy with you for a second while I check on Paul?" I asked. She nodded. Anna handed Sammy a sippy cup of milk while I went back down to the east wing.

Paul was standing in his doorway with a plaid shirt buttoned unevenly and a pair of pants printed with little whales on them. Looking down, I saw that he had chosen navy blue galoshes, and they were on the wrong feet. All the colors, however matched to perfection. "Wow, you're dressed!"

"Mommy didn't put my clothes out."

"Are you comfortable with what you picked, or would you like me to get you an outfit?"

"I like it!" he said triumphantly and stepped up by my side as we entered the hallway.

"Let's go and get you some breakfast." I approached the door to my room, noticing that my bed was empty, and the sheets were in disarray, in usual Kip-form. I shook my head and shut the door.

We arrived in the kitchen to find Sammy devouring a muffin and some cantaloupe and haphazardly washing it down with his milk. Anna turned to Paul and started at the sight of his outfit. She quickly recovered, though, and asked him, "What would you like this morning, Paul?" squatting down to his level. "Muffin? Cereal?"

"Um," he was clearly giving it some thought. "I think I want some toast with butter, and eggs." His chest puffed out, he pulled out his own chair and took a seat, crossing his arms on the table.

"No fruit? I have pineapple," Anna offered.

"Yes," he said. "Pineapple too."

Sammy watched his brother. "Pih? Pih?" he whined to Anna.

"Sure, Sammy, I'll get you some pineapple too," she told him.

I sat down next to Paul, who was looking out of the bay window. "What are you thinking about?" I asked.

Paul looked over at me and then told me, "Daddy."

"Dee Dee?" asked Sammy. I nodded in his direction.

I wanted to tread lightly on this one. I turned back to Paul, "What do you like most about your Daddy?"

"When he comes home." Paul looked back out the window.

"After work? At night?"

The sun was just peeking through the window, casting a glow on Paul's face. "No, he doesn't come home every night like Ethan's daddy. He comes home mostly on weekends."

I was unsure of who Ethan was, but that was irrelevant. "Where is your daddy during the week? Does he work far away?"

"Yeah." Anna came over and placed Paul's breakfast in front of him. He took a giant bite of toast. With his mouth full, he said, "Mommy wanted Daddy to be home more, and me too, but he had to work really far." He swallowed. "I miss him."

"I'm sure you do."

"Moe?" Sammy was holding his empty sippy cup in the air and waving it back and forth. Anna dutifully came over and retrieved his cup. "Dink you!" Sammy mumbled through pieces of muffin.

Anna nodded, "You're welcome."

"Well," I attempted to lighten the air for little Paul, "I have some really fun things planned for us today!" His eyes brightened. Sammy looked genuinely interested: he stopped chewing his muffin. "I know that you have some finger paints that your mom brought, right?" I watched Paul nod his head, and Sammy's eyes bounced from his brother to me and back again. Kip entered the kitchen, observing from the arched doorway. "Well, I have a giant piece of white card-board, and we're going to feet-paint!"

"Feet-painting! Can I play too?" Kip's exaggerated voice sailed toward us. He hopped over to us in one, large stride. Paul's face was awash with excitement. Sammy had resumed his muffin, but was now eyeing Kip curiously.

"We can all feet-paint," I laughed through the words.

When the boys were finished, I cleaned them up and took them into the entranceway where I spread a large, white piece of cardboard that I had seen and confiscated from one of the tool sheds outside. I had set out the paints in a rainbow of colors. Carefully, I rolled up the boys' pant legs and removed their shoes and socks. Kip took off his shoes, cuffed his jeans, and stood at attention. I kicked off my own, and we all walked onto the cardboard.

I dumped circular puddles of paint in each corner. While I was setting up, I explained the task, "The only rule is that you have to stay on the cardboard, and you cannot sit down. You must get your feet wet with paint of any color and dance on the cardboard until the music stops. Does everyone understand?" Kip nodded his head up and down with inflated vigor.

"Okay, Gerard!"

Gerard was standing in the wings as we set up our painting, the lines next to his eyes deepening with his cheery expression. Upon my command, he went to the switchboard behind the butler's pantry and hit a button, blasting dance music throughout the house. The boys howled with delight, and we all dipped our feet in the paint and started to jiggle with the music. Paul and Sammy were dancing and spinning all over the surface, creating amazing swirls and streaks of color. Kip, in his usual style, was grabbing me at the waist and pulling me close as if we were on our own private dance floor. I pushed him away playfully.

Gerard returned with four large buckets of water for washing up and set them on the side of the room next to a pile of towels. I noticed his sideways glances in mine and Kip's direction when he walked past us. Kip paid him no notice as we bopped back and forth across the cardboard, but I was watching. Kip grabbed my hands and started spinning me around despite my attempts to deter his advances. Gerard's gaze stung me. I remembered how he'd been when I'd first arrived, but now, after seeing my interactions with Kip, he looked at me differently.

I broke free from Kip, feeling uncomfortable, but I continued to dance for the benefit of the children. Sammy followed Paul, and the two of them wiggled around, dipping their toes into the various colors of paint, stomping and jumping, laughing all the while.

"*What* is going on?" Pippa called out over the music, from atop her scooter. The music continued to pound, but the four of us stopped in our tracks. "Do you realize that whatever that is…" she extended a knobby finger at the ceiling, "is blasting through the entire house? And what are you doing? You're going to get paint all over the floors!"

The music still bouncing and blaring around us, I walked over to the edge of the cardboard, facing Pippa. "We're dancing—feet-painting. And the paint is washable. I'll have it all cleaned up when we're finished. You'll never know we were here." Pippa eyed me up and down. Then she softened a bit as she looked at the children. Sammy was squatting and drawing in the paint with his fingers.

"Ask Gerard to turn off the speakers in the east wing, please."

"I can pull you off of that scooter, Pippa, and spin you around a few times," Kip taunted her. She narrowed her eyes and gave him her most serious you-wouldn't-dare face. Kip playfully lunged in her direction, and she sped away from us as quickly as her little scooter would take her. "I'll have the music turned down," he called out to her, but she didn't look back.

I turned around, and Sammy was now sitting in the middle of the cardboard, painting his hair and cheeks with sea blue and emerald green. I tugged on Kip's shirt, and he turned to see what I was giggling about. We both snorted with laughter as Sammy sat, oblivious to our source of amusement. Paul looked at his brother in horror. "Sammyyyy! It's *feet*-painting. You can't do that!"

"Who says?" Kip reached down and swirled his fingers around in a mass of colored paint, stood up, and dragged his multicolored fingertips along my entire face. I recoiled in shock. He reached down for more paint. I shrieked and started to run, paying close attention to stay on the cardboard. Kip began to chase me as the boys howled with laughter.

"Don't you dare!" I screamed, ducking and dodging his hands, but he caught me, fingering my clothes with paint. He wiped my face with the back of his hand.

"I'm done." Paul called out. I pulled away from Kip.

"You're done?" Kip kidded his nephew. He scooped him up and turned him upside down. "Well, I guess we'll have to use you as a paint brush! Since you're done feet-painting, now it's time for head-painting!" He swung Paul around, dangling him dangerously close to the paint.

"Nooooo!" Paul giggled, squirming around in Kip's strong hands.

With that all-too-familiar grin, Kip set Paul back down next to Sammy who now was completely camouflaged on the cardboard. "Let's go and get a bath and give Miss Allie some time to clean herself up." Kip, wiped his feet off with the water and towels. Then, unconcerned about the paint that completely covered both children, he scooped them up, one in each arm, and made his way toward the east wing.

I washed off my own feet and went to find Gerard. He showed me how to turn the music off and reset the system to include the east wing. Once we were done, I made my way back to the entranceway where our masterpiece was still drying. The staff was respectfully cleaning around the massive piece of cardboard, taking care not to disturb the paint. I carefully worked alongside them and cleaned up the paint that had dribbled off of the edge of the cardboard, and then took the artwork to an empty space at the back of the house, admiring it. The painting was beautiful in its own way.

Once I had tidied up the entranceway, I went back to my bedroom to clean myself up. My bed had been made, and my room was completely in order. I didn't get this kind of service in the yellow room. Guilt started to swim around inside me for being on this side of things. I shouldn't have the staff taking care of me in any way, and I was nearly sure that they felt the same. I was caught between two very different worlds.

I pushed a sticky, paint-soaked piece of hair behind my ear. I was an absolute mess, so I decided to leave Kip with the kids and take a shower. After a quick wash, I put myself back together and went to locate them. When I found Paul and Sammy, they were in the tub off Kip's room, up to their eyeballs in frothy bubbles that had taken on a sea blue hue from all of the paint.

"Hi there," I leaned on the doorframe, watching Kip with the kids. He was a natural with them. I decided that it was mostly because he was nothing more than a big kid himself.

Kip turned around, utterly at ease. "Hey." He stood up and walked over to me. "That was fun," he embraced me. I did wonder again how many other women he'd pursued like this. Was I just someone with whom he could pass the time while he was here? It was hard to tell, with my limited experience with these things.

"After their bath, I have a tent-making activity to do in the living room." I moved away gently. "Do you mind staying with them a moment? I just want to check that Tom McCray's okay with the grocery delivery. I'll be right back."

"Sure." Kip looked over at his nephews. Paul was amusing himself by piling suds on top of Sammy's head. Sammy was entirely unaware.

I smiled at the boys and then at Kip, and gave him a kiss on the cheek. "I'll be right back." Just as I left the room, my cell phone rang in my pocket.

"Hello?"

"Allie?"

I stopped right there in the hallway. It was Robert. What was it about Robert's strong voice coming through the line that could start me trembling all over with excitement? I stood still, trying to decide how to emote. I was relieved to hear his voice, to sense his breathing, to be connected to him. Almost like I had finally come up for air again after being under water. Because for the entire time that he'd been silent, and hadn't called, I felt like something was missing, like I couldn't quite be my whole self.

I didn't want to admit it, but in my mind, I had willed him to call, or even email. Anything—it didn't matter, as long as I could be connected to him. Anger pelted me from the inside. I could feel it burning my skin because I didn't want to feel this way. I didn't want to miss him like this. Robert wasn't even here. He was too busy trying to sell the only home his family had known for generations. So, why did I care at all about him? I had no answer, and it was maddening.

Chapter Thirteen

"Allie?" he said again.

"Yes?" I managed.

"It's Robert." He was quiet for a span of time that nearly became uncomfortable before he said, "How are you?"

"I'm fine." My voice was coming out short even though I still wasn't quite sure how to feel. The response was involuntary.

"I'm glad to hear it. How's… Kip?"

"He's doing well. He's giving Paul and Sammy a bath."

"I see."

What did he want? Why was he calling me and ruining my mood? I had been perfectly happy just two minutes before.

"I just wanted to call to let you know that I am coming home for Christmas."

What? How many times had I thought about him coming home for Christmas? And even when I had asked, he had refused. Now that I didn't really care to see him, he was thinking of coming home. Robert really was the most confusing human being on the planet.

"Why?" I asked matter-of-factly.

I could hear his exhale through the long pause that followed. "I think you're right. I should have one final memory of the house and the family before I sell."

How do I respond to that? The idea of his presence, his subtle spicy scent, made me want to burst. Would a smile swim around behind his eyes like it had, or would he look at me differently? How much time would I get with him? It all made me anxious and irritated. My head began to pound.

"Allie?"

I blew air through my lips. "Yeah."

"I just wanted to let you know that I was coming home. That's all."

"Thanks for calling." I still had no idea how to react to this news, but I noticed that my hands were shaking.

"I'll let you know when my flight will arrive."

"Okay."

"Well, take care. I'll call soon."

Ugh. Don't bother. Just stay where you are and stop putting me through this. "Bye."

"Good-bye." The line went dead.

Kip peeked his head out of the bedroom door. "Who was that?"

"Robert. He's coming home for Christmas."

I had not seen panic on Kip's face before, but I was pretty sure that I caught a momentary glimpse of it when he heard those words, and I wondered why. Even though Robert had told me right then and there that he was coming home, I didn't want to believe him. It might get my hopes up, and I'd be crushed if he changed his mind, although I didn't want to admit it to myself.

❋ ❋ ❋

Sammy was down for his afternoon nap, and Anna and Kip were entertaining Paul while I went to the east wing to check on Pippa. I needed to see how she was doing, and I also still hadn't wrapped any presents for her, with Christmas just around the corner.

When I entered her room, her medical staff were packing their things and completing the last of the paperwork for the day. Pippa was doing some sort of sewing. Needlepoint? She set it down on the table and looked up at me.

"I wanted to see if you needed any Christmas presents wrapped."

"I have a few, but let's wait, shall we?" Then she stood up and approached me with tiny, unsteady strides. "Let's go to the sitting room."

We walked slowly to the sitting room, where the larger of the two Christmas trees had been erected. It was a substantial tree, emitting the scent of spruce through the surrounding area. White lights dotted its branches, and the ornaments were color-coordinated in red, cream, and silver. An angel, swathed in folds of red and cream-colored fabric, hovered at the top. I looked at the tree the very moment I entered the room. Pippa went straight to the settee and never even glanced at it, which surprised me.

"Isn't this tree lovely?" I asked her, taking a seat beside her.

"Mmm," she responded, her mind elsewhere. "Allie," she turned to me. "I'm apprehensive."

I pulled my eyes from the tree and looked into Pippa's withered face. "About what?"

"I haven't heard if Robert has accepted the offer on the house. I'm finding it difficult to sleep at night with the thought that he may have consented to a contract."

"I wish I knew."

"Kip tells me that Robert may come home for Christmas."

"Yes." My chest constricted. Our phone conversation came to mind again. I'd been fighting the idea all day that I had been extremely unprofessional with my snippiness, and I considered calling Robert to apologize.

"Do you think that he may be coming to inform us of the offer?" Pippa was rubbing her knuckles again. Originally, I thought it may be because she had pain there, but now I wondered if it was a nervous habit.

"I'm not sure."

That familiar amalgam of irritation and humor spread over her features. "It's somewhat comical, but I think *you* may have more of a relationship with Robert than any of his family members."

Relationship. Did she have to word it that way? I could feel a headache punching its way from the back of my head toward my eyes. I blinked a few times in an attempt to keep it at bay.

"I'm sure that isn't true," I said. Punch, punch behind the left eye. Blink.

Pippa's face was nearly frowning now. "Whom did he call when he decided he was coming for Christmas? Certainly not me. Or Sloane. Or… Kip."

"When he comes for Christmas," I attempted to alter the conversation just a tinge. Maybe she wouldn't notice. "I hope that you two can have time to work out your differences. Christmas is that time of year when anything's possible." I hoped to evoke some optimism, but from Pippa's reaction, I wasn't so lucky.

"You are so young. Christmas is still such a fanciful idea for the young," she said. Then, with disdain in her voice, she added,

"Reconciliation is doubtful. We have years of differences stacked up in little invisible piles, following us wherever we go."

"He's your grandson."

"He's turned into a dreadful man."

"Ms. Marley…" It really wasn't my place, but for some reason, I felt like I could offer this to her, "I haven't known Robert for very long, and we've had only brief encounters, but…" I inhaled, my eyes throbbing now, "I think that the sweetness of the nine-year-old that you knew may still be there inside. It's just that a hardened, angry man has grown up around it."

Pippa's now full-on scowl diminished ever so slightly at this idea. She ran her hands along her skirt—back and forth—for some time before finally looking up at me. "Well, dear, perhaps you can pull little Robert back out because after years of trying, I can't reach him," she said finally. "And there's always the question of him actually coming home, isn't there? I'll believe it when I see it."

Pippa asked me to walk her to her room. Then I went back to my own room and decided I should probably call Robert. My fingertip lingered on each number, quivering and clammy at the thought of calling. Quickly, and without further contemplation, I hit the send button and put the phone to my ear.

After one ring, Robert picked up. "Allie."

I didn't wait for pleasantries. "I wanted to apologize for the way that I acted when you called this morning. It was completely unprofessional, and I'm sorry." The mattress sank beneath me as I lowered myself down onto the bed.

"It's fine."

"No, it isn't. You're my employer, and I should never have acted that way. It won't happen again." The winter draft snaked along the floor. Kicking off my shoes, I pulled my feet up onto the bed and crossed them under me. Should I say anything more? "I also wanted to tell you about Ms. Marley," I began.

"Yes?"

"I wanted to let you know that Ms. Marley is very worried about the offer on the house. It's keeping her up at night." I waited an uncomfortably long time before saying, "I just wanted you to know. She'll probably ask you about it if you come home."

"Well, thank you for the heads-up." I wasn't sure, but it seemed like Robert wanted to say something else, so I waited just a bit to see if he'd start talking. Then, he did. "You never told me how the date went. How did Kip spend his twenty dollars?"

"He bought pizza."

"How did I not guess that? Pizza may possibly be the only item that Kip is aware of in the under-twenty-dollars range."

I giggled. "He made a little game with pieces of paper where he wrote questions. We had to draw them out and answer them. It was pretty creative."

"I'm surprised. Kip? Writing? Kip doing something remotely academic is an accomplishment. You've inspired him, I think." An empty hum came through the phone before he said, "You have that effect on people." I could feel Robert softening again, and it made me a little lightheaded.

"What?" I lay back on the bed waiting for his answer. I imagined his eyes, how I could see the thought behind them, the lightness in them when he looked at me.

"You make people act differently."

"How?"

"Well, you made Kip pick up a pencil and apply thoughts to paper."

Little puffs of amusement escaped through my nose. I was smiling despite myself. "You said *people*," I forced the issue. "Apart from Kip, who else acts differently?"

"Well, you have Sloane leaving her children with you, and you're a complete stranger to her."

"Yeah, but I'm a former nanny, living in her house with her family. That's not so bad."

"Kip tells me that Pippa's chatting more to you than to the entire staff combined. That should illustrate my point entirely." I thought about Pippa and our conversations. There was something about her that I really liked. It was true, she was a difficult woman, but I wondered how much of her arduous exterior was a mask for her uncertainty about the future. Then he said, "And you've got me coming home for Christmas."

"What can I say?" I boasted. Robert chuckled, sending a little quiver of happiness through my stomach. "The Christmas trees look very nice this year," I attempted to persuade him further, unsure of my own motives. "And Anna can make her homemade hot chocolate…"

"Anna's hot chocolate is delicious. Have you had some?" he asked.

"Yes. It was very good. Kip took me sledding down the hill out back and had Anna make some when we came in." When Robert didn't respond, I checked to be sure I hadn't lost the connection. "Hello?"

"Still here," he said quietly. "So," he said as he exhaled, "What do you think about our Kip?"

"He's nice."

"How are you two getting along?"

"Very well, actually. He's not like anyone I've ever known."

"How so?"

"I'm sort of a home-body. I like to read, take walks. I go to bars in town with Megan and end up sitting at a table, sipping coffee until closing, just talking. Kip is so different from me. He tried to get me go to Paris the other day. Paris, France."

"What for?"

"To see a band. Which sounded really fun, but France?"

"So, why didn't you go?"

"I don't have a passport."

"Allie, this is the twenty-first century. You really should get a passport."

"I've never really had a need to leave the country, or the means."

"There is a very small restaurant in England—I went there on business once—where you bring your own bottle of wine. It has a fireplace and an amazing view from the window. It is the most mar-velous find. For that experience alone, you should get a passport."

"And how shall I get there? On my good looks?" I teased.

"Nonsense. You're friends with the Marleys …who have tons of money and throw it away on things like this all the time."

Allowing my eyes to roam the room, I let them wander past the photos of Robert until they settled on the clock. "Oh my gosh! I have to go. Kip's been with the kids, and I need to relieve him. Can we chat later?"

"Sure. Let's talk again soon."

"Okay."

"Have a nice afternoon."

"Thanks," I said, hopping off of the bed. "You too."

I glided across the waxy floor, nearly skidding through the door and ran down the hallway toward Paul and Kip. They were walking toward me as I passed through the grand entranceway.

"Sorry!" I huffed. "I lost track of time. I was talking to Robert."

Kip rolled his eyes. "What does he have you doing now?"

"Oh, nothing. He was telling me that I should get a passport, actually." The thought of Robert and that English restaurant swept through my mind. Even if I never got the chance to use a passport, having one would give me the *hope* of using it. And suddenly, as Robert's voice moved through my mind, I wanted one more than anything.

"That is true. You should get a passport." Kip's eyes were a little more intense than I'd seen them before. What was behind that look of his?

"Do you think you could call your friend and set it up for me?"

"Anything you want."

Chapter Fourteen

"Uncle Kip?" Paul was tugging on Kip's shirt. "Can we go watch *Toy Story*?"

"Your Mom says you can only have an hour of television a day. Is that how you want to spend your hour?"

"Yeeeesss!"

"Okay, then. Let's go down to the media room and set it up for you."

Kip reached down and clutched my hand, pulling it up to his lips and kissing the back of it as we walked down the hallway. I smiled and pulled it away, eyeing the staff. Paul ran ahead and bolted through the doorway to the room where Pippa had told me her terrible story about Kip's parents' death. When we had reached the room, Kip spun me around, then pulled me close and kissed me.

"What was that for?" I asked, looking around to be sure we were alone.

"Do I need a reason?"

There was something about him that could draw me in no matter what thoughts were going through my mind. "No. You don't need a reason." I smiled up at him, noticing the satisfaction on his face.

I liked Kip. I did. No matter what feelings I had for Robert. And I was still working. I couldn't forget that. "While Paul's watching his movie and Sammy is still asleep, I really need to check on the cleaning and maintenance staff. I have to see if there are any issues with any of them. Then I need to work with Anna to plan Christmas dinner."

Kip grabbed my waist, holding me next to him. "Nope. I've been with the boys all morning when all I really wanted to do was be with you. Now, during the only hour—maybe less—of free time we get, you are not going to do Robert's work. You are going to hang out with me."

I looked up at him through the top of my eyes. "Kip, I have to actually do some work, you know. Your brother is paying me money. I have to work for it."

Without responding to my comment, Kip pulled out his cell phone and pushed a few numbers, then placed it to his ear. "Gerard? It's Kip. Are there any maintenance concerns that have not been addressed?" His eyes were on me, a smirk surfacing on his lips. "Yes, this is for Robert. Well, Allie rather." He pushed my hair behind my ear without asking. "No? Great. Thanks." He ended the call and punched a few more numbers. "It's Kip. I'm calling on Allie's behalf. Are there any concerns or issues with the cleaning staff that need to be taken care of? Great, thanks." He hung up and put his phone into his pocket. "You're mine for one hour."

"I don't care what you say. I still have to work, not frolic around with you."

"Nobody would know."

"*I* would. And I have things to do."

"Okay, then. I need your help. There are some things that need to be taken care of concerning Ashford."

"Like what," I asked skeptically.

"I'll fill you in on it in a minute." Kip walked over and sat down next to Paul. "Hey, buddy. If you need anything, come and get us. We'll be in Uncle Robert's room."

My eyes swelled with this information. "No," I corrected, "We'll be in the sitting room next to the kitchen. By the big Christmas tree."

Paul turned his head in our direction, never taking his eyes from the television screen. "Okay" he said, twisting his head back to the movie.

Kip leaned over to Paul and whispered in his ear, "Uncle Robert's room."

In surrender, I didn't bother to retort. Paul didn't seem to be listening anyway. "I still have to plan Christmas dinner with Anna," I reminded Kip in a hushed voice as we exited the media room.

"So!" Kip turned to face me. "The sitting room." He raised his eyebrows. "Romantic."

"I'm working," I reminded him.

"When are you off the clock?"

"Technically, I'm off at five o'clock, but sometimes I take a little extra time to check that doors are locked or talk with staff. You know."

"Ugh. You and Robert! No, I don't know," he fingered my belt loops and looked down at me. "It's just a house. It shouldn't be that much work. You need to have time to live in it," he nuzzled through my hair to my bare neck, sending prickles down my right arm. I squirmed away from him.

"It's not just a house, Kip. Ninety-nine percent of people in this world do not call this a house. It's a far cry from my mother's fifteen hundred square-foot rancher." He eyed me. The impact of my statement was evident on his face. "So, should we go to the sitting room? What was it you wanted to talk to me about?" I asked.

"There's something at Ashford that needs immediate attention."

"Which is…?"

"Me! I need attention!" Kip scooped me up and threw me over his shoulder, jogging down the hallway toward Robert's room.

"Put me down!" I squealed, struggling to regain control of my body.

He bolted into Robert's room and tossed me on the bed, hovering on top of me. With gentle fingers, he brushed my hair away from my forehead and kissed me.

"You are something else, Kip Marley," I shook my head back and forth.

Before he could respond, Sammy was making noises in his bed. "Mummy? Pah? Muuuummmyyy!"

I wriggled out from under Kip and stood up. "You probably woke him with your Superman routine just now." Then I looked at him sympathetically. Kip showed genuine disappointment, looking like a child again. I cradled his head like I would a toddler when he hurts himself and needs a hug, but I quickly pushed him away when he seemed to be enjoying it a little more than I had planned. "Go keep busy with something," I giggled.

I entered Sammy's room. "Mummy?" he asked me, holding out his arms.

"Not yet, but she'll be home soon," I said optimistically. "Right now, I thought we could have a candy cane hunt! Do you know what that is?" He looked at me blankly. I walked him down to the kitchen and set him in his high chair. I pulled out a caramel-flavored candy cane and opened it, handing it to him. He licked it, and his eyes lit up. "Candy cane," I explained.

"Nonny cay," he repeated, looking the stick up and down.

Kip and Paul joined us in the kitchen. "I'm tired of the movie. What does Sammy have?" Paul asked, looking very interested.

"Nonny cay," Sammy salivated, holding out the stick of brown candy toward Paul.

"Candy cane," I translated. "Would you like one?" Paul bobbed his head up and down. "I asked Anna to hide these all over the sitting room," I explained, pulling the plastic off of the candy. We have to go and find them! But first, we need bags to collect our candy canes." I pulled out a pot of crayons and two brown bags that Anna had retrieved from the pantry for me. I spread newspaper at Sammy's and Paul's places at the table and set the brown bags on top. Then I handed Sammy a few colors and put the rest in front of Paul. "How would you like to decorate your bag, Paul?"

Paul reached into the pot and pulled out a black crayon. "I'm going to draw Mommy and Daddy on mine," he said, diligently doodling circles with arms and legs. I glanced at Kip who returned a sympathetic look.

"How about you, Sammy? How are you going to decorate your bag?" I asked.

Sammy held up his crayon. "Boo!" he beamed.

"Blue! That's right!"

Kip leaned over and kissed my cheek. "You're good with children." I shot a look toward Anna, but her back was to us.

"I had better be! I have a degree in teaching, and I was a nanny for eleven years." Then I looked at the two boys as they created their artwork. "I do love it, working with children. It's what I was born to do, I think. Nothing makes me happier."

As the boys finished decorating their bags, I wrote a big "S" for Sammy on his bag, telling him "S" as I pointed to the letter. Paul wrote his name by himself. Then I wiped the candied saliva off of Sammy and put him down on the floor. "I think we're ready! Let's go find some candy!" I called out, and off they went, screaming, into the sitting room.

Anna had done a good job hiding the candy canes, leaving bits of each one exposed so that the kids could find them. They scurried around the room, lifting cushions and poking around in drawers. Pippa rode in on her scooter. "What do you have them doing now?" she asked.

Kip turned toward her. "Candy cane hunting," he said, clearly enthralled.

Pippa climbed off of her scooter and pulled her book out of the little holder at the back. She settled on the chair nearest the fireplace and pretended to read. Most of the time, she was peering over the pages at the children as they dashed around the room, locating their next piece of candy.

"What are you reading?" Kip asked, checking out the cover of Pippa's selection.

"What do you care? It has nothing to do with lacrosse or football," she winked at him.

"I didn't say I wanted to read it. I just asked what it was," Kip said playfully.

"*The Pickwick Papers*, if you must know." Then upon recognizing confusion when she saw it, she explained, "Dickens," to which she received a comprehending nod from Kip. "You'd relate, as you can be your own Mr. Jingle sometimes." The bewilderment returned to Kip's face, and Pippa tutted, rolling her eyes. "Now leave me be and let me finish reading it."

The kids collected the candy canes until we were nearly sure that they were all found. Then we placed our bags on the kitchen table and went back to the sitting room for our next activity. I asked Gerard to bring all of the wooden chairs he could find, and Anna brought the sheets from the linen closet. Pippa watched suspiciously.

"We're going to build a tent!"

The kids cheered. Well, Paul cheered. Sammy just imitated Paul.

I began to drape the chairs with sheets, and both children wailed with laughter. Pippa surveyed the situation continually from the top edge of her book. I thought that I saw a smile although she worked hard to conceal it.

"Eeen," Sammy called out as he entered the makeshift tent. "Ot!" He exited the tent. Again. "Eeen! Ot!" Paul was pretending that it was an ice cream stand, handing us all invisible ice cream cones through the square opening in the back of a chair.

We played until dinner. After eating, the boys got straight into their pajamas, since they had been bathed that morning. Paul hung out with Kip while I read stories to Sammy in his room. "Mummy?" he asked, his pacifier dangling from his lips.

"Mommy will be home soon," I assured him. "We can do some more fun things tomorrow. Would you like that?"

"Yeah," he answered, looking groggy as he sucked on his pacifier. He placed his cloth diaper near his face and attempted to concentrate on the book I was reading.

I began to read Eric Carle's *Brown Bear, Brown Bear*.

"Wod! Wod!" he called out

"That's right! Red!" I corrected him, pointing to the bird on the page. I continued to read the book until his eyes dropped considerably. With such a short nap, he was clearly drowsy. I closed the book and picked him up. "It's night-night time, little one." I placed him in his crib, and he lay down without any prompting. Covering him with his blanket, I reached over and turned on his music box. "Good night," I whispered and shut the door.

When I got to the sitting room, Kip and Paul were folding the sheets for Anna, and Gerard had removed all of the chairs. "Paul, it's your turn. What if we read three books tonight like your mommy does? How does that sound?"

"Okay," he said, taking my hand.

Kip joined us as we began to walk down the hallway. "May I listen, Paul?"

"Sure, Uncle Kip! But you might get sleeeeepyyyy!" he warned.

"I'll take my chances," Kip tousled Paul's hair.

The three of us entered Paul's room and gathered his books. Then we lay in his bed like sardines with Paul squeezed into the middle. I read the three books, and by the end, his eyelids were droopy. He asked us to stay with him, so we stayed a little while. Kip was chatting with him about volcanoes when I interrupted. "Paul, in three minutes we're going to get up." I eyed Kip, and he concurred.

We finally said our good-nights to Paul and closed his door. "Are you officially off the clock?" he asked, turning to face me.

"I think so."

"Well then, why don't we have date number three?"

"Right now?"

"We don't have to leave Ashford. We can have our date here. I just want to have you all to myself for the entire evening. If that means that I have to burn another one of my date cards, then so be it."

"What's Anna making for dinner?" I asked. "I'm starving."

We walked to the kitchen and met Anna. In her usual form, she was up to her elbows in a bowl of something. I reminded her that we still needed to plan Christmas dinner. It was my attempt to make my presence seem like work rather than hanging out with Kip.

"I'll just give you a list of ingredients so that you can order them from Miller's Grocery," she said, eyeing Kip anyway. "Pippa always has a turkey and a ham with traditional fare." Anna wiped her hands on a towel and went through the butler's pantry to retrieve some supplies.

"Why don't you take some time in your room and freshen up, rest, read, whatever. When you come back, I'll have dinner ready for us," Kip suggested.

"Kip, you don't have to go all out or anything. Let's just eat at the kitchen table, have a drink or two, and maybe watch a movie or something," I nearly whispered.

"But it's our third date. I feel like I should put some effort into it."

"Kip, I've told you that I don't need that flashy stuff. You and your family have already impressed me enough. I'm sold. You don't have to convince me that we should be dating. Don't waste the effort on ambiance."

He leaned in closer to me, his strong hands on my waist. "Is that what we are? Dating?" The corner of his mouth turned up, and behind his eyes I could see approval.

When someone goes on more than one date, she is *dating*—but Kip seemed to be taking my comment a slightly different way. Was I dating Kip Marley? "I suppose so," I said to both his question and my own.

Chapter Fifteen

"I should not be dating you, you know," I said through bites of tortelli di zucca. I'd never had it before. "I'm supposed to be separate from the family. This is not professional and not in my nature." There was something about saying it out loud that made me feel better.

"I know. But in this house, nobody cares. Think about it: Robert was the house manager before you, and he's *in* the family."

"True." I more or less just wanted to put it out there that I was aware of how weird the situation was.

"I thought I'd pull a few movies. See what you like," Kip explained, placing the boxes on the table. "Any of these look good to you?"

"What's your favorite movie of all time? Just curious," I asked him, momentarily disregarding the choices before me.

"Hm. I'm not sure." He ate a few bites, swallowed and took a sip of his beer. As I sat there across from Kip, I felt a little out-of-place. Why was this fantastically wealthy, attractive man having dinner with me? I wondered if it was because I hadn't fallen at his feet like most of the women around him surely did. And perhaps it was simply because I was here, someone to take his mind off the monotony of being home.

"I suppose there's *The Graduate*. That's pretty darn good. I don't really have a favorite." He took another drink from his glass. "How about you? What is *your* favorite of all time?"

"Maybe *Stand by Me*?" I said, feeling a little anxious all of a sudden. What was this between me and Kip? Megan had told me about what a playboy he was, always showing up at parties with a lanky blonde on his arm. He changed girlfriends as often as I changed purses. I picked up the boxes of each of the movies and turned them over in my hand, pretending to study the contents, so that I wouldn't have to look at him.

"Ugh. Robert made me watch *Stand by Me* over and over as a kid. Thank God we didn't live near any train tracks. He may have tried to make me hike them."

"It's a serious movie, and he seems to be a serious guy." I set down the *E.T.* box and took a drink of my beer.

"Yeah…" Kip appeared to be thinking about something.

We needed to get off of the subject of Robert, for both of our sakes. The mention of him seemed to make Kip anxious. And if I thought about him too long, he'd divert my attention, and I wanted to give Kip the attention that he needed.

"I thought I did pretty well with these," he pointed to the options on the table.

I tried to smile my most flirty smile, inwardly wincing at how it had probably come off. Flirting doesn't come naturally to me. Kip seemed responsive though, grinning back at me from behind his glass of beer as he put it to his lips.

"So, what will it be?"

I studied my options, fingering the box of each one again. "How about *E.T.*?"

Kip stacked the movies on the table. "*E.T.* it is then."

After our meal, Kip got us cappuccinos. We took them with us to the room with the television at the end of the east wing. The screen swallowed up nearly an entire wall. He opened a closet door, revealing a mass of buttons and gadgetry. He popped in the movie and closed the door. With the lights off, the room was like a theater, the sound seemingly emanating from every surface.

He and I sat together on a large sofa in the center of the room. It hadn't looked like this in the daytime when Paul had been in here. However, now, with the afghan that Kip had given me and his side to lean against, the room seemed much more comfortable.

I couldn't help myself. I leaned up against him and dug my feet between the sofa cushions. We sipped our cappuccinos and set them on a little table that had been scooted over in front of us. Kip had his coffee in his left hand with his right arm draped around me.

Elliott and Gertie were discussing their Halloween costumes over dinner when Kip's phone buzzed. He pulled it out in front of him, and I caught a peek at the screen. It said, "Beth." He silenced it and placed it back in his pocket. I pretended not to wonder who Beth was. She could be anyone. I certainly didn't have claim enough on him to ask. Jealousy wouldn't describe the emotion I was having—it was more like curiosity.

As the movie went on, my thoughts veered to Kip's mystery call. It brought me to an unexpected reality: I didn't know Kip all that well. I only knew him in terms of his family. I had no idea who his friends were, the relationships he'd had, or what he was like socially, out in the real world. And the part gnawing at me the most was that I didn't know when or if he was ever going to introduce me to that part of his life. Even if he did, there was no way that I would have fit in with those people anyway. Kip was down to earth, sure, but I'd bet his friends were of a social class to which I couldn't even relate. And vice-versa.

My mind raced toward future events: Kip and I at parties where no one was talking to me, sitting alone as Kip bounced around from person to person, unaware that I was out of my element. Their private school upbringing, polo matches, weekends in the Hamptons, none of which I had ever experienced. I hadn't flown all over the country and the world, for that matter. I didn't know the latest designers or fashion moguls.

Insecurity began to consume me. What was I thinking? I couldn't really date someone like Kip Marley. I was confined to his house, a diversion for him when he was home. My Cinderella complex was still on my mind when the movie ended, and I couldn't help but feel a little anxious about how to behave once the lights were turned on.

Still snuggled against Kip when he turned the movie off, I pretended to be asleep. I offered him my most groggy expression as he turned on a lamp next to the sofa.

"Did you miss the movie?" he asked, his eyes pouring into mine.

"I think I may have," I lied. "I'm really tired, Kip. I think I might just head off to bed."

"Mind if I come?" He put his hands up. "I'll be a perfect gentleman, I promise."

I chewed on the inside of my lip. How did I get myself into this? "I think I'd be boring company. You may be better off in your own room."

He could sense an underlying message hanging in the air between us, I could tell, but I don't think he could put his finger on it. He was searching my face for an answer. I didn't know what to say or how to say it.

Before I could offer him any sort of explanation, he asked, "What are you thinking about?"

"What do you mean?" I was buying time. What do I say?

"I can tell you're thinking about something. What is it?" His face was consoling and questioning at the same time.

"Nothing. It's just been a long day." I tried to contort my expression into a pleasant one. Without a mirror, it was hard to see if I had been successful. My knees began to quiver with pent-up energy.

He stood up and walked with me into the hallway. Uncertainty was written all over his face, but I didn't know how to explain myself. I knew I must seem hot and cold. I was becoming increasingly uncomfortable, and I just wanted to go to bed.

At the door to my room, Kip leaned down and kissed me, lingering a bit longer than usual. "Good night," he whispered on my lips before kissing me one last time.

"Good night."

"I'll see you in the morning." Kip slid one finger down my cheek and then turned and walked away.

I quickly shut the door and leaned my head back on the other side of it. I was so utterly confused. Was I being ridiculous? Eventually, we'd have to deal with the fact that I really did not fit into his lifestyle at all. It was probably better if I pulled away gently now before things got any more serious.

I heaved myself off the door and walked into the bathroom where I drew a hot bath. Tipping my head back on the rounded porcelain rim of the tub, I closed my eyes to let my body relax. I tried to push any thoughts about my future relationship with Kip out of my mind. It was too much to deal with right now. As I lay there in the tub, I could hear my cell phone beckoning me from the bedroom. I ignored it. I knew that Megan was chomping at the bit to hear about Kip, but I just wasn't in the mood to go into it. Plus, she'd talk me into dating him, I was nearly sure, and then I'd have to deal with the issue all over again—just later. I slid my head under the water.

After my bath, I felt much more relaxed. I brushed my teeth, lotioned myself until my skin was soft, and slipped into my silkiest pajamas, then crawled into bed and under the softness of the feather duvet. It was heaven. I clicked off the lamp beside the bed and closed my eyes. In moments, I surrendered to sleep.

❊ ❊ ❊

It seemed like the middle of the night. The door to my room opened, and there was a shadow in the doorway. Kip must have decided to come over unannounced. What was in his hand? A bag? The light clicked on, and I sprung to attention. "Oh!"

"*Ahhggg!*" Robert nearly jumped backwards through the open door. "I'm so sorry," he said, his eyes darting around the room. "This is," the skin between his eyebrows wrinkled, "*my* room, right?"

I dragged my fingers through my hair and tried to focus. "Yeah. Sloane told me to take this room to be closer to the boys. Apparently, baby monitors don't work very well here." My plunging silk neckline was a little more plunging than I'd have liked, so I bunched the duvet up by my neck.

Robert nodded in understanding. "I apologize," he walked toward the bed. It was as if he wanted to look me in the eye but didn't feel that he should. His gaze kept fluttering over to me and then away. "Can I just get a few things from the bathroom and the wardrobe? Then I'll head over to the guest room down the hall."

I nodded, my heart reacting to his presence as he quickly pulled some clothes from the closet. It was surreal to see him. I had only seen him once before, but now, seeing him again was... interesting.

His clothes were casual, his demeanor less businesslike. He turned on the light in the bathroom. I quickly shook my fingers in my hair to fluff it up a bit, licked my lips, and rearranged my pajamas. The light clicked off, and he came back out, eyes fluttering again.

"Good night," he said as he reached the bedroom door. "Sleep well. Sorry to have disturbed you."

"Good night." I lay back on his bed, watching him as he shut the door behind him. I stared at the ceiling through the darkness.

Robert had come home for Christmas.

I couldn't stop that thought from circling in my head, over and over. Robert had come home for Christmas.

❋ ❋ ❋

It was nearly eleven o'clock, and I still couldn't sleep. I had been in bed for an hour since Robert had barged into my room. I couldn't stop myself from completely freaking out that he was here. I shouldn't be feeling this way, but I couldn't help it.

I was restless, wired, on edge, so I decided to sneak to the kitchen for a glass of milk. Pulling on my robe and cinching it around my waist, I opened my door and padded down the hallway toward the kitchen.

I entered to find Robert sitting at the table by the bay window. Heat immediately filled my cheeks. He looked up from his newspaper. "Hello," he gave a curt grin. His eyes followed me as I walked closer to the refrigerator.

"Hi. I'm sorry; I didn't know you were still up. I couldn't sleep, so I thought I'd get a glass of milk," I said, pulling the carton from the refrigerator and setting it on the counter. I retrieved a glass from the cupboard. "Do you mind?"

"Not at all. There's room for two in this kitchen."

I could feel his eyes on me still as I filled my glass and returned the milk to the fridge. I stood at the counter and took a sip.

"Please," Robert called over to me, gesturing to a chair near his. I could feel my pulse in my ears, and I was glad for the weight of the milk in the glass. It made my hand feel steadier than it was. I sat down beside him.

"I don't want to interrupt your reading," I said, gingerly setting the milk on the table.

Robert folded the paper and set it down. "You aren't interrupting anything."

So, why are you selling this beautiful house? Why did you come home for Christmas? How weird is it that I'm sleeping in your room? "So, how was your flight?" I asked aloud.

"Fine. I apologize for arriving so late. I tried to call…"

"Oh… I'm sorry that I didn't answer. I was taking a bath, and I thought you were Megan."

"Ah," he smiled, still watching me.

I dragged my finger up the side of my glass to catch a runaway drop of milk and blotted it on a napkin. "How was Spain?"

"Chilly and wet. I didn't visit Spain at the most opportune time. The property I was considering was not to my liking, so I didn't end up buying it." He shifted a little in my direction. "How's the passport application going? Do you have one yet?"

I grinned. "No."

"You really should get a passport, Allie." His eyes were softer now, and I could see humor behind them. It made my chest tighten with excitement. I took another drink of my milk. I couldn't shake the peculiar feeling of sitting next to Robert in the flesh. It made me feel like I could stay up all night, never sleep, just sit there next to him.

"So," I exhaled with nervous energy. "You came home for Christmas!"

"I did."

"What made you change your mind?"

Robert's mouth opened a little, but it took a minute for words to come out. "I just thought it might be a good idea."

"What are you going to tell Ms. Marley about the house?"

"I'm not sure. I haven't worked it out," he said, suddenly standing. "Would you join me in the sitting room?" He paused, "That is, if you aren't heading to bed."

I got up, pushed in my chair, and followed him into the room with my glass of milk.

He tossed some logs into the fireplace and poked at them with the stoker just before lighting the kindling. His shirt stretched just slightly across his broad shoulders. Making a quiet clapping noise, he brushed his hands together and joined me on the settee.

The Christmas tree was still lit, sending tiny shimmers of light across the floor. I tucked my feet beneath me to keep warm. "Do you think you and Ms. Marley will be able to work out your differences—or at least put them aside—this Christmas? She seems awfully frail."

"Probably not, after she hears the news that we're selling." He looked at me carefully as if he were watching for a reaction.

I mustered all of my will to get it out, and I was still amazed when the words actually left my lips, "I still can't believe you're planning on selling it." I tipped my head back to admire the woodwork around the ceiling.

My gaze returned to him, and I thought I would drop my glass of milk when Robert looked at me at that moment. His dark hair

showed the length of his day; the wavy locks were beginning to head
in different directions. There were lines around his eyes—stress or
laughter, I couldn't tell. He was staring straight at me with no fear.
His eyes swallowed me, and his expression seemed ragged but firm.

"Allie, this house is lovely to you, but for me, it's a weight; a
heaviness that reminds me of death and anger. The Christmas trees
and greenery, the furnishings and ambience, it all acts to disguise the
complete misery that I feel when I'm here."

I understood. Seeing it in his face, it finally made sense to me.
My eyes met his, and we held there for a time before I spoke. "So,
why then did you think that coming back would be a good idea?"

"I wanted to have an experience in the house that was… happy.
I thought that maybe this year, that could be achieved."

I wrinkled my nose in contemplation. "And you felt that coming
home to tell everyone that you're selling the house would give you
this happy experience?"

Robert's face was stoic. "I wasn't planning on that. I just wanted
to have Christmas with everyone, try not to bite Pippa's head off for
once, and say a proper goodbye to the life that I had here."

I don't know what came over me. I felt protective of Robert. I
just hadn't defined it before. I placed my hand on top of his, and
I noted a badly concealed look of shock on his face. It looked as
though he were reading my face, trying to find some hidden message within my eyes. He turned his hand under mine so that he
was holding my fingers like a rare shell at the beach, then he gently
pulled his hand from mine.

"You're up!" Kip's voice crashed into the back of my head. "Hey!
What are *you* doing home?" He bounded over to us. Kip leaned in
and kissed me, startling me. Then his eyes bounced from Robert to

me. He sat down extremely close to me, sandwiching me between them, as if staking his claim. "I thought you were asleep."

"Robert woke me up," I smirked for Robert's benefit. This only made Kip's eyes dart more quickly between Robert and me. I glanced over to Robert, but he didn't return my playful demeanor. He was staring, unblinking, at Kip.

Chapter Sixteen

I was still tired when I heard Sammy chatting in his bed at seven in the morning. Last night, I had excused myself almost as soon as Kip came in, claiming exhaustion, but lay in bed until nearly three a.m., my mind racing. I contemplated so many things: how I shouldn't have put myself in this position—mixing business with pleasure—my Cinderella complex, my feelings about Robert.

I quickly threw myself together and went to get Sammy. We had our usual conversation as I entered, Sammy asking for Mommy, and me explaining that she'd be home soon. I took him back to my room for a few minutes and let him play with my bottles of shampoo while I finished getting ready. Then we went to the kitchen for breakfast.

Anna tended to Sammy while I went to check on Paul. When I peeked in, I was taken aback to see Robert kneeling next to Paul's bed, talking with him about his mom. Robert noticed me peering in and smiled.

"Good morning," he said to me as I opened the door wider.

"Morning." I followed his gesture to sit down next to him.

"Paul was just asking me about his mom and dad and how things would work now that they weren't together." I nodded in understanding.

Paul piped up. "Uncle Robert told me that it would be different." He was using his best grown-up voice.

"That's true," I said. "Your Uncle Robert knows what he's talking about." I half-winked at Robert. "What do you think it will be like?" I asked Paul.

"I think I'll probably be with Mom the most," Paul added insightfully.

"Well, you'll probably get to spend time with both your mom and dad, but they'll live in different houses. You'll get to have two houses, which means two sets of toys and two places to play. That might be fun," I said.

"Will you like being with your mom?" Robert asked.

"Yes! She's the best mom! She does lots of fun stuff."

Paul was getting out of bed, so I reached over and pulled out his dresser drawer, handing him an outfit. "Why don't you get dressed and meet us in the kitchen for breakfast? Let's see what Anna has for you this morning."

Robert held the door by its crystal knob. He opened it wider at my approach and motioned for me to exit first. As I was leaving, Paul called out, "I hope it's pancakes!"

"Have you eaten?" Robert asked as we walked down the hallway.

"Not yet."

"Why don't you sit with me and the boys and have some breakfast?" he offered.

"That would be nice," I peered up at him, but he wasn't looking at me. He was looking down the hallway, a thought seemingly on his lips.

❋ ❋ ❋

I was on my second cup of coffee when Kip joined us in the kitchen. He immediately surveyed the table—I was sitting next to Robert, having breakfast with the boys. He walked over and stood behind me, placing his hands on my shoulders. It felt slightly uncomfortable, just a little forced.

"So, how is everyone this morning?" he asked, leaning down to kiss my cheek. In my ear, he whispered, "Good morning." I turned to greet him, and he kissed my lips. Then, with a screech, he pulled a corner chair up to the table and sat next to me.

Sammy held out his pancake and said, "Pahpake."

Paul replied, "Morming Umple Pip," through a mouthful of pancakes.

I glanced over at Robert. He had resumed that passive stare that I saw this morning in the hallway. "I'm well, Kip. How are you?" Robert asked, not really making eye contact.

"Good! Slept like a baby." Kip leaned in my direction and said in a low voice, "I'm planning somewhere for us to go. Nothing too over the top, just fun. Are you game for going out?"

"As long as it's in the country," I teased. The corner of Kip's mouth turned up into a grin. It was so familiar now. Why did this all have to be so complicated? I patted his leg. "When would we be going?"

"Tomorrow night. Busy?"

"I think I'm free." I hadn't agreed to anything beyond three dates, but I was in too deep, it seemed. Kip didn't even consider the fact that our flipping contract had come to an end.

"Great! I'll pick you up at six."

Very funny, Kip.

Robert had his head inside the newspaper, seemingly ignoring us completely.

❋ ❋ ❋

It was mid-morning, and the kids were seated at a small arts and crafts table that Sloane had brought with them and stored, folded, behind Paul's bedroom door. I gave each child a piece of paper, cut in the shape of an oval with two eyeholes cut out.

"Okay, I'm going to play some music, and you decide what animal it sounds like. Then I want you to decorate your mask like that animal. Or, you can decorate it the way you'd like. It's up to you," I explained.

I hit the button on the control panel behind the butler's pantry. Classical music began to spill through the hallways and into each room. Paul was frantically scribbling away on his mask while Sammy was deciding if he should chew on the crayon. I was helping Sammy when Robert peered into the kitchen where we were working.

"Hello," I said standing up to greet him. "I'm glad that you came in. I wanted to talk to you." I walked over toward him, the two boys still coloring eagerly behind me.

Robert raised his eyebrows. "About?" We met in the center of the kitchen by the island.

"I'm assuming that I'm house manager until you tell me differently, but I wanted to be clear to the staff now that you're home. Should they report to me or to you?"

Robert's expression dropped from amiable to more serious. "Oh. Yes. Well, I'm on vacation. So you are still on duty." A small smile emerged, and it lit up his face.

"I'm done!" Paul came running up to me wearing his mask with black and gray scribbles and one dot of pink.

"And you are?" I giggled at him.

"A cat! Meow, meow," he pawed the air.

"What do you think Sammy will be?" I asked, glancing over at his little, fat hands grabbing crayon after crayon. He had built a crayon mountain, and he was crying "Uh oh!" every time one would roll off the table.

Robert observed the three of us. Always watching. I wished that I knew what he was thinking. He was so careful with his emotions, never letting a single feeling show.

He walked over to Sammy and pulled the mask out from under the pile of crayons. It had brown scribbles on it. "Sammy, this looks like a bear. Is that what you are?"

"Beh," Sammy agreed.

Robert gingerly placed the mask over Sammy's eyes. "You look like a bear!" he beamed at his nephew.

"I have something else planned in a few minutes," I said excitedly. After clicking off the music, I asked Paul, "Do you have a clean-up song that you sing when you're putting things away?"

"Yes!" he said.

"Do you think you can sing it for me?"

Paul began to sing his clean-up song. Sammy watched his brother while placing the crayons back in the box. When the boys were finished, I folded down the table and chairs and handed them to Gerard, who returned them to Paul's room. He didn't have to help me out with my children's projects, but despite his apparent disapproval of my involvement with Kip, he was always there if I asked.

When everything was back in order, I handed each boy a clipboard with five nature colors on one side of the paper and large square boxes across from each color. "Let's get coats on! We're going on a nature hunt!"

"May I come?" asked Robert, to my complete surprise.

"Um, sure."

Robert went over to a closet in the hallway and pulled a coat from it, sliding the downy heap around his shoulders and pushing his arms through the sleeves, and then helped me to get the kids dressed in winter attire. We walked out the back door, the boys holding their clipboards in mittened hands.

"Here's what we're going to do: I want you to look for something that is a color next to one of your boxes. Then, when you find something, you can draw it or keep it in your pocket. Once we have all of the colors, we'll go inside and share what we've found." I picked up an acorn that had fallen beneath an enormous tree that I figured must have been original to the property. "See this," I held it down for the boys to inspect. "It might be something to put next to one of your brown colors."

"I want it!" Paul reached for my hand. I handed it to him and picked up another for Sammy. Sammy looked at it and threw it onto the ground, then set the clipboard down on the grass and began to run around the yard. Paul was meticulously searching for every color on his clipboard.

The frozen ground crunched beneath our feet as we walked behind the children. Robert looked at me, keeping stride, "I'd still like you to plan the Christmas family meeting if that's all right. Anna can help you."

I stopped and turned to face him. Robert followed my lead, and I tilted my head up toward him before speaking. Should I be candid with him? I might as well. "Robert, why do you call it a family *meeting*?"

"What do you mean?"

"Isn't it family *Christmas*?" I clarified.

Robert rubbed the back of his neck under his coat collar. "I suppose it could be."

"A meeting is something you do in the office, not in your own home."

I could see evidence of consideration flood his features. What was he thinking? His face was unreadable.

"For regular families it would be a family Christmas, but for a one like ours—a dissimilar assemblage of members who only share the same genetics—it is more of a meeting." Paul came running up between us and showed us a leaf that he'd found. Robert patted his head and Paul ran off. I eyed Sammy, who was digging in the dirt with a stick.

"They're not that bad," I said, the warmth of my breath puffing out in the cold. Robert studied my face for a time and then turned toward the boys. I could already tell when Robert was contemplating things—which was all the time; he was at that moment. I wanted to ask him about his musings, but I just didn't feel quite comfortable enough yet to ask. Sammy was throwing rocks into a planter on the patio as Paul studied the pebbles for their color.

"So, what do I have to plan?"

"Well, on Christmas Eve, we have an open house for friends and family. You'll need to prepare the menu and guest list for that. Anna will assist you. Just don't let her spend more than a few thousand."

"Dollars?" My voice came out as a squeak.

Robert nodded and continued, "Then we usually have a Christmas reading by Pippa—make sure that she has something prepared—and we go to the candlelight Christmas service at our local church. After that, we converge for Christmas dinner where we share a favorite holiday memory and someone does a toast. Last year it was Kip. Maybe Sloane could do it this year. Just ask her."

"Do you think she'll be up to it after just coming back from her divorce proceedings?"

"Mm. You might be right."

"Why don't you do the toast?" I pressed.

Robert exhaled loudly, and I watched his breath dissipate in front of him. "I'd rather not."

"Why?"

Robert walked for a while, and I thought he wasn't going to answer. "I don't think it would be… well-received, given my current family status."

"If it's from your heart, I'm sure it would be *well-received*."

"I'm done!" Paul cried, running toward us. "Allie, look at this!" He held out his hand, revealing a flat, smooth stone the color of chocolate with swirls of gray.

"Wow! That's really nice, Paul. Maybe that could be your lucky rock."

"I'm going to draw it when we get inside," he told us excitedly.

We collected Sammy as well as our clipboards and nature items and went inside. "Why don't we all go to the sitting room and warm up by the fire?" Robert suggested.

The boys kicked off their shoes, dropped their coats, hats, scarves, and gloves directly in front of the door, and ran in sock-feet toward the sitting room. Robert pulled out a thirty-two-piece puzzle and opened it up for Paul. Sammy had a shape bucket with blocks in the forms of the basic shapes. He was putting the blocks in the bucket and dumping them out as Robert lit the fire. The scent of tea and cinnamon filled the air as Anna appeared with a silver tea set. She prepared two cups and set them on the tray next to the settee.

I took Paul's clipboard and sat down on the floor near the fire. "Paul, do you want to show me what you found outside?"

Paul abandoned his puzzle and eagerly scooted over to me. "May I have a pencil? I want to draw some of the trees in this one," he said pointing to one of the squares.

Robert walked over to an ornamental drawer on a davenport desk that was overwhelmed by the Christmas tree sitting next to it. He pulled out a pencil and handed it to Paul who began to fill in the blank spaces on his nature paper. Then, while Paul scribbled away, Robert walked over to the silver tray, picked up the two still-steaming cups and handed one to me, sitting down next to me on the floor. I tucked my feet under me and noticed the start of a smile surfacing on Robert's lips as he watched me. I wondered again what he was thinking. He was so difficult to figure out.

I took a sip of my tea as Paul came over to show me his drawings. "This is the green tree I saw outside. The one with the birdhouse in it…" he began to interpret his illustrations. I was peering down at his paper, but I could see Robert out of the corner of my eye. He was looking at my hair, my neck, my face, and my hands on my mug. I glanced over at him, his eyes popping up to my face. Nervously, I turned back to Paul.

"Allie?" Robert leaned closer to me.

"Yes?" I said, turning my head to face him and blinking in response to how close he was to me.

Robert's mouth opened as if he were about to speak when he was interrupted. "Hey there, guys!" Kip walked into the room and sat down next to Paul. Paul immediately began showing him his nature color drawings.

I turned back to Robert. "What were you going to say?" I asked quietly.

"Nothing," he told me, his expression becoming impassive again.

Chapter Seventeen

Kip walked toward me and pulled me up by my hands. "May I steal you for a little while?" he asked, his eyes fixed on Robert.

"I really shouldn't, Kip," I said. "I have to watch the children, and it isn't Robert's responsibility to watch them. It's mine." Sammy toddled over and handed me a glass egg from one of the tables.

"Dink you!" he said as he wobbled it into my hands.

I delicately placed it back in its spot. "An employer must give breaks and lunch by law, correct?" Kip said in Robert's direction.

"You're kidding, right?" I asked.

"No, I'm completely serious!"

Robert interrupted him. "Go, Allie. I can watch the boys. It's not a problem. I'll take them to the media room, and we can build something with blocks." He looked at Paul and Sammy. "Would you like to build a giant city with blocks? Paul, you can get your cars and we'll make roads and bridges for them."

The boys agreed as Robert stood up and reached out for each child to grab a hand. As he walked past me, I could feel his eyes on me, but for some reason I felt compelled to look away. Robert left the room, and Kip turned to face me. "I missed you," he said, squeezing into the remaining space between our bodies. "I just wanted some time with you, that's all." He took a finger and lifted my chin like they do in the movies. "Wanna take a walk?"

"Outside?"

"Isn't that where most people take walks?"

"Sure." I grinned at him, and he leaned down and planted a tiny kiss on my lips. As we turned around to walk toward the grand entranceway, I discretely eyed the various doorways for any sign of Robert, hoping he wasn't witness to mine and Kip's affections. Kip grabbed a small shoulder bag that had been sitting on the floor next to the front door, and we headed outside.

We walked down the long drive to the property and turned parallel to the main road. It was cold, even with my coat and scarf. We walked for some time. In the fresh, icy air that surrounded us, I kept thinking about how I shouldn't be doing this. It was all going to end anyway, so I might as well not get into anything serious. There was something very persuasive about Kip, though. I couldn't put my finger on it, but I had a very hard time telling his charming face no.

We walked over a hill and down into a modest valley when I saw dark brown wooden fencing outlining the landscape. It framed rolling hills of grass that were dotted with the most beautiful horses I'd ever seen. One of them caught sight of us and began walking toward the fence that separated human from animal.

Kip reached into the bag that he'd been carrying and pulled out a carrot with foliage still attached that was the length of my forearm. He offered it to the approaching horse. It made soft nickering sounds and nuzzled his hand, then began munching the end of the treat.

"These are Andalusian showjumping horses. They belong to our neighbor. This one's called Daisy."

I stretched out my arm to touch Daisy, and Kip gently blocked my hand. "There's a language between humans and horses. Watch her." The horse finished the carrot and began making the sounds again, then she turned away from Kip, allowing her side to be exposed to his reach. "Pat her here," he said, reaching out and stroking her russet hair. I followed his lead. Her hair was like silk, her tail swishing gently in the breeze.

Three other horses observed Daisy's encounter and trotted over to join her, greeting us with a nearly noiseless approach. They hung their beautiful noses over the edge of the fence, awaiting another of Kip's delicacies. He obliged, handing a carrot to each, one at a time.

"The white horse here is Britches. She won first prize in a state competition a few weeks back. And this one with the dark brown hair is Andre. He is the most gentle of all of the horses, in my opinion. Then, at the end there, on the other side of Daisy is Rocco." The horses began to interact with each other right in front of us, touching noses with one another and making sounds toward each other.

Andre gently nudged the others and then placed his face quite close to me. "Keep your hands down for just a minute longer," Kip instructed. The horse grazed my arm with his nose ever so slightly. "Now, be very gentle, and he'll let you pet his face." I did, and looking at the horse's face, it was as if I could see right through to his thoughts. His eyes were like human eyes—full of friendliness.

"You are beautiful," I said to Andre, and he leaned a bit further over the fence. Still stroking Andre, I turned to Kip. "They're amazing. Thank you for bringing me here." He offered each horse one more carrot before we said our good-byes and turned back toward Ashford.

"Those horses were absolutely fantastic," I told Kip.

"Robert and I ride them occasionally."

"Really? I'd love to see that."

"Maybe you can."

After a meandering walk in the crisp air, we reached the house and climbed the staircase to the front door. Kip tugged on the brass door pull and pushed the door open, a wave of heat rushing out toward us. "Would you like to ride one day? They're very gentle." Kip paced in front of me, swinging himself around so that he was walking backwards. His expression was pleasant, but he was clearly thinking about something. It was the same look my mother would give me. Like when she said I couldn't go to the high school dance with Tommy Saunders—who was seventeen and had a car—my freshman year. I could tell that she wanted me to go, but she was scared, so her "no" was weak and quiet. "I may have to let you have Andre," he said in the same way as my mother, an unreadable expression on his face.

"Oh, I don't know. I've never been on a horse before."

"Andre would take good care of you." Kip spun back around beside me and stared out ahead of us. Then he reached over and held my hand like a schoolboy. I let him, but it felt wrong, an incorrect fit.

"Where's Ms. Marley? I haven't seen her in quite a while," I mentioned to Kip.

"She stays clear when Robert's home," he answered.

"That's ridiculous. She shouldn't feel like she has to be confined to her room."

"I don't think she feels like she has to. I think it's by choice."

Kip and I headed toward the end of the east wing to find Robert and the boys. When we got there, he let go of my hand and wrapped his arm around my waist, making me uneasy. Robert's eyes fluttered down to Kip's arm and then back up to our faces.

"I know that this is completely unreasonable, since I'm supposed to be the nanny, but I was wondering," I pulled away and turned to Kip, "if you could finish building with the boys while I talk to Robert."

What I thought to be a momentary twinge of worry surfaced in Kip's eyes, but he covered it quickly and answered. "Sure, no problem."

"Thanks, Kip." There was a slightly awkward air between us, as if he wanted to kiss me, or for me to reach up and kiss him, but I didn't really want to even pretend anymore. I didn't know how to proceed. Surely, a peck on the cheek would be a nice thank you, but I didn't. And now there was a tiny void sandwiched between us.

Robert got up and ruffled the boys' hair. "I'll be back, boys," he told them, following me out of the room. I caught him looking at me discreetly as we walked down the hall.

"Do you mind if we go to your room? My room?" I corrected. He shook his head.

We walked into our room, and I pulled the corner chair over to the bed, motioning for Robert to sit down. I sat down on the bed cross-legged. "I know that this is none of my business, but have you noticed the absence of someone in this family since your return?" I asked. He looked at me blankly. "Have you seen your grandmother since you've been home?"

"Of course I have. I check on her every morning."

"She was speeding all over this house on her little scooter until you came home. I haven't seen her come out of her room at all since."

"I'm sure it's by choice, Allie."

"That's what Kip said. I don't care. It's not right. Isn't there something you can do to smooth things over with her?"

Robert leaned toward me, his forearms on his knees. "Imagine the situation from her perspective. Her entire immediate family is gone now. She only has five living relatives, counting Paul and Sammy. We have nothing in common. So, other than the love of her grandchildren and great grandchildren, the only thing tying her to this earth is this house, which I'm selling."

"If you understand her point of view, why can't you sympathize?"

"I can, but I'm not going to waste millions of dollars—*millions* of dollars—to appease her."

That point silenced me for a moment, as the gulf between my lifestyle and the Marleys' widened. Millions of dollars. For upkeep? He was spending more money on Ashford than I'd ever see in my lifetime. But then, the Marleys had that kind of money. What better way to spend it than on preserving the family history and letting the woman who raised them live out her final years happily, in a place filled with happy memories of everything she loved?

He was starting to close up, I could tell. His leg started to bounce in agitation. I reached out and rested a finger on the side of his knee, and it became still. He was obviously tense, but intently looking into my eyes. For what?

"I'm not trying to argue with you," I told him. "I'd just like to see you and Ms. Marley enjoy each other."

I could see surrender in his eyes, and his face softened, his shoulders relaxed. "I know. 'Enjoy' is a strong word, though. I'd just wish for us to 'stand' each other. I'll give it my best effort," he promised.

"That's all I hope for," I said.

✳ ✳ ✳

Kip and Paul were outside again playing in the absolutely freezing weather against my better judgment, and Sammy was down for his nap when I went to see Anna about planning the Christmas *meeting*.

Anna was prepping dinner when I entered the kitchen. "Do you have a little time to discuss the Christmas Open House?" I asked. She stopped chopping and wiped her hands on her towel. Pulling a pad and pen from a drawer, she joined me at the kitchen table. Her pen poised to take notes, I asked, "How many people are usually invited?"

"Typically a couple hundred, but Mr. Marley asked that I keep the number small this year. He was hoping to avoid discussions regarding the sale of the house."

I consciously lowered my eyebrows. A couple hundred? "So, how many do you expect this year?"

"Mr. Marley requested only fifty. Very intimate. Casual hors d'oeuvres and a few entrees. The Marleys have already sent their guest lists and the invitations are being drawn up, so the only things we need to discuss are the food options and the favors."

"I have to decide that?"

"Well, I do have some options to choose from."

Thank goodness! "Okay, give them to me. What do you have?"

We worked out the menu in only a few minutes. I decided on a starter of lemongrass chicken meatballs—I'm sure they have a fancier name—to be passed around by waiters on trays with little silver forks. Also, there would be crème fraiche and caviar (just because it sounded impressive) with little crackers and smoked salmon toasts with capers and shallots.

The main dishes I picked were roasted vegetable kebabs for the vegetarians and individual lobster pot pies for the rest of us. Choosing the gifts for each guest was much more fun. I selected a champagne-themed gift basket. Anna and I also had time to plan the Christmas dinner for the family, which was much easier. It was really the same as most Thanksgiving meals, just served on more expensive dishes.

After I wrapped things up with Anna, I decided to go and see Pippa about the Christmas reading. Plus, I wanted to check on her. I hadn't seen her in days, and in a weird way, I kind of missed her.

Chapter Eighteen

I tapped on Pippa's door and pushed it open with my finger. It creaked as it slid ajar. She was sitting in her usual chair, her fingers laced; her hands resting on her lap. "Hello," I greeted her as I approached the bed and leaned against it. My eyes followed the substantial dark-wood poster all the way up to its ornamental tip. Then I looked back at Pippa. "Is it Christmas-present-wrapping-time yet?" She smiled, but it didn't reach her eyes. She was worried, I could tell. "Are you okay?"

"Have you heard any news from Robert regarding the sale of Ashford?" she came straight out with it.

"I didn't want to ask, so no. Last I heard, they were negotiating a final offer."

"Mm." Pippa turned her head toward the window. Then she seemed to snap out of her thought. "Well, dear, go and shut the door if you're going to be wrapping presents. I can't have the entire family knowing what they're getting."

I followed Pippa's orders and slid the door closed. She told me where she had placed her bags of wrapping paper and ribbons as well as the shopping bag full of gifts. The first item that I retrieved from the bag was a flat, charcoal-colored box. "Do you mind?" I asked, holding it out toward Pippa.

"By all means," she tipped her head at me.

I opened the box, revealing a platinum necklace with a blue pendant that was so bright, it looked electric. I traced it with my finger. "What is this stone?" I asked nearly whispering.

"It's a four carat heated blue sapphire," she explained proudly. I had no idea how much a stone like that cost—a hundred dollars? A thousand? No idea—but I knew it was substantial. "It's for Sloane. Her birthday month is September, so she wears sapphires on occasion."

I closed the box and set it down in the center of a large square of paper. Pippa looked on as I folded the edges around the box and taped down corners. "Your present wrapping rivals origami," she said. I grinned up at her self-consciously then looked back down at the present. I pulled two lengthy pieces of satin ribbon from their spools, one in silver and the other in a deep cranberry and tied a traditional bow on the front of the gift. With an unnecessarily heavy pair of scissors, I snipped the ends of each ribbon into a dovetail.

"That is beautiful," Pippa said.

I set it down on the table beside her and pulled the next gift from the bag. Another jewelry box. This one was a perfect cube of black leather. I peeked inside to find a stainless steel Swiss Army watch. With the watch still holding my view, Pippa said, "For Kip." I didn't know how much it cost either, but I was guestimating that what Pippa had spent in two presents would rival at least a month of my salary. I hadn't even gotten to the last gift in the bag.

Once Kip's watch was wrapped, I drew out a tiny, flat box with a clear top and a coin nestled in black velvet. I pulled it close to my face and squinted at the picture. *Buffalo nickel?*

Pippa interrupted my speculation. "It's a Nineteen Eighteen-D Eight over Seven Buffalo Nickel. If you look very closely, the eight in the date has been printed over an original seven." I analyzed it more closely to make out the error. "It's for Robert. He collects coins."

I looked up. "You're kidding me," I didn't even attempt to hide my complete surprise.

Pippa looked over at me quizzically. "No," she said slowly, her voice going up at the end of the word. She pursed her lips and watched me as I studied the coin. "Why is that such a revelation to you?"

"Well… I'm sort of the exact opposite of a coin collector in a way." Pippa questioned me with her eyes. "My grandmother used to buy me coins, but I never saw the point in collecting them. So, my sister and I would unwrap them…" Pippa pulled in a large breath in indignation. "Yeah, we unwrapped all of them and played with them. I couldn't even tell you where most of them are.

"Why do you think Robert collects coins? I've always wanted to know why people collect things like coins…" I continued to wrap. "I mean, they aren't particularly striking in any way and most people—well, the people I know—don't have room to display them. They may be worth something, but if you never sell them, then they aren't worth much, in my opinion. They don't do anything except take up the extra space in your closet."

Pippa politely allowed me to finish before she responded. "Once Robert opens his gift, so as not to spoil the surprise, you see, you'll have to ask him why he collects coins. It is an interesting story, but one I'm sure he'd rather tell." She broke eye contact and peered out of the window as if she were thinking about something in particular. I carefully finished covering the coin in silver paper and adorned it with a ribbon bow, then set it on her table next to the other two.

"Are there any more to wrap?" I asked, obviously pulling her out of some thought.

"That will be all. The children will have a gift that isn't wrapped."

"Do you mind if I ask what they're getting?"

"I'm having Gerard and the staff work overtime on Christmas Eve to erect an enormous wooden play set outside here at Ashford." I felt a stab of sadness knowing that the house would not be in their possession long after the holiday. It was a waste of time and money to build something like that, but it wasn't my place to say anything.

❄ ❄ ❄

I had an enjoyable afternoon with the boys. Paul and I tacked early reading sight words all over the media room and played a great game of "Sight-Word Safe"—a game I created for Nathan when he started to learn to read. Paul seemed so articulate; I thought I'd give it a try. I taught him the five words that were on the cards, put them up on the wall in various locations, called out a word and tried to tag him before he could reach that word in safety. Sammy had absolutely no idea how to play, but enjoyed chasing Paul.

I was delighted to see that, while reading bedtime stories, Paul found the words "and" and "the" six and eight times respectively in his story. I couldn't wait to teach him more words.

I knew, in the back of my mind that Sloane would be coming home soon. I really missed being a nanny, and I was a little sad that she was returning, although I knew the kids would be happy about it.

Anxiety swelled within me as I realized that once the house sold I would have to leave this family and return to… what? What would I do? I wouldn't have any reason to contact the Marleys except possibly Kip if he was still pursuing me—which I had to wonder if he would when I was no longer shoved in front of his face every day. To take my mind off it, I decided to see if I could get any dinner from Anna.

When I entered the kitchen, Anna was wiping down the counters. I strode in and leaned against the counter across from her.

"Oh, here," she said, pulling a large opaque envelope from her bag. "This is your official invitation." She handed it to me. I slid my finger under the flap and pulled out a piece of cardstock that looked more ornate than any wedding invitation I'd ever received. "It's for the Marley Christmas Eve Open House," she explained as I scanned the calligraphy.

"*I'm* invited?" I didn't take my eyes off the invitation. It had my name in curly script at the top. "Why?"

"You're Kip's date."

"What?"

"Aren't you two dating?" Did I sense a slight bit of sarcasm slipping out in her words?

I tucked the card back into the envelope. "Well, I guess so."

"Wouldn't you know if you were dating a Marley?" she huffed. "All I know is that Kip gave me his guest list, and you were guest number one."

I knew that I could never ask her, but I wondered, not why I was number one on Kip's list, but whether I was any number at all on Robert's.

"Do you have a dress?" she interrupted my thoughts.

"What kind of dress should I wear?"

"Well, it's usually black tie, so something relatively elegant."

"I can't say that I brought anything like that to be a house manager. I guess that means I'll need to buy something."

"Buy what?" Kip popped in, as he always managed to do somehow.

"A dress for the party," Anna said over my head in Kip's direction.

"Do you need a dress?" Kip asked, now standing directly opposite me.

"I suppose I do. I'll just run out and get one after Sloane comes home."

Kip grabbed both of my hands and held them out like the wings of an airplane, looking me up and down. "I'll call my friend Alex. She's about your size. She has tons of dresses."

"That's okay, Kip, really."

He was already texting away on his phone. "No worries! She won't mind at all! How tall are you?"

"Five seven."

"Favorite dress color?"

Black? Isn't that what everyone likes, though? It would make me look the thinnest. "Any color is fine."

"Pick one. She probably has every color."

"Um, red?"

"Perfect." He hit a final button on his phone and slid it back into his pocket.

I leaned in closely toward Kip. "Don't I need to work at the party?" I asked.

"Not when you're with me, you don't. You're my date." He pulled his phone back out of his pocket, checked the screen, and looked into my eyes in a very odd and direct way. Then he typed something on his phone again.

"What are you doing?"

"Alex just texted me back and said she has loads of red dresses, and she asked me what color your eyes were. Hazel, right?" he asked, poking his face back into my personal space again.

"Yes."

"She said that you're welcome to any of her red dresses, but she has a champagne-color dress that may go very well with your eye color." His fingers were moving across his keypad a mile a minute. "Look, let's jump in the car and go over to her place, so you can check them out."

"I was just coming to get some dinner," I said, nerves ravaging me instantly at the thought of meeting someone who was probably very rich, a friend of Kip's, and nothing like me. All of a sudden, I felt very small.

"No problemo. I'll get you a bite to eat first if you'd like."

"What about the kids? I need to be here for them."

"They're asleep! Plus, I'm sure Anna wouldn't mind checking on them. We'll be right back." He surveyed Anna's expression. She shrugged and waved us off. "See, she's fine."

"Okay then, I guess."

"Great!" Kip was rubbing his hands together as if he were making fire with an invisible stick. "Get your coat. I'll pull the car around."

❈ ❈ ❈

After we ate a quick bite at the most elegant *casual*, as Kip had described it, soup and sandwich place I'd ever been, we began driving through an area of the city that I'd never seen before. I supposed that it was because no one I knew, or would ever know, could have afforded it. Absolutely charming terrace apartments were nestled into this perfect little section of shoreline on the bank of the James River. We parallel parked along a brick path that skirted around the water. I tried not to gawk as we made our way to the entrance of the building.

A man wearing a uniform and white gloves opened the door for us, tugging on brass door handles that were the size of a baseball bat. Kip nodded a thank you in his direction and guided me through the door first. I stood in an extremely new modern lobby, full of dark wood furniture with clean lines and brushed nickel accents. One wall contrasted with the rest of the interior, made of exposed brick that looked weathered and historical.

The entire lobby was more elegant than any I had ever seen. I was trying not to let my eyes roam in the ridiculous way that they wanted to as Kip pulled me into an elevator and hit a button for the top floor.

My hands began to sweat as the elevator slid up to our floor. Kip looked over at me and winked, wrapping an arm around the middle of my back and pulling me close to him. The doors opened, and we exited into a hallway that was endlessly long, and nearly as wide as the bedroom I'd been sleeping in for the last month. Kip walked down to the third door and knocked, still holding on to me. When the door opened, he dropped his arm so that he could kiss Alex on the cheek.

Even in her obviously casual clothes, she was more glamorous than anyone I knew. Her long, blonde hair was curled just at the ends and bounced back and forth from one side of her shoulders to the other. She had a perfect body, her breasts pushed up in some kind of must-be-wonder-bra that gave her cleavage under her v-neck t-shirt. She was wearing diamond stud earrings the size of M&Ms and a bracelet to match.

She reached out and grabbed my moist hand with both of hers. "You must be Allie," she beamed. "It's so nice to meet you! Come in!" She let go of my hand—thank God—to allow us entry into her apartment.

Alex's apartment was no less striking than the lobby downstairs. I tried to glance at each room as we made our way to her bedroom.

On her four-poster bed, complete with white gauzy fabric draping from the top and pillows in some sort of absurdly perfect silky material, she had five dresses laid out. The champagne-colored dress was the first in the line. It was lightly beaded, giving it a shimmery look, with simple lines and a forgiving shape. I immediately loved it. Alex picked it up by its substantial wooden hanger.

"This is the one that I thought would be just perfect." She held it under my chin. "And it goes with your hazel eyes and brown hair perfectly!" She handed the dress to me. "Try it on! Over there's the bathroom."

I clasped my fingers around the top of the hanger and smiled my most I'm-not-anxious-at-all smile and headed to the bathroom. As I was leaving, she draped herself over Kip's chest and whined, "It's been so long since I've seen you! I missed you so much!"

I hung the dress on a hook near the shower and leaned against the granite counter. After a few deep breathing exercises, I pulled myself up, leaving two wet palm prints on its surface. I undressed and slid the gown over my head. It fit like a glove. I looked in the mirror and did a twirl. Kip knew what he was talking about. This dress was perfect! I wasn't sure how I could fit a garment that a perfect female such as Alex would fit, but I didn't care. It was lovely. I opened the door.

Kip's eyes devoured me as I walked into the bedroom. Still looking me over, he handed me a flute of sparkling wine. "For you," he said, his cheeks rosy. "You look amazing."

"Thank you," I said, feeling bashful, as I accepted the beverage.

"Oh!" Alex clapped her hands together. "You look great!" She swept behind me and yanked my hair up onto the top of my head. "You *have* to let Franco do her hair!" Then she dropped my hair in a pile on my head, leaving me to shake it back into place, and ran over to a large armoire. She pulled out a box and opened it, revealing a delicate strand of linked emeralds and a matching pair of teardrop earrings. "You can borrow this! It will go so well with your eyes."

"Oh, I couldn't," I said, placing my hand on my chest more to steady my palpitating heart than anything else.

"Nonsense! Kip can return them after the holiday. It's no biggie." She snapped the box closed and laid it on my coat.

"Thank you."

"It's nothing." It probably really was nothing at all. I'll bet she had loads of dresses and jewelry like those. That gown was probably just an ordinary dress to her. Even if I won the lottery, it would still be a fancy dress to me. I returned to the bathroom, knocked back my entire glass of sparkling wine in one gulp, and took off the dress, returning it to its hanger.

❅ ❅ ❅

There was something very alluring about the look of Kip, walking through Ashford with my garment bag slung over his shoulder. For a brief moment, it felt like all of this was real somehow. I couldn't believe that I would actually be attending the Marleys' party—and, I might add, I was not oblivious to the fact that I would be taking home one of those gift baskets I had ordered.

Kip and I walked side-by-side into the sitting room. As he tossed my dress over the edge of the settee, I noticed Sloane sitting in a chair in the corner, a box of tissues in her lap. Kip gave me a unifying glance, and we both walked over to her.

"You okay, Sloane?" he asked, kneeling beside her on the floor. I wedged myself between her chair and the Christmas tree and sank down onto my knees on the floor next to her. She was sobbing into her hands.

She ripped a tissue from the box and pressed it against her eyes. Her nose was red and her lips had those little chapped lines in them as if they had been stretched and snapped back to their original size. She was a mess. "It's done," she sniffled through the tissue. "He's seeing someone else! Already!" She began to heave large sobs into her now soaking tissue. I pulled another from its box and handed it to her.

Kip rubbed her back as she blew her nose and handed him the wad of used tissue. He looked as though he were swallowing utter revulsion and took it in his palm. Robert walked up behind us, clearly distraught at his sister's grief, and handed her a cup of tea. She reached out and took the steaming cup, knocking the tissue box off her knees. I caught it and placed it back in her lap.

Robert retreated to the settee and sat down, inhaling deeply, exhaling slowly. His discomfort showed in his rigid stance. Sloane flapped her hands in the air, one hand still clutching a balled tissue. "Stop fussing over me! It's driving me crazy," she wailed. "I'll get over it. It'll be fine. I just need to let it out."

Robert, still sitting tensely on the settee, eyed the garment bag, then looked over at Kip and me before settling on the view of a blank space on the wall. I attempted to make eye contact, but he didn't look in my direction. His chest went in and out with his breath before he got up and left the room, an annoyed expression on his face.

Chapter Nineteen

Sammy was giggling and chatting in his bed, and I wondered if I was the first to hear him. Sloane hadn't gone to bed last night until she'd stopped crying which had taken a considerable amount of time. She'd probably been so exhausted that she slept straight through Sammy's noises.

I got up and went into the bathroom to brush my teeth and wash my face. Once I was ready, I opened my door to find Sammy still in his bed. Sloane's door was closed. As a friendly gesture, I decided to get the boys ready for the day for her.

They were still unaware that their mother had returned home when I took them into the kitchen for breakfast. Anna looked at me knowingly as I entered the room with them. "Shall we have yogurt and fruit today, boys?" she asked in her most put-on chipper voice.

"Okay," Paul said with a satisfied look.

Sammy was attempting to crawl up to his seat on his own. I assisted him and then pulled out a chair for Paul. Anna placed a bowl of fruit and yogurt in front of each of the children, and she gave me a cup of coffee fixed just as I like it. With the boys now settled, I thanked her and took my coffee into the sitting room for a moment.

For the first time in ages, I saw Pippa perched there by the fire, drinking her own cup of coffee. Anna must have been in a good mood today, I thought. I sat down next to her. "Sloane's home," I said, sipping from my own cup.

She nodded.

"She was really sad last night."

More nodding.

We sat quietly beside each other drinking our coffee for quite a while. The only sound in the room was the crackling of the fire. "Divorce is a tricky business," Pippa broke the silence. "Marriage is not something to enter into lightly. I told her that when he proposed after only a few months."

"There's no way of knowing how it's going to turn out. We just have to make the leap, don't we?" I took another sip of my coffee.

"Young people these days don't see the honor in it anymore. The complete servitude to each other…"

Yikes. Servitude? I guess she was partially right about my generation. It was more about whimsy and love at first sight these days.

"Robert was engaged once."

I nearly choked on my sip of coffee. "What?" I managed through small coughs and throat clearing.

"To a woman named Alice. She was the youngest child of the MacDonough family and heir to an enormous fortune. Her family had a conglomerate of retail stores." She looked at me down her nose. "Alice was quiet. Polite. Robert was foolishly affectionate toward her." Pippa shook her head at the memory.

I tried to imagine this and couldn't. There was this quality about Robert that was warm and loving, but I had never seen him excited about anything, so the mental picture was difficult.

Pippa continued, "He proposed, and in the middle of their engagement, she broke it off. He was devastated."

"Why did she break it off?"

"She never said. Only that she was unhappy, and she thought they both were better suited for other people."

"Do you think he still loves her?"

Pippa took another sip from her mug. "I don't think so. It was a long time ago. I do think it broke him though. He hasn't dated anyone seriously since."

"Do you think he'll bring a date to the Open House?"

Pippa chuckled. "I doubt it." She looked at me, still smiling. "I think he has all he needs right here."

I was too afraid to wonder about Pippa's comment, so we sat together until I finished my cup of coffee, and I used that as my exit.

As I left the sitting room, I literally ran into Robert, thumping right into his chest and jumping with fright.

"I'm sorry!" he said as he grabbed me by the top of my arms. "I didn't know you were there."

Obviously.

He looked down at his hands on my arms and quickly let go. I decided to follow him into the kitchen where Anna was wiping the children's mouths with a washrag. "Morning, boys!" he said in a chipper voice. They returned his greeting. Then he looked back at me. "Sit with me?" he asked.

Surprise involuntarily surfaced on my face. "Me?" I poked my chest.

Robert grinned. "Yes," he said. "To whom would I be referring if it weren't you?" Robert was in good spirits today. I was not sure how to successfully respond to his mood swings. Placing my empty mug on the table in front of me, I cautiously sat beside him. He set the newspaper down and didn't open it.

"So, what will you do after this?" His gaze roamed the room as Anna refilled my mug and helped the kids down from the table. "After Ashford is sold?"

"I don't know." I looked straight at him, and he looked back at me. It was so clear and perfect—like we could communicate without talking—and I was surprised by it. I broke eye contact first, peering into my mug as I took a drink. I swallowed, using forced energy as bitter black liquid filled my mouth. Keeping my eyes on my coffee, I was afraid to look up for fear that I might have to answer to the look we just gave each other.

"I suppose I'll look for another job. Maybe as a teacher," I said quietly and then took in a breath to calm my nerves. Robert scooted a little closer to me, making me just slightly more nervous. I used all of my courage to meet his eyes again and smile up at him. "Could I put you down as a reference?"

"Mm." He looked out into the room as if contemplating something, but as usual, didn't divulge what he was thinking. He then seemed to emerge from his thought, and said, "Of course," in reply to the alarm probably written on my face at his lack of response. "I'll just go check on my sister, shall I?" he said more than asked as he stood up from the table. Anna set cream and sugar in front of me, so I added some to my cup and stirred with a shaky hand. I continued to study the creamy swirl in my coffee mug until he had turned away from me. Only then did I glance up to watch him leave.

❊ ❊ ❊

I was drawing with the boys when Robert entered the sitting room. "Do you mind speaking with me a moment in the hallway?" he asked, his eyes oddly tired.

I helped the boys choose their next crayon and directed them a little to buy some time before joining Robert in the hallway. He looked…unsure? I couldn't figure out his expression. He was fiddling with his watch and chewing on his bottom lip. "Do you think you could go and see Sloane?"

"Me?"

"Well, you're a woman… I don't think I'm sensitive enough to console her."

I allowed the confusion on my face to soften. "I doubt that's true." And there it was again—that look between us. It was starting to make me crazy. What was he trying to say to me? *Just say it!*

"I tried. She won't open up."

"I'll do my best," I said. Robert placed his hand on my upper back. It was different than when Kip did it. Robert's was more firm, less flirty. It was still startling, though, because it was unexpected coming from him.

He walked me to Sloane's door. "Good luck," he said and left me there.

"Go hang out with the boys," I called after him.

"Of course," he said over his shoulder and then began walking further away from me. I could hardly pull my eyes from him.

When I knocked, Sloane didn't answer, so I let myself in. She was curled up in a heap under her white duvet, face down in her pillow, her dark hair spread out like a giant sea creature over the sheets.

"Sloane?" She didn't respond, so I walked over to the bed and sat on the edge. "Sloane?" Still nothing.

I rubbed her back. "I know that I'm not your family, but I have a sister, and I... understand. I don't mind being a sounding board."

Sloane slowly turned her head around on her pillow exposing one side of her face. Her eyes were crimson on the edges, and the pillow under her was wet from tears. Her neck was splotchy. "I. Can't. Keep. Going." Tears surfaced at the bottom of her eyes and spilled over the edges. She sniffled through a pink nose.

Sloane wasn't my sister—far from it—but I felt the sisterly instinct come on in full force. "Tell me about it." I said.

She sat up, her hair sliding off of the pillow, and looked at me. With shaking hands, she stretched her fingers out along the satin fabric of the sheets. A tear slipped off of her chin, dropping a gray spot on the sheet next to her thumb. Sloane shook her head, her lip quivering.

I remained on the edge of the bed, my hands now in my lap. I'd give her time and let her collect her thoughts. The sound of shoes clacking down the wooden floorboards in the hallway outside the door rose to a crescendo and then dissolved back into the silence that surrounded us. I looked down at my knees, waiting.

"I'm fine," she finally said.

I turned toward her and waited again. She and I both knew that she wasn't fine.

After an excruciating number of seconds, she slumped in defeat and said, "It's all so overwhelming."

I rubbed her back again, and Sloane took in a jagged breath. I wanted to fix things, make it all better, but I knew that I couldn't. So instead I would listen. I'd give her all the support I could give.

"All of my money went into this marriage—the house, the vacations, keeping up with a certain standard of living—and now, it's all dissolving right in front of me. Now I'll have to work," she sobbed, "I've never worked before. And how can I when I have the boys? They'll never see me. And God knows, they never see their father…" She balled the sheets up in her fist. "Our family is broken. I don't know how to make us a family. I don't know how to smile when they talk about their father. I don't know how to teach them how to be good men. How will I afford adequate schooling for them? Childcare? How will I do it? I can't!"

I knew all too well about the single mom with two children scenario. The difference was that her kids were used to a wealthy lifestyle, and this may be a big change for them. And her. I recognized what she had ahead of her, but I was living proof that it can be done.

"These things find a way of working themselves out. Take the challenges one at a time ."

"I don't know how to do it," she sniffed. "I'm not strong enough."

"You don't have to be strong enough to do it all at once—no one is. You just have to be strong enough to do *one* thing. That's it. Then you rest, and when you've regained that strength back, you tackle the next thing."

"What if I can't? I don't think that I can keep going."

"I'm not going to tell you that you can keep going," I said, "but I *am* going to tell you that you have to, because there are two amazing little boys who have been asking for their mommy back. You're going to have to turn off Sloane for a while and stuff it down inside. You need to be just Mommy right now. Ignore the rest. Let that be your *one thing.*"

Sloane perked up a bit at the mention of Paul and Sammy. She wiped her eyes with her hands and then smeared the wetness onto her bed sheets. I sat beside her quietly for support. After a few deep breaths, she pushed the duvet off of her legs and swung her perfectly pedicured toes over the bed onto the floor. "You're right," she sniffled. "I have to get myself together." Then, nearly knocking me over, both literally and figuratively, Sloane hugged me. I braced myself on the footboard with one hand. "Thank you," she said, pulling away to look me in the eye.

"I can't say that it'll all be okay because nobody knows the answer to that, but I can say that you'll go on, and you'll grow from this. It will change you, teach you. And I hope it will be for the better."

We sat in silence for a moment, Sloane staring ahead as if collecting her thoughts. Then, she looked over at me. "It's so nice to have you here, Allie. I've never had another woman to talk to about things like this. Pippa would worry too much, judge the situation, so I've never burdened her with my feelings." She smiled for the first time since I'd come in. "You're an old soul, you know that? Are you sure you're with the right brother?" she winked, her eyes still cloudy with tears.

Even though she was kidding, the comment hit me like a foot in the gut. Blood filtered through my cheeks as I pondered her question. Was I with the right brother? I couldn't deny anymore that there was something between Robert and me, but it was so weird that I couldn't define it. It was as if I knew exactly who he was, but at the same time I knew nothing about him.

I tried to center my thoughts on Sloane. "So! What will help you pull yourself together? Coffee? Ibuprofen? Whiskey?" I asked her.

Sloane giggled a little and picked up the phone. She punched a few keys and somehow contacted Anna. Like Double-Oh-Seven. As she spoke into the phone, she fumbled around in a bag on the floor, pulled out my coin and tossed it onto the bed. "Here. Thanks!" she whispered to me, holding the bottom of the receiver at the back of her head. She quickly repositioned the phone, ordered a glass of red wine, and gestured to me that she'd see me later. I slid the coin into my pocket and waved as I left the room.

※ ※ ※

I was finished with my duties for the day, so I decided to finally pull out the book I'd brought and read a little. I took my book into the sitting room where I found Robert doing exactly the same thing. He eyed my book. "How's Sloane?" he asked.

"She's okay."

He nodded appreciatively.

"Mind if I join you on the sofa?"

"Not at all," he said, scooting over to make room for me and the personal space that would be required for two people like us.

I sat down and tucked my feet under my legs to keep them warm. I noticed Robert glancing over, attempting to hide his view with his book. A grin twitched at the corners of his mouth, but I didn't mention it.

We read together quietly for a while before he spoke. "Forgive me if this is forward of me…" He waited for some sort of approval, so I looked up from my book in anticipation of his thought. "You look like you belong here. You're so… comfortable all the time. I grew up here, and I don't think I'm as comfortable as you seem."

Believe me, I'm not comfortable. I'm ridiculously nervous with you sitting next to me. I'm still a little afraid of your grandmother, I'm sort

*of dating your brother who's a little more ostentatious than I'd like him
to be, and I'm emotionally tired from consoling your sister so no, I'm not
exactly comfortable.*

"Really?" I said aloud.

Something else was about to leave his lips, but he censored it,
I could tell. "What were you going to say?" I asked him. I couldn't
believe I just did that. Why didn't I just look back down at my book
and keep reading?

"Nothing."

Of course.

On second thought, I was not going to let this go. "No, tell me,"
I pressed.

"Some things are better left unsaid."

Now I was intrigued. I scooted a little closer and put the bookmark
in my book. "Now you have to tell me." The corners of his mouth
turned up just a little, and I could, for the first time, see his resemblance
to Kip.

"I didn't intend to bait you. I'm sorry."

"Robert," I scooted even closer and tossed my book onto the
floor. "Tell me."

"No."

"Robert?"

He pushed air through his lips, but I could tell that he wasn't
as annoyed as he was trying to look. "I was just thinking—I can't
believe I'm saying this out loud—that…" He broke eye contact.

"What?"

"Had I seen you sitting on the settee like this a few weeks ago, so
comfortable, I may have reconsidered selling the house."

"Why?"

"You give the house a different... personality. You make it seem livable."

A wave of misery enveloped me. I could see myself here. Even though the house was cold and drafty, and it had enormous spaces that were lost at the ends of snaking hallways—nothing like the kind of house I would ever have dreamed of having—it was oddly livable. Perhaps it was because I hadn't really had a home of my own, so I had nothing to compare it to.

I couldn't explain, though, the immediate connection I felt with this family. Even little Nathan who I'd raised for eleven years didn't seem to affect me like the Marleys.

"I'm sorry, I've embarrassed you."

"No, it's fine."

I watched him draw into himself. He was closing off because of my reaction. "I'm not embarrassed," I scrambled, "I'm reacting to the fact that I *feel* comfortable here. It's weird though, isn't it? To feel comfortable in a house that isn't mine, with people who aren't family?"

"I suppose so, yes."

"Why do you think that I feel so comfortable here?" I was stepping out on a limb, but he seemed to have relaxed again.

"I expect that it's your temperament. You are able to keep Kip in line, calm Sloane, converse pleasantly with Pippa, and..." he grinned, "make me say things I usually wouldn't."

"I like it when you say things you usually wouldn't." I couldn't help but feel a little giddy when I saw the smile that broke out on his face as he looked back down at his book.

Chapter Twenty

"Here you go!" Kip gently tossed a stack of papers secured with a paperclip onto the table where I was sitting with a glass of water and a pack of crackers that I had smuggled into the house a few days ago.

"What's this?" I asked, sliding it over toward me.

"Your passport paperwork. All you have to do is get a photo, and fill in the info and I'll take care of the rest." I noted that Kip didn't mention the monetary requirement. I wasn't taking any handouts, but I didn't say anything out loud.

"Thank you, Kip." I folded the wad of papers and set them next to my place at the table. He leaned down and kissed me, just missing my mouth and landing below it. We tried again awkwardly and succeeded with a little peck on the lips. I had to stop this. In more ways than one. Truthfully, any hope that a passport created was nothing but a dream. Because the reality of the situation was that I was not like the Marleys, and no matter how much I wanted it, I'd never have what they had: a family steeped in history, knowledge of a code only shared by others with such wealth. I'd never be able to live up to that.

"I'm going out, by the way. I'm going to meet a few friends to talk about a trip they're taking to Sydney. I might like to get in on that!"

I certainly had no right to require any permission for such an excursion, but I found it odd that Kip would consider it without even wondering how it may affect me. We weren't a couple, exactly, but we were dating exclusively—at least I was. But this was exactly what I meant by such a code. Flying to Australia was not even in my realm of understanding. "How long will they be visiting Australia?" I asked.

"For a year, I think," he answered casually.

A year? "So…" I considered the best way to ask this without saying *What in the world are you thinking?* "You would plan to be gone for a year as well?"

"That's why I'm going to see them. I need to know if I'd have accommodations that long, etcetera, etcetera." He was gesturing with his hands. What was he trying to do? Was he trying to break up with me? Did he care what I thought? How was I supposed to ask *What about me?* without sounding like a complete moron? A thought came to mind that I might be just like all of those other women to him. Perhaps it had never occurred to him that we'd be dating after my employment was over.

"Would I visit?" I asked carefully.

"No! You can come with me! Why do you think I got you the passport paperwork? You said you'd love to visit Australia."

"Kip," my face fell, "I can't come with you."

"Why not? There's nothing tying you anywhere. Your job here will end as soon as the house is sold. You don't have anything lined up here. Why wouldn't you come with me?"

"Because I don't want to. I don't want to live in Australia for a year. It doesn't even remotely interest me."

Kip looked like a little boy again. I had just stolen his lollipop. "Well, I don't have to go. It was just an idea…"

"Kip, go and see your friends. Find out about the trip. You don't have to decide right here, right now. It's fine. Really."

He kissed my cheek. "Okay. I'll be back around four to get ready for the open house. I'll meet you downstairs at five. How does that sound?"

"That sounds great." He caressed my back with his hand in the way that he always had and pulled me in sideways for a sort-of hug. Then he left for the day.

✻ ✻ ✻

"What do I buy for people who have everything?" I asked Megan as we strolled down the street, Christmas shopping. I stopped and peered into one of the windows of a men's clothing store and then continued walking.

"Buy for Kip first. You know him the best," Megan suggested, tugging at a purse on an outdoor rack and flipping over the price tag.

"Do I?"

"Well, he's your boyfriend!"

"He's not my boyfriend," I rolled my eyes. Was he my *boyfriend*? "The thing is, I can't afford anything that he would like." I pulled my coat together in an effort to keep the cold from slithering down my shirt.

"Yeah, I know. So, you have to get creative." She flipped over another tag on a brown satchel and then dropped it as if it had caused a burning sensation.

We walked along until we came to a store selling unique kitchen accessories. "Hold on," I grabbed Megan's arm and went inside, "I think I see something for Kip." I walked over to a display table at the front of the store and picked up a pint glass. "It's an English pint glass with the Queen's seal etched on it! He'd love these!" I handed two to Megan and carried two myself, and we headed toward the checkout.

"See? Easy! Now, are you getting Robert, *your boss*, anything?" she asked with mock seriousness, setting the glasses down on the checkout counter.

"Well, I kind of already know what I'm getting him." Megan's eyes widened suggestively. "I just know what he would like, that's all."

"That's why I'm making the face. You have no idea what to get your boyfriend, but you know exactly what to get your boyfriend's brother…"

I handed a wad of money to the checkout clerk who wrapped the glasses in paper and put them into a boutique bag. "What should I get Sloane?" I asked, attempting to divert the attention elsewhere.

"Don't know. What are you getting Robert?" A cowbell jingled as the door's movement knocked it against the door. Megan wasn't going to let it go.

"An antique record."

"Of?"

"Louis Armstrong. He said he liked it, and he doesn't have it. He uses a borrowed copy."

"Interesting choice. What's he, like, seventy-five?"

I pursed my lips in annoyance. "No," I said defensively but pulled back on my tone almost immediately, trying not to suggest anything. That's the thing about being sisters, we catch on really quickly. My "no" sounded protective, and I knew she had heard it. "It has his late parents' favorite song on it, if you must know." That shut her up. I didn't bother to tell her that I had ordered it days ago and paid extra to have it shipped to the music store in town so that

I could pick it up. That would have just sounded crazy, wouldn't it? "So… Sloane. What should I get her?"

"Maybe you could get her a book or something," Megan offered.

"That's a good idea."

❄ ❄ ❄

I walked through the grand entranceway with my shopping bags as the staff was dutifully decorating for tonight's open house. When I got to my room, I tossed the bags under my bed. I headed back toward the front of the house, and I got a glimpse through a window of the delivery truck beginning to unload what seemed like millions of the champagne gift baskets—the ones I had ordered. They looked amazing from a distance.

Soft, instrumental holiday music was humming above my head from all of the speakers in the house. The candles were lit in every room, giving the air a scent of cranberry and vanilla mixed with the aroma of spruce from the Christmas trees. A fire danced in the large stone fireplace in the sitting room. The house was absolutely amazing.

The only thing keeping me from the joviality of the moment was the fact that Gerard had said that Pippa wanted to see me. I had an hour before Franco was coming to do my hair, and I'd rather have something than nothing to do, so I went to see her right away.

When I opened the door to her room, Pippa was sitting in her regular chair near the window, looking more frail than usual. She turned in my direction and stood. With both hands extended, she clasped mine. Pippa's grip was cold and dry.

She led me over to the door and then grabbed my arm. "Let's walk, shall we?" We strolled down the hallway and carefully climbed the long staircase to an area of the house where I hadn't spent much time. It was on the second floor and on the front of the house. The room looked like it must have been a sewing room years ago. Pippa was obviously winded from the walk upstairs, so she sat down on the first available chair then motioned for me to sit in the chair opposite.

"I've been dreaming of Henry every night for a week," she began, rubbing her knuckles with her thumb.

"Henry? Mr. Marley?"

"Yes." She peered up at the ceiling as if she were looking for him. I sat quietly, wondering what this was about. "Either he's calling me home, or I'm a crazy old bat—the latter could be entirely true..." She toyed with the hem of her sleeve. "I've let a lot go in the last few days. I'm not angry with Robert about the house anymore. I'll get my home soon enough." She stopped fidgeting and looked at me with interest. "I have a feeling about you."

What? Was Pippa losing it? I watched her, waiting for more explanation. She didn't offer much.

"I want you to consider your choices very carefully." I waited for more, but nothing came. Should I say something? What should I do? I sat, staring at her as she looked away.

"What do you mean by that?"

"I mean," she exhaled with impatience, "You will blink. Literally, blink. And you will be me, on the edge of life and looking back on what you've done with yours. Don't sail through it. Make each decision as if your life depended on it. Don't just flit through your years with choices that mean nothing to your future."

Was she lecturing me? What the heck?

"There are choices before you that could change you forever. I just wanted to kick you in the bottom a bit." She allowed a little smile.

"Can you elaborate?"

"I'm not trying to be vague, dear, but I don't want to spell it out for you either. I'd just like to make you think. That's all."

There was a hushed atmosphere between us as we sat opposite each other. What was she talking about? Choices? I racked my brain. Was she talking about Kip? I was already giving that a shot. She couldn't be talking about Robert. I didn't have any current choices with him. I stared at my knees.

"You are clearly confused by my advice," she said. Then she blew air through her nose making a quiet whistling sound. "My three grandchildren are all very different. Some of them are more forthright than others. Just don't discount anyone who may not be as outspoken."

She *was* talking about Robert. What did she know that I didn't know …if anything? She was probably just a crazy old bat, as she had put it.

❋ ❋ ❋

Franco was shorter than me, spoke with an accent I didn't recognize, and blinked his eyes a little too often, making it difficult to maintain eye contact. But he was amazing with hair. He swept mine up like some sort of supermodel's in loose, gentle waves, piled up with perfect strands on top of my head. My hair was still soft, yet held the style flawlessly.

"You're amazing," I confessed. Franco affirmed my opinion with a proud nod of his head. Then, against my objections, he helped me get into my dress and apply my makeup.

I found myself wandering downstairs through a ton of people I'd never met. Gerard was in a tuxedo letting people in through the front door. Despite his usual disapproval, he winked in my direction as I made my way into the sitting room. It was nearly five o'clock, so I hoped to see Kip soon so that I wouldn't have to stand alone. I passed a waiter who handed me a glass of champagne with a strawberry suspended in bubbles at the bottom of the glass.

"Hi," came from behind me, and I turned around. Robert had never looked so relaxed, and he was dressed in his tuxedo. How strange is that? Seeing him filled me with calm. Usually he made me edgy, but tonight, among all of these strangers, I was actually excited to see him.

"Hi!" I reached over and laid my hand on his chest. "Look at you!" I said, smoothing the white V of his shirt that was exposed beneath his tuxedo jacket and thinking yet again how unlike these people I was.

Robert placed his hand on top of mine, pulling it from his body. He held it for a minute before letting go. "Look at *you*," he said, shaking his head back and forth just slightly. His eyes scanned me from head to toe. "You look incredible."

"Thank you." I tipped my drink back and drank as much as possible without having the strawberry tumble down the glass toward my lips. Then I handed it to a waiter who happened to be walking by. He replaced it with another. This one had no strawberry, thank goodness.

"You seem relaxed tonight," I pointed out.

"Yes. Well. It's Christmas."

"Yes. It is." I didn't like to think about that. Soon, the house would sell, and I'd have to leave. But, I promised myself I'd ignore that fact. My hands were shaking a little.

Robert must have taken notice of my tension. He pointed to my glass of champagne. "Drink that and you'll feel less anxious," he said.

The warmth was already flooding my neck and face as the overhead music melted away and a band began setting up in the corner of the room. Within a few minutes, they were playing live music. "This is great!" I bellowed over the music. I wondered who had planned that. It certainly wasn't me, but it was a pleasant surprise.

Robert affirmed, raising his eyebrows and nodding. We drank a little more of our drinks as we listened—drums tinging, saxophone whining. I suddenly wanted to leave with Robert, get out of there, just the two of us. It was an odd sensation to have, and I couldn't stop it from overwhelming me.

"Do you know what my most favorite instrument is?" I offered.

"What?" He looked down at me, questioningly.

"Steel drums. I just love the sound of them." My mind was wandering. I thought about Robert, relaxed on a lounge chair, the sea air swelling up around us. I took another sip and called out over the music, "Have you ever been to the Caribbean?"

He shook his head back and forth.

"Why not? If I had your money, I'd go."

"I've never needed to go to the Caribbean," he said above the music, still looking in the direction of the band.

I touched his arm, sending his eyes directly to my hand, but I ignored it. "That's the thing about the Caribbean. You don't have to have a *need* to go there. You just go!" I remembered the restaurant he had told me about in England. There were so many places that we could go together… Why was I thinking this way? The alcohol and the fire were heating my skin, and I was sure that my cheeks were bright red.

Robert's eyes roamed my face. "Well, maybe I'd go if I could go with someone."

"There you are!" Kip's hand found my lower back, and he leaned in and kissed me, knocking my grip on Robert's arm loose. "You look amazing!" Kip told me, holding my hand and spinning me around. I glanced at Robert, but he didn't seem to be bothered by it.

Before I could get a word in, three women came swooping toward us like screeching gulls, sucking my attention toward them. It was Alex and two others. I watched as they swooned over Kip. He handled it with dignity, turning to introduce us. "Allie, Robert, these ladies are Olivia," he nodded toward a brunette, "Keegan," he eyed a blonde, "and you know Alex." Robert graciously greeted each one. I offered a tiny wave in their general direction and then eyed a waiter for another drink. The girls pulled Kip aside, leaving me with Robert once again.

"So!" I turned to Robert. "Ms. Marley tells me that you collect coins." I was desperate for conversation and slightly interested as well, so I brought up the topic.

"Yes. How did the subject present itself?"

Yikes. I couldn't mention the present. That's why Pippa had told me to wait to ask him. Ugh. Think… "Well, I'm sort of the anti-collector." Robert looked at me, obviously perplexed. "My grand-mother used to buy us coins—Megan and me—but we never really saw the value in collecting them, so we took them all out of their wrappers and played with them." Robert shook his head, his expression scolding me as if I were a two-year-old. "What's the point in collecting them? They aren't particularly pretty and, unless you cash them in, they don't give you any money. Why do you collect them?"

"It's a story for another day, perhaps."

I let it go. He was talking, that was the point. "Do you have any coins here at Ashford?" I asked, gladly taking another glass and plac-ing my empty one on the tray. That was what, three glasses? I had to slow down. Where was Kip? I'd lost him in the crowd.

"Yes, I have some coins in my room—the one you're staying in."

"May I see them?"

"Now?" He looked around as if seeking approval from someone.

"Yeah."

He hesitated. "I suppose so." He took my hand, and we walked out of the crowd toward the east wing. As we made our way down the hallway, we encountered Pippa on her scooter all decked out in a red cardigan set and an ivory skirt. She smiled at us as we passed; never even asking why we weren't walking in the direction of the party. "Good evening," Robert greeted her. She tipped her head and sped along past us.

We entered the bedroom, and Robert dropped my hand. I had forgotten he was even holding it. He opened the bottom drawer of his dresser and pulled from it a wooden box the size of a formal silverware caddy. When he opened it, I marveled at the pristine coins that were displayed there. Some were in boxes, others in sealed packages. I carefully pulled one of the smaller ones from the caddy. It was in a tiny plastic box the size of a matchbox. "Take this one, for instance, what do you think it's worth?"

"Quite a bit." Robert walked closer to me and stood just behind me to peer at it. I could feel his breath on my neck.

"Okay, *quite a bit*. But right now, sitting in our hands, it's nothing but a coin. You'll probably pass it along to your kids and so on, and it will never give anyone anything in return. It will just sit there screaming, 'I'm expensive!'"

"Your point?"

"What good is it?" I set it down and picked up one in a baggie and pinched it with both fingers like I was about to open a bag of chips. "What would happen if I opened this?"

"You wouldn't."

"And if I did?" I held it up, taunting him.

"Why would you want to?"

"Well, Megan and I used them as flipping coins. We could flip for something."

"Like what?" he asked suspiciously.

I looked around, thinking. The alcohol was giving me more courage than usual. I was a little tipsy. Reflecting on Pippa's advice, I suddenly wanted to test the waters. "Heads, you get your room back tonight. Tails, you stay in the guestroom."

"Where will you go if I get my room back?"

"Oh, I didn't say anything about me. I'm not going anywhere."

Robert's eyes widened in surprise. I was proud of myself for being so forward. He needed a little kick in the bottom, as Pippa would say. I held up the coin again.

"Maybe we should flip for that tomorrow," he said unpersuasively.

"Why?"

"We've both been drinking, Allie." He looked down at me, a warm expression playing around his eyes. "I wouldn't want to put you in an uncomfortable position. You may have a different opinion about this conversation tomorrow."

"Nope." I pinched the bag at both sides.

"NOT that one!" Snatching the coin from my fingers, his shoulders relaxed. He studied the box. Then he picked up another coin that was also packaged in a small sealed bag. "How about this one? It's half the value of the other one," he grinned a crooked grin.

"You sure?" I asked as I placed my fingers on the bag and began to pull. Robert closed his eyes, squinching up his face in preparation. One tear and the coin dropped into my hand. In a hushed voice, I asked, "How much is this one worth?"

"It was worth about four hundred dollars. Now, it's worth much less."

I held the coin in the center of my palm and stroked it with my forefinger. It was different than the coins that we had gotten from Gram. It was more significant somehow. I thought I could see hope in Robert's eyes as I placed the coin on my thumb. He didn't blink once when I flipped it into the air, caught it, and covered it on the back of my hand. My heart was thumping. How would I explain this to Kip? *Who cares*, I thought. At that moment, it didn't matter. It was done.

Robert inched closer to me, completely invading my personal space. His nose was somewhere near my forehead and if I wanted to, I could turn my face up and touch his lips. The thought occurred to me. Instead, I just repeated, "Heads you get your room back."

"Let's see." Robert placed a hand on my back and this time, it was a little different. It was like an embrace. I lifted my hand, revealing the coin.

Tails.

Robert pulled away and plucked the coin from my hand. He set it on the dresser and turned toward me. "We should probably get back to the party."

Chapter Twenty-one

"Where have you two been?" Kip came walking over to us as we approached the grand entranceway. "I've been looking all over for you," he said, pulling me near him, his eyes darting over to Robert.

"We were flipping coins," I smirked and tried to give Robert a playful glance, but my eyes could only go as far as his shirt before I lost my nerve and looked at the floor.

"I was showing Allie my coin collection," Robert said.

"Robert, let her enjoy the party. Don't bore her with that coin collection of yours."

"My apologies," he nodded in my direction, his look nearly giving us away. I shifted my weight nervously in response. "I'll let you two have some time together since I've monopolized her for the entire start of the party." Robert gave me one more fleeting look and then walked away.

"Hey! You don't have a drink!" *Oops*, I thought. I had left it in the bedroom. "I'll just go and get you one." Kip touched my arm and gave me a quick grin before leaving me standing at the edge of the entranceway with no one to talk to.

Alex and the other gulls were standing a few groups away. I thought about joining them, but I didn't want to interrupt, so I just listened in on their conversation instead. Maybe they'd say something that would prompt me to come over and say, "I couldn't help overhearing but…" I hoped so.

Alex caught sight of Kip as he walked over to a staff member for our drinks. "Isn't he delicious?" I heard her say. *Delicious?* "He brought their employee over to my house the other night to borrow a dress. I think he may have taken her out. Isn't that so odd?" The gulls nodded their heads in concurrence. "I knew he was having a fling with the help, but I didn't know he'd take it this far. Well, you know how Kip is…always saving little puppies. He probably feels sorry for her."

That might have been an opportune time to enter with, "I couldn't help overhearing but…" but I decided against it. It was starting—my Cinderella complex. All that I had feared, it was actually happening to me. Insecurity overwhelmed me at that moment, and I suddenly felt like a peasant dressed up for the night. I didn't belong with these people. My throat tightened with emotion, but I swallowed it away.

Kip returned with two glasses of wine. "Hey there," he said as if he'd just stopped for the first time to look at me. He handed me my glass.

"Hi," I smiled, but I knew that he noticed something new lurking between us. He downed his drink and set it on a silver tray nearby. Then he grabbed me by my waist and slowly pulled me toward him. I looked up at his face, my mind racing. I didn't belong with someone like him. Alex was right. We were all wrong for each other. I was just a fling. And I couldn't stop thinking about flipping that coin with Robert. I don't think I'd be a fling to him, but he was raised just like Kip. The problem would be the same. Kip leaned down to kiss me, and I barely returned the kiss.

Pippa rolled up on her scooter, scrutinizing the two of us. "I wanted to let you know that I'm going to the Christmas Eve service at church. The open house is still quite lively, so let's not cut it short on my account. I'll be home around seven o'clock. I told Anna to have dinner ready by then."

I hadn't really figured out what I was doing at Ashford on Christmas Eve anyway. It was suddenly exhausting being here.

I had spent every single Christmas of my life with my family. I'd never missed a single one. The feeling of seeing Mom's face light up at the front door when I arrived, Megan's hugs, seeing Gram... Anything else was inconceivable. There was something magical about it, about us. At Christmas, I could count on being with the only people in the world who knew me inside and out. And, no matter what may be going on in our lives, all was well for those few days because we had each other.

As we started to walk back toward the crowd of people, I turned to Kip. "Kip, can I ask you something? Should I go home for Christmas?"

"Why?"

"Well, I don't think I'll have much work to do tomorrow. I'll be the only staff member around, and I'm not a part of your family. Even if we were dating under regular circumstances, I wouldn't necessarily spend Christmas with you and your family. I just don't want to impose."

"You are not imposing! This family has come together in ways that we never have before. And I think it's because of you, to be honest. Robert wouldn't even be here if it weren't for you. He told me that himself. But let's not get on the subject of Robert..."

Robert had come home because of me. Had he come home *for* me? *Don't be ridiculous, Allie*, I said to myself. He barely knows me.

"I don't want to be this non-family member intruding on your holiday."

"I want you here. How about that?" The lift in his features shifted, and suddenly, his face became serious as he gripped my shoulders. "Stay with me tonight."

What do I say? After the scene I made with Robert about flipping for the room, there was no way that I could turn around and stay the night with Kip. "I'll stay for the holiday, but I'd like to sleep alone if that's okay." I stole another lollipop.

* * *

The dining room had been transformed into a picture from that movie I kept recalling. The people had all gone with their gift baskets and their fancy clothes. Kip instructed me to change into something a little more casual, but I did leave my hair in Franco's style so that I wouldn't have to mess with it. I was standing alone in a perfect dining room, looking around at a table that had seen generations of this family every Christmas. What was I doing here?

Anna came in and started when she saw me. "Oh! Here, take a seat. The others will be here shortly."

I pulled out a chair and sat down. A dark red tablecloth with a gold and cream colored runner dividing the table into two halves stretched out before me. The china was a simple pattern: cream-colored with platinum edging. The stemware sparkled in the light of the crystal chandelier that hung low over the table. Candles were lit along the runner, sending flickering lights across the reflective dishes and the fresh greenery with red berries that snaked through them. I sat alone, taking in the beautiful scene.

The chair beside me moved, and I jumped as Robert sat down next to me. "You scared me." I placed my hand on my chest.

"I'm sorry," he said, scooting his chair under.

"I was just taking in this gorgeous table." Then, to my surprise and delight, I noticed a plastic booster seat peeking out from one of the chairs. "I'm guessing that Paul and Sammy will join us tonight?" I pointed to the seat.

"They get to stay up late for this. It will be better anyway since Santa's coming tonight. That way, they'll be a little more tired than usual, and we won't have anybody getting out of bed."

Santa! I suddenly became so excited at the idea that I was around children again who believed in Santa! I hadn't helped with Santa in years! I planned to offer my assistance. Maybe I'd try and bring it up during dinner.

"I have to help Sloane set the things up for Santa later tonight."

Maybe I wouldn't have to bring it up at all! "Do you think she'd mind if I helped?"

"I doubt she'd turn away two capable hands. You haven't seen what Santa brings these boys yet." He looked at me. "You know, you're really wonderful with the boys. You would make an astounding teacher."

"I should have been a teacher, but I took a nanny job instead. After this, I'm going to look into being a preschool teacher. I'm still certified."

Kip walked in and came up behind me. He put his hands on my shoulders and kissed my bare neck. "You look nice," he beamed, pulling out the chair on the other side of me.

Pippa rolled in behind Kip, pulled a weathered Bible from a pouch on her scooter, and sat opposite Robert. She cleared her throat and eyed the three of us. "Church was inspirational tonight. We had the candlelight service, and we caroled at the end. I absolutely enjoyed it."

Robert nodded at Pippa in response while Sloane came in carrying Sammy. Paul was behind her, tugging on his tie. They took their seats, Paul sandwiched between Pippa and Sloane, with Sammy at the end of the table.

Anna placed cards on each of our plates with a Bible verse typed in elegant font. Pippa grabbed the table with both hands and used it to assist her as she moved into place to address us.

"For tonight's Christmas reading, I'd like to quote from First Corinthians." Pippa opened her Bible, removed a delicate rose petal bookmark, and set it on the table in front of her. She read the verse, and I followed along on my card.

She looked at all of us as if she were appraising us as her family. "Tonight on the night of our Savior's birth, I wanted to remember love. In our recent history, we have not shown love to one another—myself included. But, if love is, indeed, to endure *all* things, then it shall endure the loss of loved ones, the unresolved anger and resentment we have, and the differing opinions we possess on the exchange of our family assets. I want to say that I love you all, and I'd like to move forward under that premise." She sat back down, her legs wobbly as they lowered her into her chair.

Just as fear swelled inside my stomach at the recollection that I was supposed to organize a family member's speech, Robert stood up with his glass. "Kip did his duty last Christmas and Sloane, I thought you may need a pass this year," he discretely winked in my direction, "So I thought that I'd offer to do the speech."

Robert cleared his throat and raised his glass. "You all have reentered my life this season in new ways. You are a part of my happiness, and, thanks to Allie, our newest and most valuable friend, I think I finally understand what family should be. He raised his glass in the air, and we followed suit. "To the Marley family and its newest friend. May we all find love in our own lives and within our family."

The moment that we took our sip of wine, the staff descended upon us with dishes of sweet potatoes, mashed potatoes, grilled asparagus, buttered squash, fresh bread, and dressing. In the center of the table, Anna and two other staff members carefully placed a ham and a turkey, both displayed on silver trays.

"That was a great speech," I whispered to Robert as I received the bowl of mashed potatoes from Pippa. I scooped a spoonful and dropped a dollop onto my plate. "When did you think that up?"

"Just now."

"You're kidding!"

"No." He took the stuffing from Pippa, scooped some out, and handed it to me. I passed the potatoes to Kip, ignoring his interest in our exchange. I was too busy thinking about the unsettling fact that Robert, who had just spoken about love and family, was still planning to sell their home right out from under them.

Could I divert the attention? I already felt close to this family, oddly almost a part of it, and I hoped that what I was about to say was acceptable for this dinner. "I know that you all usually share a holiday memory, so I'd like to share one. Would that be okay?" All eyes were on me.

"Yeah!" squealed Sammy and we all laughed.

With the Marley family poised, I began to tell my story. I remembered it as if it had just happened. I was nineteen, and I'd just come home from college for the holidays. The winter wind blew snow around us like a swarm of white butterflies, each snowflake draping itself on the nearest surface. Neither Megan nor I had our own car, so we'd both bummed rides from other students heading in our direction. I got home before Megan and went inside. When I first entered the house, I hadn't noticed, but as I looked around for Mom, a realization finally solidified. Mom hadn't decorated for Christmas. There was no tree, no stockings on the mantle.

Decorating the Christmas tree was Mom's favorite tradition. She started pulling boxes from the attic at least three weeks in advance to sort and clean all of the ornaments before she put them on the tree. She always bought the biggest live tree she could find, and spent an entire day arranging its wares, taking ornaments off and on, and moving them around. But this year, she had nothing. Why?

The Marleys were all looking at me, heads cocked, cordially waiting to know the answer. I quickly jumped back into the story so as not to lose my nerve. Especially with Robert looking at me so intently. My mind went back to that day.

I could hear the washing machine going down the hallway just as Megan came in the front door. She noticed faster than I had because her eyes slid around the room before locking with mine. "Where's the tree?" she asked.

"I don't know."

We walked past the folding doors that hid the washing machine and dryer. Mom wasn't there. Megan and I looked at each other, both of us clearly confused by the situation. Then, finally, we saw a note. Sitting on the kitchen table in my mother's awkwardly slanted handwriting was a message that she'd run into town to the bank. She wanted to get there before it closed. She said she'd be home in a few minutes; she just had some errands to run afterward. So we settled in.

Not long after, Megan called me into the living room. She was standing at the small desk where Mom kept all of our most important paperwork. Her bank statement was laying out for all to view, and it was clear that she was only just scraping by. As we scanned the debits to her account, our two tuition payments had given her very little left on which to live.

Sammy interrupted the story, asking Sloane for more squash. She dished him some without taking her eyes from me as I continued.

I looked at Megan, thinking what I was nearly sure that she was thinking. "Do you think we can find a tree in the woods down the road?" I asked, more telling than asking.

"Get your boots. Let's give it a shot."

Megan and I trudged through the snow-covered woods that ran along the edge of our neighborhood, Megan holding the small saw she'd gotten from the shed out back. The forest trees looked like black silhouettes against the absence of color in the sky. The cold had seeped through my gloves, and the tips of my fingers were starting to burn just as Megan put an arm out to stop me. Nestled against a larger tree, as if seeking shelter from the storm, was a baby spruce only the size of a small child.

"I can probably get the saw through its trunk," Megan said, her breath dissipating in the frigid air. "And it doesn't have much snow on it."

I held the tree tightly by its center as Megan pulled the saw across the trunk—back and forth, the snow falling around us, covering us from head to toe—until the tree came loose in my hands, causing me to stumble backwards. The motion shook the snow from its branches, revealing the bright green of last summer's new growth. "It's perfect," I said.

We steadied it in the tree stand by wadding old magazines around the base. It didn't matter, though, because the tree skirt covered it well. I put my presents for Mom and Megan underneath, and Megan did the same. We had pulled the boxes of ornaments from the attic and picked out our favorite ones, putting them in a pile on the recliner near the tree just as Mom got home.

She walked in, and her tired face lit up. She looked back and forth between me and my sister without saying a word. That was the first time I'd ever seen my mother cry.

Pippa clapped a hand over her mouth, and everyone at the table sat in silence. Robert was looking straight at me, and it was as if he were talking to me with only his eyes. *I understand*, he seemed to be saying. I had no idea, given his background, how he could understand, but somehow, I knew that he did. I took in this moment with all of the Marleys together and me with them, and I knew that this would be my second favorite Christmas memory.

"So," I continued, "It was, by far, my most memorable Christmas ever. I've never again had a Christmas as good as that one."

"There's no way that I can top that." Robert said. "Anyone else?" Even through his affable expression, I thought I saw contemplation on his face.

"Absolutely not, no way." Sloane said as she eyed Robert.

"Oh wee!" cried Sammy. Then he burst into fits of laughter.

The mood changed around me—I could feel it. Every time I looked over at Pippa, her face was thoughtful, her eyes on me. I felt pretty relaxed, so I decided to carry the conversation further. "So! Now you know something about me. Tell me something about another person at this table that I don't know." At once, every person at the table began looking at one another.

Kip was the first to pipe up. "Sloane had to buy a second copy of *Twilight* because she read it so much, the cover fell apart. And, if you look in the top drawer of her dresser, she has an Edward poster." I knew I liked Sloane.

Sloane replied to Kip's comment with, "Kip has to watch himself brush each tooth in the mirror when he brushes his teeth! He has an electric toothbrush, and it spits white foam all over the mirror, walls…"

"Okay, okay…" Kip was playfully shooing her off.

"Robert is an artist," Pippa said.

There was a hush, and I looked over at Robert. He took a sip of wine and made eye contact, his face now somber.

"Is this true?"

He shrugged it off. "I do a little painting now and again."

"A little painting. Please," Pippa snapped. "He can do line drawings that rival that Richard fellow. Do you know him? Oh, what's his name? He's wonderful."

"The artist or Robert?" I asked, grinning.

"Both are equally wonderful," she smiled in return.

I swiveled in my seat toward Robert. "Do you have anything that you could show me?"

"Oh, no…" he shook his head. "I don't keep any of my art."

Pippa's eyes narrowed and she looked as though she were urging him to admit something. Robert caught her eye and added, "Well, I do have a sketch that I drew of my mother. It's how I remember her anyway."

"If you'd ever like to show it to me, I'd love to see it," I said, placing my hand on his arm.

"I do more than spit toothpaste on mirrors," Kip interrupted. I spun around in his direction, dropping my hand from Robert's arm.

I was obviously ignoring Kip. Guilt swelled up from the pit of my stomach because Kip had been nothing but wonderful to me and I was supposed to be doting on him, not Robert. I should be talking to *him*, putting my hand on *his* arm… So, why wasn't I?

"I play guitar," he said, looking a little defeated.

"What kind of music do you play?" I asked.

"My own stuff mostly. I write music as well." He looked at me warily.

"Before Santa comes, maybe you could play for me," I suggested. A peace offering for not letting him stay in my room.

Pippa sat up. "Let him play now! Kip, your plate is empty. Go and get your guitar and play something for us while we finish eating."

By the end of the dinner, Kip had played us a handful of songs. They were really good. Robert had loosened up, leaning back with his arm around my chair. I had to go to the bathroom, but I didn't want to disturb his position. Pippa had her elbow on the table and her chin in her hand talking to Sloane, who was wiping Sammy's mouth and Paul's hands. I'd never seen Pippa this relaxed.

The Marley Christmas dinner was more of a family atmosphere than I'd expected. Growing up, it was just my mom, Megan, Gram and me—four girls, three generations—trying to have a holiday like everyone else. It was funny, but the Marleys with all of their troubles were the best example of an extended family I'd ever seen, and they weren't even aware of it.

"Okay, boys," Sloane stood up, clapping her hands, "Let's get our cookies and milk for Santa and then it's off to bed. We have to go right to sleep or Santa won't come to visit."

"What if Santa leaves our presents at Daddy's house?" Paul worried aloud.

"He won't," Sloane reassured him.

"How do you know?"

Sloane mentally scrambled for an answer.

"Because!" Kip jumped in, "His elves tell him. Look! There's one!" he pointed to the corner of the room. The boys' heads wheeled around in that direction. "Ohp! You missed him." Sloane pulled Sammy from his booster seat and Paul crawled off his chair. The two boys followed Sloane out of the room, chattering away about the elves, leaving Pippa, the guys, and me.

"Well," Pippa blotted the edges of her mouth with a linen napkin. It had the letter "M" monogrammed in a deep cranberry color. "That was lovely. Thank you for your generous anecdote, Allie. It was truly charming. In all of my ninety-two years, this has been the most amusing Christmas dinner I've had." Her face was alive, her eyes sparkling. "And now I'm off to bed." Kip helped her to her scooter, the motor coming to life, and she exited the room.

"Wait!" I called out, and she rode back in.

"Yes?"

"What's something about you that I don't know?"

Everyone waited in silence. With an air of confidence, she said, "You don't know that I am actually an optimistic woman." And then she whispered something very personal in my ear.

Chapter Twenty-two

It was just the three of us: Robert, Kip and me, left at the table. Robert seemed to notice the change in atmosphere and suddenly became aware of his arm, discretely moving it off my chair. Kip leaned around me to address Robert. "Do you know what Santa's bringing the boys?"

"I've heard that it may require two grown men to assemble," Robert complained. "And possibly two grown women." He winked at me.

"Well, let me hit the ladies room and change into some comfortable clothes, and I'll meet you in the sitting room. Is that where Santa's leaving his loot?"

Kip nodded affirmatively as he stood and returned his guitar to its case. Then the three of us went our separate ways.

❄ ❄ ❄

It was amazing how the sitting room had been completely reassembled as if nothing had happened mere hours ago. The staff was just finishing the last of the cleanup effort from the open house, polishing and wiping down furniture before they all went home to their own families.

Piercing white light shone through the windows of the sitting room, illuminating Gerard and the staff while they finished the children's swing set outside. The frost glistened underneath their feet as they turned wrenches and lifted timber. I wondered if Anna would be making them any of her hot chocolate. I was glad that I had bought Gerard a new quilt, and I had left it on his bed as a surprise. After spending the evening out in the freezing cold, he may need it.

"What in the world are they building out there?" Robert asked over my shoulder. I turned around and had to bend backwards against the frigid windowsill to keep from bumping into him.

"Ms. Marley is having them construct a play set for the boys."

The smile fell from his lips as he watched. "It's wasted effort for only the few weeks that remain for us here at Ashford."

I nodded. It was only a second, but I felt as if the two of us were somehow unified by our thoughts, and it made me feel strong and happy and wistful all at the same time.

Sloane and Kip entered the room carrying so many boxes that their view was nearly obstructed. Kip dumped his onto the floor in front of the fireplace. Sloane carefully bent her legs and lowered hers to the floor.

"Robert," Sloane said, "go and stand guard in the hallway. We'll take turns."

I plopped down cross-legged next to Kip. My head became woozy from my body dropping down so quickly. I'd had so many glasses of wine between the party and dinner that I'd lost count. "What is this?" I asked, referring to the giant, rectangular box sitting in his lap.

"It's a play tent that has replica artwork from the 1880 Barnum and London Circus," Kip explained, pulling three large red rods from the box and flattening the assembly manual, which was the size of the New York Times, on the floor.

"*Barnum* from Barnum and Bailey?" I asked, holding one of the red rods while Kip screwed on a large red ball at one end.

"Apparently. Sloane has riding toys that are models of the circus animals to go around it when it's finished." He opened a bag of nearly 100—I swear—nuts and bolts and dumped them in a little pile between us.

I pulled a large canvas tarp from the box and unrolled it on the floor like an enormous yoga mat. Kip took it and threaded one of the red poles through a narrow pocket on the edge of it.

Robert peeked his head in. "How's everything going so far?" The three of us looked up at the same time. Sloane gave a thumbs-up. "Can someone get me my book or something?" Robert asked. "A pillow would be nice as well."

"Where is it?" Sloane asked.

"The pillow is on the settee and my book is over on the table there," he shook a finger toward the end table next to the settee. Sloane sat up onto her knees and scooted over to the table. She picked up the book and tossed it through the air. It slid on the hardwood floor and landed at Robert's feet. He leaned down to pick it up and, before he could resume an upright position, a pillow smacked him in the head.

"Thanks." He grimaced at Sloane and left the room.

Kip continued to thread and connect and secure until he was down to the smallest bag of nuts and bolts at which point he began a frenzied turning of pages in the manual. Then, in a few instances, he unthreaded, unconnected and unfastened, breathing louder each time. Finally, after much inhalation and exhalation, he told me to go and get Robert.

I walked into the entranceway to find Robert sitting on the pillow at the mouth of the east wing, his back against the wall, knees propped, reading his book. He looked up as I approached.

"Kip needs you."

"What's wrong?" he asked.

"He can't get the tent together."

Robert chewed on a smile as he placed his bookmark in his book and stood up. "Trade places?" he asked me.

"Sure." I sat down on the pillow, taking his book as he offered it to me. Then Robert left the room, and I was alone. I opened the book and tried to read the first chapter, but the words kept sliding around on the page. My eyes were feeling heavy, and fatigue was setting in from the alcohol. I tried once more to read through waning consciousness.

✳ ✳ ✳

I woke up, still in my clothes, lying on my back on the bed in my room. The sun was seeping through the curtains that had been drawn. Did I draw them? I tried to focus on the fuzzy dark blobs that were floating around on the ceiling, and I realized that it was just my vision. I closed my eyes, and the room spun ever so slightly. Then, without opening them, I remembered flipping a coin in this very room with Robert. I put my hand on my mouth to stifle the panic that was escaping through my lips. Did I offer to *sleep* with him? Then my thoughts wandered to another vague memory.

It was of being scooped off of the hallway floor.

By Robert.

I opened my eyes and stared at the fuzzy blobs again as dread whirled around in my stomach. I couldn't go into the sitting room with a family that wasn't mine, on a holiday in a house in which I did not live, and look at Robert after making a pass at him last night! Did he tell Kip? Oh my God!

After I'd had a complete mental breakdown, I decided that I'd have to face the music. I pulled myself out of bed. My mouth felt dry and wooly, and my head was like cement. I brushed my teeth, washed my face, applied enough make-up and primping to hide the way I felt, dressed, and then walked out of my room toward the sitting room.

When I entered, the room looked like a toy wonderland. The tent was erected with miniature animals surrounding it. There were riding toys and balls, hula hoops and dress-up clothes. I'd never seen anything like it. A track snaked through the circus scene with a giant toy circus train that the children could actually sit in.

It took me a moment to realize that the only person in the room besides me was Robert. He was sitting on the sofa, a newspaper spread across his lap, smiling up at me. "Good morning, Sleeping Beauty."

Anxiety flooded every cell in my body, prickling my skin and sending icy waves of tension through my limbs. I walked over and sat next to him. "Robert, I woke up this morning and remembered…" I tried to find the words. "making…" How do I say this? "…a pass at you."

Robert laughed out loud, causing me to jump, my heart slamming around inside my chest. "You made a pass at me? I wish that I had realized that. The outcome may have been different." he joked.

"When we flipped the coin…"

"Ah, I see. You weren't planning to sleep on the floor?" He was clearly enjoying this.

I narrowed my eyes at him. "I just wanted to say that I'm sorry." I swallowed, my mouth drying out again. "And I'm sorry for falling asleep in the hallway."

"It's fine."

"Where is everybody?" I asked, looking around, trying to change the subject.

"Outside with Pippa's new play set." He folded the paper and set it on the end table. "Are you hungry?"

"Starving."

"Do you like omelets?"

"Yes…"

"Okay, I'll whip one up for you," he said, standing up. "Anna's off on Christmas Day, so we have to fend for ourselves," he said over his shoulder as I scrambled to follow behind him.

"No, no! You don't have to…"

"It's fine, Allie," he turned around and faced me. He was oddly familiar—the square of his shoulders, the tone of his arms through his shirt, the compassion in his eyes—as if I'd known him my whole life, or as if I'd been meant to know him. "It's Christmas," he continued. "Enjoy yourself, and let me cook you breakfast."

I sat on a bar stool at the large island, across from the prep counter as Robert reached into the fridge and pulled out a few eggs and some diced peppers. He cracked the eggs into a stainless steel bowl and whisked them in tight little circles. His hands looked powerful somehow, strong. "How did you sleep?"

"Like a rock. I could hardly get up this morning. I don't think I've had that much to drink in a long time." I got up and walked over to his side of the counter. "Mind if I make some coffee?" Robert shook his head and poured the egg mixture into the pan. He helped me find the supplies and get the coffee started. It was a relief to hear the gentle drip of the coffee pot when it percolated.

We didn't talk much while he cooked, but it was comfortable, easy. It would be so effortless to slide my hands around him and look up into his face.

"I wrapped up a little gift for you," he said, shimmying the omelet onto a plate.

"Oh? Well, I have something for you too."

Robert slowly turned in my direction as if registering this piece of information. "Is that so?" he asked, his eyes all glittery and happy again. I kept waiting for him to snap out of it; to flip the switch and be Mr. Closed Off again. I knew that it would happen eventually. It was probably just because it was Christmas.

I took a bite of my omelet and set my fork down. "Um hum," I said, pouring a cup of coffee. I added the cream and sugar and took a sip. "The omelet is really good. Thanks for making it for me."

Pippa came rolling in on her scooter. She took us in for a moment. "Well, aren't you two pleasantly domestic this morning?" Robert grinned at her, but also took a step away from where I was standing. "Don't stop on my account! Carry on your little tête-à-tête." She wriggled her hand in the air.

Neither of us said a word. I sipped my coffee, and Robert started to wash out the dishes in the sink as Pippa made conversation. "I couldn't stay out there very long. I'm already frozen to the bone!" She made a shivering motion and then rolled over to me. "Go on, make me a cup of coffee, dear." I looked at Robert for approval, but Pippa rolled between us. "It's Christmas! You had better," she waggled a finger at me.

Pippa was talkative this morning. She kept chatting as I poured her a cup. "The boys want to go riding later! I won't be able to stand it out there in that bitter cold."

"Riding?" I looked at Robert for an explanation.

"On Christmas, usually in the afternoon, we go riding over at Sheldon McCormack's farm."

"On the horses?"

"Yes. That would be the most obvious animal to ride, wouldn't it?"

I glared playfully at him. "Kip took me to see the horses. They were magnificent."

Robert dried his hands on a kitchen towel, refolded it, and placed it on the counter. "Will you go with us?" he asked.

"Yes! But can I have Andre? Kip said I should ride him. He said Andre's the most gentle."

"Kip offered you Andre?" Robert's brow furrowed.

"Yes, why?"

"Well, Andre's my horse. Not mine actually, but I always ride him. I'm surprised he didn't tell you to ride Britches. Kip usually rides her."

I tried to recount Kip's exact words. "I might have to let you have Andre," he had said, or something like that. Was there some sort of double meaning?

"In a few minutes I'd like to call everyone in to open presents. Would that suit you two?" Pippa interrupted. Robert and I both nodded, and he walked Pippa out of the room.

I finished my omelet, refilled my coffee, and walked with Robert into the sitting room. Pippa sat down next to me on the settee as Robert left to call everyone else in. I'd seen her sit here before, but only now did I really take in how small she was. Her legs only just reached the floor when she sat on the edge. The sofa looked as though it would swallow her small frame if she sat back on the cushion.

Kip walked in and sat down between Pippa and me, rubbing his hands on his jeans. "Good morning," he beamed and kissed me on the cheek, glancing over at Robert. His lips were like ice. "How are you feeling, you little party animal?"

"I'm fine, thanks. I'm sorry I fell asleep."

"You did?"

"In the hallway."

"What?"

Robert cut in as he reentered the room, "She fell asleep," he tipped his head in the direction of the boys as they came into the room, "in the hallway, but I… helped her to bed. It was no problem." To everyone else, it just looked like any other conversation, but I was in tuned enough to Robert's expressions that I thought I noted a sense of rivalry between him and Kip. It was almost as if the two of them were staking their claim or something. The idea of Robert possibly competing for me made me happy beyond belief.

Like little ducklings, the boys followed Sloane into the center of the sitting room, their ears and noses red from the cold. They sat down next to the tree, Paul pulling out presents and setting them in his lap.

Sloane reined him in and picked up the first present. "This one's for Allie," she said, turning over the tag. Sloane handed it to me.

I read the tag aloud, "To Allie. Love, Kip." I pivoted my legs to the side so that I was facing him. Setting the tiny gift in my lap, I pulled back the paper at the seam until it was free from the box that it had been concealing. The paper wadded easily in my hand as I passed it to Sloane, who placed it in a trash bag. Gently, I removed the lid of the box. Inside was a note written in Kip's elongated, scratchy handwriting. It said, "Hold on a sec." He stood up and exited the room after shooting a wink in my direction.

A minute or so later, he returned, wobbling into the room behind an enormous rectangular object obscured by brown paper. It was thin in width but extremely large, and it seemed quite heavy as he set the bottom down at his feet with a thud.

"What in the world is this?"

"Tear off the paper and you'll find out." Kip looked obviously proud of himself.

I grabbed a corner of the bulky brown paper and began to pull it off in wide, haphazard strips, revealing a framed piece of artwork. Upon further scrutiny, I realized what it was and let out an involuntary squeal.

"It's our feet painting," Kip explained to the rest of the family. Paul and Sammy both hopped up to inspect the picture. They were pointing and giggling at the streaks of primary colors encased in the most regal frame I'd ever seen. "It's museum quality, you know," Kip said, turning to me. "I had my friend Beth help me get it framed. She runs the fine arts museum in the city."

I remembered Beth. The cell phone caller from movie night. Shame overtook me as I recalled my trepidation regarding that call. My Cinderella complex... Had it all been just insecure paranoia? I stood up, heat flooding my cheeks, and put my arms around Kip. My face brushed his and his cheek was soft like a baby's skin. He had very recently shaved. "Thank you," I whispered in his ear. He pulled back and gently placed his lips on mine.

Sloane interrupted our moment as she pulled a second gift from the tree. "This one's for Robert," she stated. "It's from..." she peered at the tag, but I knew the answer. "Allie," she said and handed it to him.

My hands began to sweat as Robert reached out and took the gift from Sloane. I held onto The Feet Painting for support. Robert pulled the corners loose from the scotch tape that I had applied, and slid his finger beneath the overlap of paper and ran it along the length of the gift until the paper fell loose in his hand. My heart pounded as he turned the record over in his palm.

"Louis Armstrong."

I heard the words come out, but they weren't Robert's. He was still studying the album cover. The words came from Kip who was trying to be subtle about his irritation, but it was painted across his face like a red stripe. My thoughts went immediately to the pint glasses. I wanted to pause time, slip under the tree, steal them and exchange them for something meaningful, but I knew that I couldn't. I would have to watch Kip unwrap beer glasses after I had just given Robert the song of a lifetime. After Kip had given me the best piece of artwork that I knew I would ever own.

Robert was still peering down at the cover. "Thank you," he said without looking up.

I couldn't look at him. It was too awkward, so I turned my head in Pippa's direction. She was attempting to conceal a grin beneath her shell-pink lipstick. She gave me a miniscule nod of approval and then, said aloud, "Who's next?" gesturing to Sloane.

Robert ignored Pippa and leaned over toward me, seemingly unaware of Kip's clenching and unclenching of his jaw. "Really. Thank you," he said, kissing me on the cheek. His scent of spice and laundry soap assaulted my senses, making me a little light-headed.

"You don't need to borrow Anna's anymore. I just figured..." but I never finished the sentence. Robert was nodding his head in understanding.

"For Pippa! From Kip!" Sloane called out.

Chapter Twenty-three

The pint glasses sat in the corner of the room, nestled in the now crumpled red and green paper in which I had concealed them. Kip had been gracious about my gift. After all, I'd bet that he probably couldn't have come up with anything better. But I did worry about the message that I sent with my gifts. How could I explain that I just knew what to get Robert?

Adding to the awkwardness, Robert decided to wrap up the flipping coin that we had opened the night before. He placed it in a box, heads-side-up and said, "Just in case you ever wanted to know what heads looked like…" I was getting fed up with all of the passive aggressive flirting. And why would he do that when I was dating Kip? But then I remembered that I was the one who dragged Robert into the bedroom for that ridiculous game of heads or tails.

I sat on the settee while the boys were off getting dressed in their riding clothes. We were all going to Mr. McCormack's to ride horses. All of us except for Robert and Pippa. Robert had abruptly changed his mind, saying he had some business he needed to finish. On Christmas Day? And Pippa said it was just too cold. I didn't blame her.

Kip drove us to the stables in his car. The Marley family and I got out like a herd of cattle and walked in a huddle of bundled bodies to where I had first met the horses. Kip held the swinging wood-rail gate open so that we could enter. As we neared the barn, which was painted in traditional red and white, his boots scuffed the bare, frozen ground.

Sloane and I took the kids over to the horses while Kip retrieved the riding equipment. Paul and Sammy fed carrots to Daisy and Britches. "So…" Sloane spoke quietly in my direction, "Robert seems aloof this afternoon." I knew it was only a matter of time before his mood swung in the other direction. Christmas was over for the most part, so he was jumping right back into work again, surely.

Kip returned with a saddlecloth for one of the horses, set it on a bench outside the barn, and began to assemble the rest of the equipment. I pretended to watch him, but my mind was still on Christmas. I hoped that I hadn't made Robert uncomfortable with that record. I was just trying to give him something meaningful.

Andre meandered over to Kip as he emerged with the saddle and bridle. He draped Andre's back with the saddlecloth, slung the saddle over it and began fastening the straps. "Are you all ready?" he asked the kids, tightening the girth on the horse's belly with a few short tugs.

Paul sprinted over to Kip with Sammy stumbling behind him. "I'm first!" Paul shouted.

Gently, Kip led Andre over a few steps to the mounting block and pulled on the reins, instructing the horse to stay put. Paul stepped up onto the block and held the horn of the saddle. With his left foot in the stirrup, he swung himself up onto the horse's back. Kip handed him the reins, but kept a firm hold as well.

Sammy had returned and taken a seat next to Sloane on the bench. I joined them, crossing my arms around me in an attempt to trap what little heat was in my coat. We watched Kip and Paul make their way across the field.

"Will you be going with Kip to Australia?" Sloane asked.

"Did he actually decide to go?"

"He told me this morning. I wondered what Robert would do for a house manager if you and Kip ran off together." Sloane hid her hands in her coat pockets.

I was dumbfounded. It took me a second to make myself form the words, "No, I'm not going to Australia." I watched as Kip tilted his head up at Paul. Paul was riding Andre like he'd done it all of his life. And then I realized that he probably had.

"Why not? I hope it's not because of this job."

"No," I shook my head, "I'm just not the kind of person who jet sets like that. It's not in my nature." The thought that I'd been pushing off, holding at bay, trying never to think about came rushing in, slamming me hard. I was not like this family. I did not belong here. I was not a jetsetter, or a person who lived in mansions and rode horses on Christmas Day. I turned to face Sloane. "Did he say how long he was staying?"

"I think he said a few months," Sloane answered, but her thoughts seemed to be elsewhere. She refocused from whatever she had been contemplating and asked, "So, you'll have peace and quiet then in a few days."

"Why?"

"Well, I'm moving into our home on the river, Kip's going to Australia, and Robert told me just before we got in the car that he's going back to New York as soon as he can get a flight. Looks like it will just be you and Pippa."

My feeling of humility dissolved under a flood of anger. I may not be like this family, but I knew how to *be* a family. Here they were, scattering again at their first chance! No wonder none of the Marleys got along; they wouldn't stay together long enough to work anything out.

Sammy hopped off of the bench. "My tun!" he toddled toward Kip and Paul who were walking toward us with Andre. Before I could grab Kip's attention, he had turned away, helping Sammy up onto the horse. I decided that it wasn't the time anyway and sat silently stewing about the days ahead.

*   *   *

When we returned to Ashford, Kip and Sloane were getting the kids out of the car as I walked briskly up the enormous staircase to the front door. It was unlocked, so I let myself in and marched straight for Robert's office. I had become increasingly irritated about Sloane's comments as the hour had worn on. Kip wondered, I could tell, when I hadn't wanted to ride the horses, but I didn't care.

I barged in and walked straight over to Robert who looked up at me questioningly from the desk.

"You're going back to New York? When?" I demanded.

He didn't change his curious expression as he said, "Tomorrow." With a few clicks on the mouse, he shut down his computer and swiveled in my direction.

"Why?" My annoyance withered into disappointment. I caught myself and straightened my shoulders to hide my feelings.

"I have some things to take care of."

"Like what? You've sold the house already!" I threw my hands up in frustration and let them slam back down at my sides. "What more could you have to do?"

Robert stood up, and he was so close that he had to look down at me to make eye contact. "Allie, I buy and sell property for a living. Not just this property."

"You and Pippa finally had a good night, and the family seemed to be happy. Now, everyone's leaving again."

Kip walked into the office, and we both turned to look at him. "What's going on?" he asked coming closer to me. Robert took a step back.

The exasperation returned, and I whacked Kip on the chest with my hand. "I'll tell you what's going on," I began, my hand still on his chest. "This entire family is bailing. Everyone's leaving! And when were you planning on telling me about your trip?"

Kip's cheeks flushed. "Can we talk about this privately?"

"No. What's the point?"

"Look, I asked you to go with me and you didn't want to..."

Robert cut in, "You don't want to go to Australia?"

The aggravation that was originally pecking at my insides was now gnawing through my body. "No! I don't! I don't want to live out of suitcases half way across the world for months in a city that I don't know with people whom I've never met. That doesn't sound interesting in the slightest!" I could have said more, but I could see Kip's face looking more miserable with each remark, so I stopped there.

Robert placed a hand on my arm. Kip seemed to notice, but didn't react. "Well, do you mind living out of suitcases just a while longer? I'd like you to stay on for the first few weeks in January to help organize things while I'm gone."

I should have been ecstatic to have employment, but I really didn't feel that way at all. "Sure," the word came out as nearly a whisper. Wetness built behind my eyes, but I blinked it away. Robert was rubbing my arm up and down in little strokes. If he kept doing that, I might have a full-blown tear fest, so I pulled away from him.

I suddenly needed a break from the Marley family. I wanted to go home. "Do you mind if I excuse myself? I'd like to call my sister." I left both men standing in the office and headed toward my room.

Chapter Twenty-four

Megan picked me up, since I didn't feel like driving, and we made the thirty minute commute to Mom's, chatting the entire way. After hearing the latest in my Marley saga, Megan was more than ready to give her thoughts on the matter.

"Kip's hot. You should go with him to Australia."

"Megan!" I tried to stifle my amusement with a straight face, but was unsuccessful. "Nothing about traveling is comfortable. It's so stressful. You know that's just not my thing." The heater was blowing air straight at me, so I reached over and turned the vent down toward the floor of the car.

"And what, exactly, is *your thing*?" she asked. "I'd love to hear what you like to do with your free time other than meddle in other families' business."

I gave the question some thought. Shifting my feet around the Christmas presents that I'd brought for Megan and Mom, I turned to face my sister. "I'd just like to be… settled."

"What?" Megan pulled out a small bag of red and green jellybeans from her purse that was wedged between us, opened it, and offered me some. I declined. "What do you mean?" she asked, popping a red one into her mouth.

"I've lived at home, at college, with the Andersons, and now with the Marleys. I've never had a home of my own or a steady boyfriend… I just want to be in one place with someone I care about. I don't need to go anywhere or do anything special." Reconsidering, I reached over and dipped my two fingers into the bag of jellybeans and grabbed one.

There went the belittling sigh. "If you don't care what you do, then just go to Australia."

"It's not the same. I'd at least like to be in my own country." I tossed the jellybean into my mouth and chewed. It tasted like strawberries, an odd flavor choice for Christmas candy. "And, I can't put my finger on it, but with Kip I feel…" I tried to find the correct way to describe our relationship. "…like I have to work at it."

"Girl, I would not have to work very hard to date Kip Marley. What's wrong with you?"

"I don't know," I leaned on my knees with my elbows and buried my face in my hands. "Am I over-thinking it?" I asked into my hands. I looked up and Megan was moving her head up and down in an exaggerated motion, her lips pursed in disapproval.

"He's too rich for me."

"So, when I sell enough homes to make that kind of money, you'll stop talking to me?"

"No. It's different. We didn't grow up the way he did. Sometimes I feel like I can't relate." I was getting it all off my chest now and it felt good.

"Does he ever do or say anything to make you feel like you can't relate?"

"Not really. I just feel like it's a little forced, that's all."

"Then let him go to Australia and move on to someone new when the opportunity presents itself," Megan clipped. She always got bent out of shape about my decisions. To her, I consistently made the wrong ones.

"And what should I do about Robert?"

Megan's eyebrows rose, giving her forehead three wide creases. As her face oscillated from the road to me, she asked, "Is there something *to do* about Robert?"

"He's like my own personal project. I just want to make him feel something. He's so closed off. I've seen a glimmer of the real him— that I know is in there—over the past few days, but I don't think I've even scratched the surface with him. I think there's so much more to him than he's showing us."

Megan offered the bag as I reached over and grabbed another jellybean—green this time. It had a mint flavor. Mint and strawberries. Ugh. "Where did you get this candy?" I scowled.

"Robert Marley isn't one of your students, Allie. You don't have to fix him, or teach him, or… Whatever. Just let it go. Why do you care?"

I couldn't answer that, so I looked out the window. The only sound between us was the quiet growl of the engine. Megan turned on the radio; the station was broadcasting a Christmas classics marathon. "Let it Snow" was finishing. As the disc jockey began talking, the tune continued to bounce around in my head while I watched the trees, trying to keep my eye on just one as we passed it. It was a little game I had played since I was a kid.

"You know, you overanalyze everything," Megan blurted out over "Silent Night." I pulled my eyes from the window and looked over at her. "You've always been in your head too much." She reached out and turned down the volume. "Silent Night" was now a hum coming from the backseat. She continued, "When you got out of school, you kept thinking and thinking about what job to take. It was exhausting! And what happened? You didn't take a job at all!" Megan punched the volume button on the car radio with her finger, silencing "Silent Night."

"And then there was Travis Nelson. Remember him? I tried to set you up with him when you were living with the Andersons. You found something wrong with him… What was it?" Megan snapped her fingers repeatedly with one hand as she asked the question, her other hand gripping the steering wheel. "Oh! I know! He said he really liked you and you weren't sure you liked him as much as he liked you." She rolled her eyes in disgust as she pulled the car onto an exit ramp. We slowed to a stop at the next traffic light. "Now you're telling me that you have to try too hard with Kip Marley. Are you sensing a theme yet?" The light turned green, and Megan accelerated. "You're claiming to have this need to fix Robert Marley, but I think it's just a clever way to push Kip out of the picture. Robert Marley is an insensitive, haughty man. It would be just like you to use him to sabotage the first good thing you've had in a long time."

I looked back out the window without responding. Was she right? I tried to consider the situation objectively. Maybe Megan was making some sense. As I watched my hometown slide into view, I pondered the idea of going to Australia with Kip. My focus moved from the scene passing by to the spots of dried precipitation on the window, but I was only partly conscious of it. I was too busy weighing my options.

❄ ❄ ❄

Mom's Christmas tree looked even smaller after seeing the Marleys'. She had strewn tinsel on all of the branches. Colored bulbs that looked like multicolored robins' eggs bulged between the evergreen needles. Wafting scents of turkey and sweet potatoes penetrated the air inside the house. I removed my coat and draped it on the recliner. The house was unusually warm. It was probably because the oven had been on all day.

"Girls?" Mom's voice beckoned from the kitchen. "I'm so glad you're here! Come in and wash your hands. We need some help with the potato salad."

We entered to find Mom and Gram, both apron-clad, preparing an unreasonable amount of food; so much that it barely fit on the laminate countertops. Megan stuck her finger in the mashed potatoes and scooped a little glob. As she placed it in her mouth, Mom scolded, "Wash your hands! This is sick season, you know."

It was so good to see Gram, so familiar, so comfortable. I realized just then how much I'd missed her. She was looking at me with that smile that I knew so perfectly that I could recreate it at will. I kissed her on the cheek. Her familiar scent of lilac saturated the air around her. "How are you, Gram?" I asked, stepping just far enough away from her to relieve my nose of the floral aroma. Seeing her now filled me with relief that I was home with the ones I loved.

"Not so bad," she said as she peeled a potato. "My hands are hurting a little more these days, and I'm not getting around as quickly, you know." Gram shrugged off her own comment and continued peeling the potato. She peeled the potato in one, long, continuous strip that dropped like a spud slinky into the black-bag-lined trashcan below her hands.

I turned on the water and got my hands wet. Megan had grabbed a dinner roll and was picking pea-sized pieces off of it and popping

them into her mouth. I pumped some soap into the palm of my
hand and lathered.

"I didn't think we'd see you for Christmas dinner tonight, Allie," Gram said, her face still turned down toward the potato in
her hands.

"I thought you all were going to do dinner on Christmas Eve,"
I said.

Mom wiped her hands on the front of her apron. "We waited so
that Gram could join us. She wanted to go with her friend Eloise
to church on Christmas Eve, and it was too much to try and come
here too."

I rinsed. "I'm so glad it worked out. I'm starving." I flicked
the excess water from my hands and wiped them dry with a
kitchen towel.

"Well, you'd better get to cuttin' if you want to eat tonight.
We've got to get things moving if we're gonna do presents after,"
Mom said. Megan washed her hands, and we both started chopping
potatoes into neat little squares. "Megan tells me you've found a
boyfriend," Mom mentioned, adding a layer of pecans to the sweet
potato casserole.

I continued chopping potatoes into squares as I answered, "I
wouldn't call him my boyfriend, but we're dating."

"Caught yourself a rich boy?" Gram chimed in.

I made eye contact with Megan, my insecurities stinging me
again. I hadn't *caught* anything. Here I was with three generations of
women who all had their own versions of life: Megan just starting
hers with her fantastic job and apartment; Mom, who had made
her own career and raised two daughters; and Gram, who had lived
a full life, including work, children, and then grandchildren. I was

still taking handouts, and Kip had just sort of fallen into my lap. I hadn't pursued anything, achieved anything.

"Gram, I don't care if he's rich."

"I didn't say you cared, honey. But it can't hurt, can it?"

We continued cooking dinner, never responding to Gram's comment. But I was thinking about it. Can it *hurt* to have all of that money? Sometimes, I think it can. The Marleys' troubles seemed to all revolve around their money. Had they not had something as grand as Ashford, Robert may not feel compelled to sell it, and he wouldn't have to hurt Pippa. If Kip didn't have his inheritance to fall back on, he'd have to figure out his life, and he wouldn't be so irritating to Robert. If Sloane hadn't had the Marley fortune, she'd have probably found herself a career of some sort, and she wouldn't be in the turmoil that she's in now. And, I had to consider how their money isolated them from the world in which I lived, how different it made us. So, back to the question: Can it hurt? I'd seen a lot of hurt over the past weeks, so yes, I think it can.

As we chopped and stirred, Megan talked about the latest reality show she'd been watching, and Mom went on and on about an email she'd received with a video of a dog saying *I love you*. She swore it was the funniest thing she'd ever seen. Eventually, the oven timer went off—three long beeps—and Mom pulled a dish from the oven with two oven-mitted hands. "Let's get the table ready to eat, ladies."

The kitchen table was located approximately three paces from the oven. Gram moved the long cutting board from the tabletop, balancing it across the sink. She wiped the table's surface with a rag before setting a pile of plates on top with a heap of paper napkins. I helped Megan pass out the dishware and fill the cups with ice. Gram took a seat, laying one hand on her fork and the other on her knife. I sat down next to her and Megan next to me.

Mom came over with a few serving dishes and set them in the middle of us. "You'll have to get up if you want the potatoes and the green bean casserole. They're on the counter. Megan, turn the oven off, would you? It's stifling in here." She cracked the window a bit to allow the warmth to escape just as my face began to fully radiate heat.

As I looked around our small but happy table, I wondered what the Marleys would think of this. It was a far cry from the lavish spread I'd enjoyed the other night. They had so much, and Robert was just throwing it away. He didn't even realize what he had. It was infuriating. Also infuriating was the thought that, with or without Ashford, the Marleys could be as happy as my family had always been if they'd only let themselves. My own thoughts consuming the sounds around me, muting the voices of my family, I watched as Gram said something to Megan, making her laugh, throwing her head back, her chest convulsing in amusement, Mom's face alight with joy, the steaming food nestled between us, squeezing our plates to the very edge of the table. It was simple but perfect. The intimacy of it was its perfection, and it didn't matter that the table was small or that the kitchen was hot—nobody here noticed that at all. What mattered was that we were together—a family—and we were enjoying each other.

Once we had said grace and we all had our food, Mom said, "So, Allie… What do you have planned after this job is finished?" She looked over at Megan as she stabbed a green bean with her fork. "That big house is sold now, isn't it, Megan?"

Megan nodded as she chewed. "Nearly," she said, her hand concealing the bite of roll in her mouth. Mom looked back in my direction.

"I don't know. I was thinking I'd look for a preschool job." I twirled my fork in my mashed potatoes.

"Maybe Megan can find you something else," Mom said, scraping her spoon around the edge of her mashed potatoes and dipping each bite into the little cavity of gravy that she'd created in the center. I think she was trying to be helpful, but it came across to me as condescending. Reaching across Megan's plate, I picked up a roll and buttered it in silence.

"I think you should look into teaching again. You've always had a natural ability with teaching children," Megan said. I knew she was trying to be supportive, but I was feeling more depressed by the minute. I knew my own strengths; I didn't need Megan to point them out as if I were a child. So why couldn't I find a way to use them? People got jobs all the time, one after another. Why was it so hard for me? What was wrong with me that I couldn't just go out there, fill out the applications and get the calls? My life was slipping away with every day and I'd made nothing of it. I quietly agreed, outwardly acknowledging Megan's comment, my mind still reeling.

Then I turned to Gram and attempted to change the subject. "Gram, where did you live growing up? Have you always lived here?" I speared a piece of turkey with my fork.

"Yes ma'am. I've been here since Daddy moved us when I was only two years old. I grew up here, raised my babies here and now, I'm having a lovely Christmas dinner with my grown grandchildren here." She smiled.

Gram was obviously one who enjoyed being settled in one place. Mom also has liked being settled in the same location. Maybe it was some ancient genetic pull that made me still, with all of the mental energy I could emit, not want to go to Australia with Kip. "It's nice here," I said, as I placed the piece of turkey into my mouth.

It *was* nice here. This house, this town—all of it—was me. It was exactly who I was.

❆ ❆ ❆

When morning arrived, I woke up in my childhood bed. I closed my eyes and rolled over onto one side, wadding the bedding up around me. When I opened my eyes again, I tried to focus on my blue and gold cheerleading trophy. It looked smaller than I had remembered.

I wanted to get out of bed because I could smell the scent of scrambled eggs wafting into my room, but I was suddenly aware that my nose was an ice cube, and I had every blanket on my bed, including the scratchy purple and white ruffled bedspread, yanked in a tight line up to my neck.

Hurriedly, I pounced from under my covers and grabbed the new robe and slippers that Mom had given me for Christmas, tying the belt tightly around my waist. I slid the slippers onto my feet and stepped into the hallway to check the thermostat. When I reached the little box on the wall, I cupped my hands in front of my mouth, with the robe's tag still hanging from the sleeve, and breathed out in a feeble attempt to warm them. The temperature read sixty-two degrees. Sixty-two degrees?

"Mom?" I called, entering the kitchen. Oh, thank goodness, she'd made coffee. "Why do you have the temperature set at sixty-two degrees?"

Mom slid a pan full of eggs onto a platter and lightly dusted them with salt. "I heard the cooler temperatures help you sleep better," she said.

Gram added, "And it saves on the heating bill. Good thinking." She tapped her temple with her index finger. "Lower bills'll help you sleep better too, I imagine."

I giggled in Gram's direction just as Mom rolled her eyes, a smile sliding across her face. I raked my fingers through my hair and itched the back of my head. "Well, it's absolutely freezing." I poured some coffee into a mug the shape of a pig, sweetened it, added some cream, and stirred. Setting the spoon in the sink, I picked up the mug by its curly tail handle and took a sip.

Mom scooped a pile of eggs from the platter, dropped them onto a small plate, and handed it to me. The steam from them danced its way into the air, warming my face as I took the plate and set it down on the placemat in front of where I was sitting. Just as I was about to eat, my purse—that was still hanging on the back of my chair from when I'd put it there yesterday—began to buzz. I recognized the ring to be my cell phone, so I began rummaging around, attempting to locate it.

Upon retrieving the phone, I peered at the screen. It was Robert.

"Hello?" I said, pushing the chair under the table and exiting the kitchen.

"Allie. I was hoping I'd get you. How was Christmas with your family?"

"Fine, thanks." Both Mom and Gram were attempting to see around the corner in my direction. I walked into my bedroom and shut the door.

"I'm actually on my way to the airport," he said. "I got a flight out this morning, so I'm going back to New York."

I assumed that a comment from me was what he was waiting for, but I had nothing more to say about Robert going back to New

York, so I sat there, the sounds from the kitchen stirring behind my closed door.

He continued, "The sale of Ashford is nearly complete, so we need to go ahead and begin to pack what we'd like to keep. I want you to organize an estate sale for the items with which we'd like to part."

"Okay." I sat down on a pile of ruffles.

"We're estimating the actual closing to be in two weeks' time, so you'll have to move quickly to get it all done. I'd like to advertise in the local paper, and I'm not certain of the timeframe they employ, so you'll have to do some checking on that."

"Okay." I wasn't sure what else to say. I wondered if I'd be able to utter only the word "okay" for the rest of the conversation. His leaving annoyed me so much, I decided to try.

"I'll be in New York the entire two weeks." I couldn't believe that he was leaving. It was so infuriating.

"Okay."

"Once the sale is final, I'll consider that your last day of employment." I noted a small exhale that made its way through to my end of the phone line.

"Okay."

"Have you ever considered the possibility of working for us in the future?"

Darn. "Okay" wouldn't work. Then I thought about his question. Would I work for the Marleys again? The memory of Robert kissing me on the cheek with the Louis Armstrong record in his hand came flooding back to me.

"Would you at least consider it?"

Yes! "Okay."

I grinned.

"Allie…" Robert started to speak, but I cut him off. My head was muddled with my own thoughts.

"I have to go," I said.

"Allie…"

"I really have to go."

✳ ✳ ✳

When I walked back into the kitchen, my eggs were spinning under the orange light of my mother's microwave. "I thought they may need some warmin' up," Mom said. The timer dinged, and she removed the plate, setting it back in front of me.

"Thanks," I said, taking a bite, chewing through the heat of them, and swallowing the burning bits of fire down my throat. "I have to be quick. I want to get a shower and get back to Ashford. Is Megan working today?"

"No," Megan answered from the hallway. She was wearing flannel pajamas and thick gray socks that bunched around her thin ankles as she walked.

"Can you take me back to Ashford today? My car is still there, and I have no way back."

Megan poured herself a cup of coffee and sat down next to me. Her Busch Gardens mug had a picture of a roller coaster looping around its entire black ceramic surface. It made me think of sledding.

"Can I have a few minutes to wake up?" she asked.

"Of course. I have to get a shower anyway."

"Getting ready to see Kip?" she asked, suddenly more awake than she had been.

"No, I have to shower because I'm going to work and most people shower before work." I cut my eyes at her and sipped my coffee.

❀ ❀ ❀

On the way back to Ashford, I contemplated having "The Talk" with Kip. I brainstormed ways to explain my feelings and I went over all the choices mentally:

1. Kip, our lives are very different. We shouldn't drag this out any longer than we have.
2. Kip, I feel like our relationship is strained.
3. Kip, we are two very dissimilar individuals.
4. Kip, I want to break up.
5. Kip, I think I might want to see where things go with…

"What are you thinking about over there?" Megan's voice ripped me from my list-making. She was driving with one hand and applying lip balm with the other. With her knee steadying the wheel, she capped the stick before tossing it into her open purse that was, once again, wedged between us.

"Nothing." I turned on the radio and hit the seek button just to kill time. The truth was, I was going back and forth between breaking up with Kip and going with him to Australia. The two choices were ridiculously juxtaposed. My mind was clouded with thoughts about the kind of person I knew I was and the kind of person I could be. Should be? I didn't know.

"Well, you're awfully quiet." She punched the seek button, tuning to a pop station that I'd never listened to in the entire time it had been broadcasting.

"I think I might stop seeing Kip." This time, I hit the seek button.

"What?" Megan reached over and turned off the radio. Her head went from me to the road and then back to me. "You've got to be kidding me, Allie!"

"Megan, deep down you know that the kind of person who goes to Australia with a guy she's just met and spends a considerable amount of time traveling around with him probably wouldn't even be friends with me. So what am I doing trying to be that person? It isn't me, and you know it."

Exhale. The look.

I turned the radio back on, and we continued to drive without talking.

Chapter Twenty-five

I arrived at Ashford midmorning to find my itinerary waiting for me. The house was completely vacant, so I decided to see if Pippa was allowing anyone into her room. A nurse wearing blue scrubs that puddled around her bright white shoes greeted me as I entered. Pippa was sitting in her chair, scowling at an open book in her lap, as someone took her blood pressure.

"Hello, Ms. Marley." I kneeled down beside her so I could be at eye-level. "Did Robert tell you about the sale of Ashford?"

Her head swung in my direction and then back to her book. "Yes."

"I have to organize an estate sale. Do you mind helping me tag the items to be kept and those to be sold?" I leaned close to her chair, trying to be more personal, and smiled up at her. It didn't seem to work. She was obviously ignoring me, so I put my hand on her arm. "If you tell me what I should save, I give you my most solemn promise that I'll make a personal effort to keep it in the family." She looked up.

The medical staff scrawled some numbers on her charts, packed their things, and left for the day. It was just Pippa and me in her room now. Her eyes were moist as she said, "I leave in two days for Birkwood Assisted Living." With her feeble hands, she slammed the covers of her book together, startling me with the loud bang. "So, if we're going to sort out my belongings, we'd best get a move on." She stood up and mounted her scooter.

❊ ❊ ❊

Pippa had decided that since the storage areas were the most annoying to clear out, we should start there. In the end, it would be much easier for a third party to sort the house furniture, but the boxes of postcards and old photos, letters and mementos would be much more taxing. We had cleared four boxes for trash, three for keeping, and we had six more to go.

Pippa asked Gerard to pull a wing chair into the hallway as I dug through the boxes in the storage area that was just off the east wing. She watched as I pulled the next box onto my lap, clapping my hands together in an attempt to rid them of the dust. I pulled off the lid, revealing another box of photos. They were thrown haphazardly into the box, so I reached in and pulled one out. "We should sort these by era first. Then chronologically if you know the date."

I turned the photo around in my hand and had to hold in a tiny fizz of happiness. It was a picture of Robert at around eight, sitting by the brook at the bottom of the hill outside, the white rose bush in full bloom. He was perched on the bank, his knees drawn up, and his back to the camera, but he'd turned toward the person taking the picture, and he was smiling. I studied it for a long time before turning it around for Pippa to view.

She shook her head. "That was the summer before his parents died." She was looking past the picture. She was remembering. "He was so happy then."

"Did he spend a lot of time here?" I traced the brook with my finger.

"Every now and then. But it was this time that I remember the most. His mother took that photo."

His expression seemed clearer than it had before. I could make out the love for his mother radiating though his features. I'd seen that same smile a few times over Christmas, and I remembered it perfectly. The look of happiness that was captured here, frozen in time, was the same one I had seen on Christmas Day.

"Why don't we sort the photos by the person in the picture? That might be a better idea," Pippa said. "That way, we can pass along the photos to the person who may be most interested." She leaned in more closely to me. "You can start a pile for Robert in front of you, beginning with that one." I could have sworn that I saw a glimmer in her eye as she said it.

❋ ❋ ❋

I had been sorting photos with Pippa until the afternoon. We had a huge pile for each of her three grandchildren, one for her and a larger pile that would have to be split between all of them—photos of Samuel and Carolyn Marley at various stages of life as well as ones of other family members. I dumped the piles into giant freezer bags and wrote the name of the person on the front with a permanent marker. The grandchildren had four bags each and Pippa had two.

My knees and ankles ached as I stood up in the hallway and shut the storage door. I supported my back with my hands, bending backward to relieve the built up pressure.

"We still have a ton of boxes in there," I said, letting my head drop to one side to relieve my aching shoulder. How long had I actually been sitting?

"Call Gerard for me, love, and ask him to come help me label them. I'll decide which boxes we need to sort out and which ones we can just discard. There's no way that we'll be able to sort through it all in the days we have remaining."

Two days. That's how long we had left together. I had grown fond of her in the short time I'd known her. She seemed as close to me as my own grandmother in a way—maybe more like me even. I couldn't quite describe the feeling. She was testy at times and not always pleasant, but I didn't mind anymore.

"Is there anything you'd like me to help you pack before you go to Birkwood?"

Pippa looked thoughtful. Then, as if something had just occurred to her, she said, "Yes, actually, there is." We walked together to her room. The sun was beginning to set, casting shadows on the wooden floor. Pippa clicked on a lamp near the closet and opened the closet door. "Do you mind reaching way at the back and pulling out the first of those flat canvases?"

Her closet was not a simple walk-in. It was L-shaped, and I had to wade through boxes and bags to get to the back of it. My nose began to tickle from the collected dust as I pushed further into the recesses of the closet. I stretched my hands out in front of me, searching, nearly blinded by darkness, at the back. Feeling what I thought to be canvases, I wrapped my finger around one and tugged at it lightly. It slid from its space easily, so I lifted it above the clutter and walked it into the light.

Setting it down on the floor against the side of the bed, I turned it around to view the artwork and my breath caught. In gray and black brushstrokes that were so thin they resembled pencil lines, facing me was a winter rendition of Robert's brook. "Did Robert...?"

I had to consciously pull my gaze from the canvas. Pippa was practically glowing.

I let my fingertips slide down the surface of the painting, feeling its rough texture. "When did he paint this?" I asked, sitting down cross-legged at its base. I tightened my focus until the picture sharpened so much that it revealed the fiber of the canvas itself. I felt my throat close with emotion.

"When he was in his twenties." Pippa sat down on a chair near the bed. "Lovely, isn't it?" She rubbed her fingers as if she were using imaginary hand cream.

"I'd like to part with this one, I believe."

My head popped up. "What?"

"I saw you sitting there one day from the kitchen window. It looked just like this painting that day." Pippa's eyes fell onto the canvas. "I'd like to give this painting to you."

"Please forgive me, Ms. Marley, but is it yours to give? I mean, since Robert painted it?"

"He doesn't find the value in his art," Pippa said, her face hardening slightly. "He had set this one out with the trash, but Gerard brought it to me."

"Why?" I looked from Pippa to the painting, my face crumpled in disbelief. "Why would he ever think this is trash?"

"*You* seem to understand him better than I," Pippa chuckled. "You tell me." Her limbs fell loosely at her sides, and she shook her head. Then she looked over at me, her expression gentle. "Please keep it for me."

"Of course," I managed, still looking at the painting. My cell phone rang in my pocket, pulling my attention away from the painting. I looked down at the screen. "It's Robert. Do you mind?"

I asked, gesturing to the hallway. Pippa fluttered her fingers at me, and I quickly exited the room, answering the call at the same time.

"I was just making sure that the preparations were going smoothly."

"I'm helping Ms. Marley sort her things for the estate sale."

"How's everything going?"

"I've seen your entire childhood in photographs."

In his usual fashion, Robert took some time to digest what I had said before speaking. Finally, he said, "I don't think anyone is going to buy our family photographs."

"Probably not. But they're sorted now. The storage closet at the end of the hallway in the east wing is nearly organized…" I decided quickly to add, "and I've seen a certain painting of yours."

"Oh?"

"Of the brook out back. During the winter."

From the way he quietly coughed, it seemed like he was a little uncomfortable. "Where did you find *that*?"

"Ms. Marley kept it after you tried to throw it away. Robert, why would you ever throw that away?" The phone hummed with emptiness in my ear for a considerable amount of time. "I really want to know. Please tell me." I waited without speaking just hoping he'd tell me something in response.

Then, to my surprise, he explained. "I paint as a form of expression. So, when things bother me, I paint them. Then, to rid myself—in a way—of the feelings, I discard the paintings."

"What was so awful about that brook?"

"It wasn't the brook."

I slid down the wall and sat on the floor of the hallway, my knees up at my chest.

He continued, "My parents used to take walks with me down there, and we'd talk about all of the things we saw—the deciduous trees in that area, the life we saw growing in the brook…" I thought he was finished, but he kept on going. "The day I painted that picture, it was the eleventh anniversary of their death. I was particularly sad that day because of the realization that one, I would never take that walk with them again, and two, that it had been over a decade since I had."

I had to swallow the lump that had formed in my throat. "Ms. Marley gave the painting to me. Would you mind if I kept it?"

"Whatever for?"

I bit my lip. The brook had taken on some importance for me, but how did I explain it to Robert? I wasn't even sure why it had any significance to me, but it did. "I…" I sat up nervously. "I just really like that brook. I wish I'd had the chance to see it in the spring."

"It's lovely in the spring."

"How's business?" I changed the subject abruptly. "Are you glad you went back to New York?" *You should have stayed here. You should have kept the house, you big jerk.*

"I'm getting my project off the ground, yes."

"Will you come back to Ashford?"

"Only for the final sale. I do have a little business to do there in town. I'd like to oversee an investment in that area, but I may not stay very long."

The door opened next to me as I sat on the floor, causing me to drop the phone in surprise. "So are you going to sit and shoot the breeze all evening, dear, or are we going to sort more of my things?" Pippa asked as I scrambled to pick the phone up off the floor.

"Robert?" I put the phone back to my ear.

"I can hear her. I'll call you back this evening if that's okay."

"Okay," I said, not wanting to hang up. "Bye."

He returned a good-bye, and then the line went empty. Pippa was already walking back into her room, her back to me. I put my phone back into my pocket and followed her.

Chapter Twenty-six

I had been so wrapped up in sorting things with Pippa that I completely forgot to inquire about Kip's whereabouts. Where was he? I resolved to have The Talk in the morning.

Robert's painting was leaning against The Feet Painting on the wall opposite my bed. I left a small light on so that I could see it as I lay down to sleep. I wasn't looking at it, though. I was watching the ceiling, trying to sort out what I was feeling.

I had one more day with Pippa. Then she'd go to a home for the elderly. The house would be sold off piece by piece in the next week or so and then, the shell of the Marley family, the Ashford Estate, would be sold as well. I would have no income and nowhere to live.

How did I get myself into this? I should have been on my way up professionally, but I wasn't. I've never even really had a career of any kind. I did, however, have two very nice pieces of artwork for when I did sort out my life, I mused.

I got out of bed, pulled my Susan B. Anthony coin from my purse, and rolled it around in my hand. For so long, I thought this was my lucky charm, but now I was starting to wonder if it was actually bad luck. I'd relied on chance many times in my life and look where it had gotten me. Megan was right. I don't know how to make my own decisions. I dug out the box that housed Robert's Christmas-gift-coin and opened the small lid. Wedging my Susan B. Anthony coin inside, I snapped it shut and put it back into one of the inside pockets of my suitcase.

The crisp bed sheets were cool on my skin as I settled back into bed. Pulling the duvet up by my chin, I vowed at that moment not to allow anyone but myself to determine my life choices. No more handouts from Megan. No more coin flipping. I would complete some preschool applications and live at home with Mom until I was financially able to live on my own.

My head began to pound with the tension from it all. I switched off my phone, setting it on the bedside table. The sheets slid around beneath me as I turned on my side and looked at Robert's painting. I stared at it until sleep overtook me.

❄ ❄ ❄

The kitchen seemed larger and emptier without the Marley family present. It was just Pippa and me now. I walked over to Anna, who was making breakfast for us. A cup of coffee awaited me on the counter.

"Good morning," I said, taking a steaming sip.

"How are you?" she asked, her hands inside a ceramic bowl full of dough.

"Well, thanks." I added one more sugar cube, dropped a spoon down into the mug, and walked over to the kitchen table. It was just far enough that we could still talk without yelling. "Have you seen Kip?" I asked after taking another sip.

"I believe he stayed at Miss Hardinson's so that they could plan their trip to Australia."

My eyes widened in response. Alex? The dress-lending-saving-puppies-*delicious*-uttering Alex? "He spent the *night* with her?" *And he's going to Australia with her?*

"He has spent time with her before," Anna said, looking down into her dough, kneading it with plunging fists.

I took another sip of coffee and let the warm liquid slide down my throat as I thought about this development. Kip and Alex? Kip was far too mannerly to do anything as obvious as shack up with another girl without properly ending things with me. I knew that much to be true. The nagging thought hanging before me in the air, dangling in front of me like an annoying sibling dangles a toy, taunting and annoying, was the question of whether the idea of Kip and Alex bothered me or not. Indifference shifted around within me, and I found myself working very hard to push it away. I should be outraged. Or at least bothered by it.

But I wasn't. My need for The Talk was not just because we were too different or because he was too rich; it was because I didn't have feelings for him.

"Do you know when he'll be home?" I asked, wrapping my hands around the mug and swinging my feet back and forth under my chair in an attempt to push some warmth into my toes.

Anna lightly dusted the countertop with flour and said, "He'll be back by noon. I know that much because he's asked me to prepare lunch for him." She dumped the little glob of dough onto the floured counter and pushed it flat with a wooden rolling pin.

"I'll just go and check my itinerary in the office," I said, having never bothered to eat breakfast. "When you see Kip, could you ask him to come and find me, please?" Anna nodded as I grabbed a banana from a fruit basket nearby, took my cup of coffee in the other hand, and headed toward the office.

The signed receipt of payment had just come up with the email when I saw that I had another message, so I opened it:

I tried to call you back last night, but I got your voicemail. I didn't leave a message.

Hope you slept well. —Robert

Almost involuntarily, I clicked the response icon, my fingertips poised to type. Pulling my hands back toward my body, I stopped. My mind reeled as I attempted to draw my thoughts together. I slid out the desk chair and sat down, placing my hands on the desk, the empty response box displayed before me. My fingernails rapped on the surface with nervous energy. After a moment of thought, I typed, "Turned it off so that I could go to sleep. I slept like a baby. Thanks. What's New York like today?" Send.

Immediately my phone rang, and I pulled it from my pocket. Was he waiting there for me to respond? I answered, "Hello."

"It's snowy here." Then he sat quietly on the other end.

"It's gray here. My toes are freezing even in my socks." Despite my effort to squelch it, a feeling of happiness began to bubble its way up from my stomach as I talked to Robert. "Where do you live in New York? An apartment or something?"

"You could call it an apartment, yes," he said.

"What's it like? Is it new, or is it historical like Ashford?"

"It's new. And warm." I could sense him smiling on the other end.

"Do you think you'll end up there after you sell Ashford?"

He was quiet again. Then he answered, "I'm not sure." After a moment, he asked, "Where will *you* go after I sell Ashford?"

"I'm going to live with my mother until I can get a job. Then I'm going to find a roommate and an apartment in town."

"So, it's a definite 'no' for Australia then?"

"Yes," I giggled. "I do *not* want to live in Australia. I'd like to visit sometime for maybe a few weeks, but I'd rather live in my own country."

"So, things with Kip…?"

I didn't want to tell Robert about my thoughts regarding Kip before I had had a chance to talk to Kip about them. That wouldn't be fair. "We'll just wait and see…"

I heard a light knock on the doorframe of the office door. "Anna said you wanted to talk to me. Tell me you're not talking to Robert," he shook his head in disbelief.

I ignored the fact that Robert was on the line and said back to Kip, "I thought you weren't coming home until noon."

"Alex had a hair appointment." He made a face. Okay, so he wasn't hiding the fact that he stayed with Alex.

"I am talking to Robert, actually. Where can I find you in a few?" I could hear Robert begin to protest and attempt to end the call, but I told him to stay put. I wasn't going to let Kip ruin another conversation with Robert. Kip mouthed the words, "The sitting room," and I waved him off sweetly with a smile.

"So!" I said back to Robert. I didn't know what else to say, but I didn't want to get off of the phone either.

"So."

"What's my actual last day of employment here at Ashford?" I asked. I didn't know what else to talk about, and I was genuinely wondering, so I figured this time was as good as any to ask.

"January twentieth."

The rest of the staff would also be ending their employment soon. "What about Anna? Gerard? What will happen to them?"

Robert's manner returned to the way it had been when I'd first met him. It was abrupt and without feeling. "I've given the staff a memo detailing their final weeks of employment at Ashford. I've explained to each of them that they can, if they so choose, interview with the new owner to seek employment with him. Each member of the staff has a personal letter of recommendation from me on file with him."

"Do you think they'll like working for the new owner? Is he going to change anything?"

"I'd say so. He's planning on tearing it down to build his dream home."

"What? You've got to be kidding me! Robert!" For the first time in this whole ordeal, I really felt the full impact of what was about to be lost. My head dropped down onto my forearm, and I focused on the wooden grains of the desk's surface below my arm.

"I've upset you. I'm sorry." Robert's tone was softer now, back to the way it had been earlier in the conversation.

I rubbed my eyes with my fingers. "I just don't understand how you can let this magnificent home go. I thought I did, but I really don't." I opened my eyes and surveyed the surroundings. "It isn't the house's fault you've had a lousy life here. It isn't the rest of your family's fault. But, because you were dealt a bad hand in childhood, you're going to take the blood, sweat, and tears of the family members before you and throw it all away. People can be happy here, Robert. They can. I've seen it—at Christmas!" I took a breath and steadied myself. Then I looked down at the desk again and drew an imaginary line back and forth on its surface with my index finger. "But I suppose this speech is in vain because the deed is done."

"The deed is done."

This wasn't my battle. I had to keep telling myself that. "Well, I have to go and see Kip. I haven't seen him since I went home, and I need to talk to him."

"I understand."

※ ※ ※

The fire was going in the sitting room as I walked up to Kip from behind. He turned and looked over his shoulder.

I sat down next to him on the settee. My hands were a little shaky, so I slipped them under my legs. Before he could start making small talk, I blurted out, "I need to talk to you."

His forehead wrinkled, but his face was still pleasant. "Sure," he said, placing a hand on my thigh.

"Kip, I want you to go to Australia without any worries about me." He looked a little confused. Maybe he hadn't planned to worry about me. I shifted uncomfortably. "I think that we shouldn't see each other anymore."

"Ah." He nodded. There went the light bulb. His face turned serious, and he removed his hand from my leg. "I thought this might be coming."

"We're just too different, Kip. And I'm not talking about the money."

"I, too, have been noticing the differences between you and me. I've realized recently that you'd be much better suited for…" he hesitated, "someone else."

Did he mean to say Robert, or was I imagining it?

"You sure were quick to shoot me down on the trip to Australia."

It was true. He was right. Had it been Robert who'd wanted me to go, would I have been so quick to say no? I already knew the answer to that.

His face turned serious. "It would've been fun, you know. You might have enjoyed yourself."

"Maybe." I didn't have the heart to argue. "So, when do you leave?"

"Tomorrow."

"Wow." Then my mind wandered from Kip leaving to the empty house, and I thought of the auction. "Have you marked the furniture and other things you'd like to keep before we sell everything in the auction?"

"I've taken everything I want to keep besides the house itself."

"So you *do* want this house?"

"I want the house, but not for myself. What would I do with this house? I'd never live in it. I don't want kids or a family… It needs a family."

"I know." Kip and I just sat with each other, both thinking. The fire popped and sizzled. "Well, I should go. I have a lot to do to get the house ready."

Kip stood up, hugged me, and kissed me on both cheeks. "Even if we aren't dating, please keep in touch. I feel like you're a part of the family. Really. I'm not just saying that."

"Thank you." I left the room, my chest filled with elation that Kip Marley felt like I was family. Speaking of family, I had to check on Pippa. This was her last day at Ashford.

Chapter Twenty-seven

Pippa's room was stark and empty when I arrived. She'd had the staff box up most of her belongings for Birkwood. There was an odd sort of peacefulness about her. Closing her book around her finger, she marked her place.

"Is there anything else I can help you with before you go tomorrow?"

She reopened the book, peered down at the page number, as I'd seen her do, and then pulled her finger from the middle, setting it down on an empty bedside table. "I don't think so, dear. Thank you for asking. Robert has arranged for Tom McCray to deliver meals to Birkwood, you know."

"That's…" Nice? I wasn't sure how to define that gesture, so I let it go and looked around the room. "Is there anything more that we should tag before the auction?"

"I don't need much with me… I believe that the kids have all tagged what they're taking." She rubbed the back of her hand with her thumb. "Is Robert keeping anything?"

I frowned with uncertainty. "He hasn't asked me to tag anything for him."

"Perhaps you had better ask him then."

"I have to email him anyway," I looked at my watch, "in about ten minutes, so I'll ask him then."

"How are you two getting along?"

Odd question. "What do you mean?"

"Is he being nice to you?"

"Of course. He's always nice to me. He's my employer."

"Being an employee doesn't guarantee you a pleasant disposition from Robert Marley, dear. You have to consider his motives."

I eyed her skeptically. "Ms. Marley, he's very professional."

"For God's sake, child, call me Pippa. It's grating to hear you continuously refer to me by my surname. I hope Robert allows you to call him by his given name."

"Yes, he does."

"Well, go and email him or whatever it is you kids do these days. Ask him if he'd like any shred of his life to remain after this sale. And, if he does, go and tag it for him quickly before he changes his mind."

I nodded at Pippa. "I will. Come and find me if you need me."

"Allie?" I turned to face the matriarch of the family once more. "Remember what I said to you on Christmas Eve."

"I remember." I gave her one, final smile and left the room.

❊ ❊ ❊

I opened my email and had no messages, so I composed one to Robert: "Do you want anything from Ashford tagged as your personal property before the auction?"

Response: *No, thank you. I've removed everything that belongs to me already. How's the sorting going?*

"I've sorted almost everything that I could with Pippa during the time that I had. I think Gerard and Anna also helped her organize some things. She looks completely packed for Birkwood. Who will take her there tomorrow morning?"

Response: *Her driver.*

Her driver? Really, Robert? "I'd like to take her." Send.

Response: *You?*

"It would be a bit more personal than having a driver take her." Send.

Response: *Oh? So,* you *would be more personal than the driver that she has employed for fifteen or so odd years?*

"I think so. She asked me to call her Pippa today instead of Ms. Marley. What does he call her?"

Response: *I believe that all of the staff, apart from you, apparently, refer to her as Ms. Marley. She must favor you.*

"Can we just talk on the phone, please?"

My phone came to life in my pocket.

"Thank you." I said into my phone and heard a little puff of laughter on the other end.

"So, what have you been up to with Pippa to suggest a first-name relationship?" he asked.

"Nothing out of the ordinary. She just told me that it was annoying when I called her Ms. Marley, and that I should call her Pippa." I fiddled with the cuticle of my thumb. I was full of nerves all of a sudden.

I was attempting to place the feeling when Robert said, "She likes you."

"Well, I like her too. So, Robert, you aren't tagging any of this beautiful antique furniture to keep as your own? Not even this desk?" I asked, pulling open the top drawer. I was taken aback to see that it was completely empty. "What happened to the sticky notes?"

"What?"

"The sticky notes? And there was a stapler. Where did they go?"

"Are you snooping?" he teased.

I shut the drawer quickly. "I… I… needed a pen once and now… It doesn't matter. Where is your stuff?"

"I told you that I've cleaned it out. Do you think that the person who buys that desk is going to want to have a used stapler and some stationery?"

"I guess not."

"So, have you scheduled the auction?"

"Yes." Why did he have to sell Ashford? It was utterly ridiculous.

"When will it be?"

"In two days."

"And did you advertise?"

"Yes. I did just as you said. There's an ad in the local paper. It will run tomorrow through to the next day. I've mailed you the bill."

"Perfect. Thank you. You really are a wonderful house manager."

I tipped my head back and looked up at the ceiling. "Thanks."

"Allie, I'd like to help you find your next job."

"What? No!" Did Robert see me as a charity case? I wasn't going to be some poor little girl that he helped put back on her feet. My blood ran hot in my veins. "Absolutely not." There was no response. Had anyone ever said "no" to Robert Marley? Well, I wasn't backing down.

"I didn't mean to offend you. I just thought…"

"Well, it doesn't matter what you thought. I don't need your help to find a job."

"I know you don't *need* my help, but I'd like to offer you help. As a friendly gesture."

"No, thank you."

"Where will you be looking for a job? Do you plan to stay in the area?"

"That's the idea."

"And are you still looking for employment as a preschool teacher?"

"Yes. I've kept my endorsement up to date by taking a couple of classes every five years. And, it's what I love to do. I miss being with kids."

"You're excellent at it. I've seen you in action." Robert's voice was light, causing a little flutter in my chest. "Allie," his voice was as smooth as silk, "won't you let me help you find a job?"

"Robert, I want to do this by myself."

"Okay. It's just that I know…"

I cut him off. "I don't care. Don't say it. I'm a big girl. I'll find myself a job."

"If that's what you want, I'll leave it alone then."

"Thank you."

Chapter Twenty-eight

Those department stores in New York City that have the revolving doors where people keep coming and going, going and coming, and the thing spins around and around like a merry-go-round, never stopping, that's what the auction day reminded me of. I watched as people came in, devoured Ashford's massive square footage and carted away all of the family belongings, claiming them as their own. They squabbled over pricing and criticized amazing pieces in attempts to offer lower bids.

In the end, it was just me and an empty space. My bed—Robert's bed—was gone. The dresser, gone. The settee where I had had such good memories, gone. Throughout the day, which was broken into tiers according to price range, the remaining pieces were sold. So I sat, at the end of the auction, cross-legged on the empty floor in the hallway of the east wing, letting my eyes roam the carved names on the woodwork. My feet were tired and my shoulders ached.

I heard the sound of footsteps echoing down the hall. With the back of my hand, I wiped the wetness from my forehead. The footsteps were loud now—*clack, clack, clack*. I didn't turn around.

"Allie?" The voice came from behind me, and the clacking stopped. There was a hand on my shoulder. I knew that voice, and I remembered the touch of his hand.

I turned around to face Robert. I looked a mess. I was dirty from moving furniture all day, and I was nearly sure I had no make-up remaining on my face. It didn't matter, though because that was how I felt. Awful.

Seeing Robert at that moment brought back all of the memories of Christmas and the kids and the horses and the brook at the base of the hill out back...

"It's done," he said.

"It's done," I attempted to smile. "And, with all of the commotion today, I can't find my feet painting. I think someone may have bought it."

"I'm sorry."

I didn't let on, but I was sad not to have the feet painting. That day wasn't the beginning of the sadness that I had experienced. A few days prior, I had packed Pippa into her car after her refusal to let me drive, and watched her speed away, against my better judgment, to some God-awful place. I had seen her tears as she packed her few bags and couple of boxes. I caught a glimpse of her as she touched the glass protecting a photograph of her three grandchildren, and I held her hand as she stepped around the staff and the disarray of furniture that was about to be stripped from her possession.

How much longer did she have, really? That was not how she should spend her final days. I hoped that she could squeeze out another decade. It could happen.

The staff had said their goodbyes earlier that day. Anna's uncle helped her move her things into a U-haul while she sniffled and balled up tissue after tissue in her jeans pockets. Gerard had gnawed on his sadness all day, pushing it back with a tight jaw and gritted teeth. One by one, they went away until there was no one left but me.

I was aware of Robert caressing my back. His familiar scent floated toward me. He was so close. If I reached up, I could wrap my arms around his neck. I wondered what would happen if I did.

"Look, you're tired, and you've worked all day. Let me take you to dinner. Since... This is your last day with us."

Was he asking me out? "I'll need to freshen up."

"Take your time. The water's still on. Take a shower. Whatever. I'll wait for you."

I walked a few doors down to my room where the only items left were my two suitcases, Robert's painting, and a duffel bag. There was an airy smack as I tipped one of the cases over on its side and unzipped it. I removed a fresh outfit and a towel and zipped it back up, then I took the items and my duffel bag into the bathroom so I could take a shower. About twenty-five minutes later, I emerged fresher on the outside, my insides still wobbly from the last few days.

Robert was waiting against the bar in the kitchen. One single lit chandelier hung above him. The rest of the room was dark. He walked over to me when I entered the room. Making a conscious effort to straighten up my shoulders and hold my head up, I set my bags down at my feet and leaned the painting against the wall. Exhaustion was creeping up on me.

"You know, you seemed to enjoy this old house more than most of the Marley family," he said.

I attempted a smile. "I never really had anything like this growing up. I don't mean the size of the house; it isn't that. But the story of it. There's something so compelling about Ashford's story."

Robert looked anxious. He laced his fingers and bent them out-ward, cracking his knuckles. "I'm sorry that you were here to wit-ness the end of Ashford." He smiled weakly, thoughts still obvious behind his eyes. "Where would you like to eat? I could try Bonacci's and see if they can get a table ready for us."

I was already shaking my head back and forth. "Please, not Bo-nacci's. I wouldn't want you to spend that kind of money." If lunch was a hundred dollars, I could only imagine what dinner would cost.

"Allie, it's fine, really."

"What are my options?"

Robert looked into the air in front of me. "Well, there's Hillsview Market. They have gourmet take-out and a few tables, Bonacci's, obviously, and—what's that pub called?—The Black-bird."

None of the choices were hitting the mark, but I found myself leaning toward Bonacci's. I really didn't want to ask Robert to drop that kind of money on me. Oh, what the hell… "Bonacci's, I sup-pose. Why not." Robert gave me a little smirk and placed his hand on my back to lead me out of the room.

"I'll drive. We'll get your car after dinner." He clicked the light switch, sending us into complete darkness. Once my eyes adjusted, I could see the grand entranceway of Ashford. It looked hollow and lonely. Robert opened the front door and allowed me to pass through it. He pulled my belongings out onto the front steps, then, with a cold clink, he shut the door for the last time.

We headed toward his car without looking back. I'm not sure why *he* didn't look back, but I knew why I didn't. I wanted to afford the home its dignity. It was not at its best, and all of my memories of the house were warm and full of life. I didn't want the current state of the house to cast a shadow on what it really was—brilliant. He let me into the car and tossed my bags into the trunk.

We drove quietly down the winding road to Bonacci's. Robert had secured us a table at the height of the dinner hour with one phone call. The black night slid past my window. I'd never been outside of Ashford with Robert before, but it felt natural to be with him.

Once we arrived, and the pleasantries were finished with the wait staff, we were sitting across from one another, a small square table nestled between us. I had a chance to really look at Robert. He smirked at me, his eyes searching my face. He seemed to have so much to say, but wasn't saying any of it. Typical.

"So," I attempted to make small talk, "how does it feel to be rid of the house? That was a huge undertaking…" It felt good to be with him, but strange without Ashford around us. I wanted to run back there, wrap up on the settee, and light a fire in the fireplace.

"Well, I'm not officially rid of it until tomorrow. Allie," he looked at me with sad eyes, "you don't have to make light of the situation…" he trailed off as if unable to find the words.

"I shouldn't even have an opinion of Ashford. It wasn't mine. I was only there a short time. But the lives of so many people have changed so quickly… Let's not waste the night talking about it," I said.

"You're right. Let's not talk about that," Robert said, taking a sip of his water. "A far more interesting topic to discuss is what exactly Pippa said to you at Christmas dinner."

"I'm not telling."

A playful expression crept across his face. "I can't stand it. Tell me."

"I won't. At least not… yet. Maybe down the road."

Robert's eyes grew round and bright. "So," he waggled a finger between us, "we will be in touch down the road?"

"I would hope so."

"And Kip?"

"Well, he's your brother. I hope you'd be in touch down the road."

"Very funny." His face grew more serious. "Will he be in touch with you? In the future?" The waitress brought us bread and refilled Robert's water. He took a sip and tipped his head at her, never removing his gaze from me.

"Maybe a friendly call now and then." The tea light candle between us was flickering with the movement of the wait staff around us. My eyes met Robert's. He was looking at me, an unreadable expression on his face.

"I'm sorry," he said finally.

"I'm not." I looked directly into his eyes. Excitement bubbled inside me as I said it. It was then that I actually admitted to myself that I had completely fallen for Robert Marley.

He seemed to be contemplating something. Nerves consumed me, and I was suddenly too uneasy to say anything else. Thank God, the waitress brought us two entrees—apparently preordered by Robert.

We made small talk through the meal, and I was thrilled to find out how much we had in common—pastimes, movies, likes, dislikes. By the end of the meal, I didn't want to leave him. I wanted something to happen, something to keep us together, but I knew that there was nothing left.

❄ ❄ ❄

The grounds at Ashford were pitch black when we returned. The house looked cold and abandoned. Robert escorted me to my car, his own headlights lighting the path. He opened my driver's side door, and then propped his arm on it stiffly.

"Can we get another bite to eat sometime soon?" he asked.

"I'd love to." I stood as close to him as I could without being uncomfortable. I wanted him to lean in and kiss me, but he was still standing too far away and it didn't look like he was going to attempt it. "You have my phone number, right?"

Robert tapped his temple with his finger. "Got it."

"Thank you for dinner. It was really nice."

"You're welcome," he reached out and took my hand. "It has been… so nice getting to know you over these past months. When can I call you again?"

Tomorrow! Call me tomorrow! Better yet, I'll go home with you tonight!

"Anytime."

Robert let go of my hand. "I'll watch you go. Make sure you get onto the road safely." I got in, and he shut my door. He placed my bags in the trunk and closed it. Knocking on my window with his knuckle, he mouthed the words, "I'll call you soon."

I nodded. He took a few steps backward and raised his hand to say good-bye. I maneuvered the car down the driveway and headed home with Robert, his hands now in the pockets of his coat, fading away in my rearview mirror.

Chapter Twenty-nine

Moving back home with my mother at thirty-two years of age was probably the lowest point in my life. It didn't help matters any that Megan was about to close on the largest home of her career and could stand to make enough money to upgrade her studio in the city. I had thought about moving in with her, but she had told me that I'd have to pay rent, and since I didn't have a job yet, I chose to stay with my mother who offered me my high school bedroom, complete with purple floral wallpaper and trophy accessories, for the nominal price of zero dollars.

When I arrived at Mom's, she was asleep in the recliner, the television snapping off frames of before and after photos for an infomercial claiming to offer results in days if I would just drink their green shakes and exercise using traditional Aboriginal dance. I latched the front door shut and turned the bolt without my mother even stirring at my arrival.

The short hallway leading to my old room was dark, so I clicked on a dusty overhead light that was original to the house. It probably hadn't been removed and wiped down since then either. When I got to my room, I closed the door with my knee and set my bags down in the available floor space beside my bed.

The first thing I did was to remove the framed beach scene print from above the bed and replace it with The Brook. It looked out of place against the purple wallpaper. I slid the ocean print under the bed and, without changing clothes, I kicked off my shoes, crawled under my ruffled blankets, and cried myself to sleep.

* * *

"Good mornin' sunshine," Mom called over her shoulder as she pulled the carafe from the coffeemaker and poured herself a cup. She turned around, "Whew, you look like a sight!" I stood in the doorway, still in my clothes and last night's makeup. I had no idea what my hair looked like, but I'm sure it was reflective of the way I felt inside.

"Do you have to work today?" I asked, ignoring her assessment of me.

Mom slurped a sip off the top of her coffee then licked her lips. "Yeah, I'm doing a shift this afternoon for Pam." Mom was, and had always been, a labor and delivery nurse. She loved her job. When Megan and I were little, and she was raising us on her own, shift work was more than difficult to manage, but her supervisor had given her days as much as possible to allow her to be home with us when we got off of the school bus. Some nights, our neighbor, an elderly woman named Cynthia, would come over and stay with us until my mom could get home.

Mom did her best to give us what we needed, and we never felt cheated—not once—but, with the costs of childcare and general living expenses for three people, there hadn't been anything left over to save for retirement, so she'd be working for the foreseeable future.

It was a good thing that she liked what she did because she'd be doing it for many years to come.

"How about you?" Mom asked. "Do you have anything lined
up for today?"

"I think I'm going to follow up on some of the applications I've
submitted."

"Sounds like a plan."

"I feel like something good *has* to come along, you know?"

"It will, honey. It will." She put her hands on my face and kissed
my forehead.

Mom left the kitchen to get ready for the day, and I made myself
breakfast and headed back toward my room. I balanced my plate on
a shelf near the window and sat down cross-legged on the floor to
unpack my suitcases. My cell phone buzzed on the night table and
I nearly leaped to get it, hoping it was Robert. It wasn't though; it
was Megan.

"Hey. What's up?" I answered.

"You will not believe this!" She was squawking into the phone. I
winced and pulled the receiver away from my ear.

"What?"

"You'll never guess who is opening a preschool!"

"Megan," I warned, "please don't try and find me another job. I
can do this myself."

"Yeah, but they want a preschool teacher," her voice went up and
down like a mother coaxing her child to do something.

"Megan…"

"I can take you over there today."

"Megan, do not tell them anything about me. I'll check it out
and apply, but please do not say anything to them regarding me.

And I don't want to know anything but the phone number. I want to get this job by myself. Promise me."

"But…"

"Promise me!"

"Okay, but you had better check it out. This could be big."

I wrote down the details for the new preschool on a teacup note-pad that my mother had given me for Christmas, then I ended the call and walked down the hall to the bathroom for a shower, only to find that it was occupied. So, I decided to retrieve my breakfast and a book and read while I waited.

❄ ❄ ❄

I parallel parked my car along the narrow street in front of the preschool. It was like something out of a storybook. The façade was painted in rustic colors to match the exterior buildings in that part of the city, but it had two uncharacteristically large pic-ture windows. When I peered inside, the space was constructed as an enormous room, and it was decorated like a classroom.

I could tell that the decorating wasn't complete, but from what I could see, it was going to be amazing. There was an en-tire dress-up and pretend corner with costumes of every size draped on pegs of varying heights. Another corner was covered in shelving with reams of paper in an array of colors and textures. Matching bins containing brightly-colored blocks and building materials littered another set of shelves. There was a carpet in the center with the letters of the alphabet. Circling the carpet were tiny wooden tables and chairs. In the center of the room I saw a big, cushy chair with numbers embroidered on the back. I was in heaven already.

A cluster of silver bells jingled as I opened the door and walked inside. A thin woman with a pleasant demeanor walked out from a small office at the back and met me in the center of the space.

"Hello," the woman greeted me, extending her hand. "May I help you?"

"I'm here to inquire about the teaching position." I shook her hand. "My name is Allie Richfield."

"Tamara Eastwood," the woman said as she led me over to one of the miniature tables and pulled out a chair. "Are you free right now?" she asked. I nodded. "Have a seat. I'll just go and get a pad of paper and a pen." The woman returned with the paper and a pen capped with an enormous elephant.

"I'm looking for someone who meets the qualifications to be the teacher of the preschool. This," she waved a hand through the air, "as you can see, is set up sort of Montessori-style, with one room for everything."

My interview transpired effortlessly. I explained my qualifications as well as the experience that I had as a nanny. Mrs. Eastwood seemed very interested and said that she'd call me in a few days to let me know the status of the position one way or the other. I left with a feeling of optimism that I hadn't had in a long time.

I decided to go and visit Pippa. I knew that it hadn't been very long since I saw her last, but, then again, no one knew how long she'd have on this earth, and I wasn't going to waste any time. While on a high from the interview, I made the decision to treat myself to a cup of coffee and a muffin and then go and visit my old friend.

Birkwood was closer than I had expected. I pulled into the parking lot within twenty-five minutes of leaving the coffee shop. I shook the crumbs from my lap as I stepped out of the car. With my coffee still half-full, I balanced it on the hood while I retrieved a smaller cup for Pippa. I figured I'd try and smuggle some in for her.

The atmosphere in the lobby of Birkwood was friendly and inviting. It looked like a well-run establishment. I sat down in a leather chair and finished my drink before gingerly hiding Pippa's in my purse, wedging it between my wallet and the inside wall of the bag. Carefully, I made my way to reception, and they buzzed me in.

The hallways were bright and cheerful—not the clinical white I had imagined. The whole place had the personality of an old-folks' Trump Towers. I couldn't help but wander slowly through the hallways as I admired the artwork on the walls and the flower arrangements that adorned the cherry wood Queen Anne tables. At the end of a very long hallway, I finally arrived at Pippa's door. After knocking twice, I set my hand inside my purse to steady the coffee.

Pippa answered with her usual pearls and perfectly pressed outfit. Her face lit up, and she threw her frail arms around me, causing the coffee to slosh up through the hole in the lid onto my hand. I gently pried her off and, like a special agent, my eyes darting down both sides of the hallway, led her inside the room to reveal her prize. She was tickled to see that I had remembered her favorite treat, and she shut the door quickly to hide our deception.

"You would not believe my luck," she said, removing the lid from her cup and sipping the beverage delicately. "I have not had this much fun since I was a young girl. Did you know that they have social hour every evening, and they serve wine? As long as I am on the doctor-approved list, I can have wine! And there's this wonderful man named Arthur who tells me about his years as an airline pilot. He spent three years living in whatever destination he pleased when he was a young man. His stories are fascinating."

"Pippa, you're positively glowing," I said, shaking my head. "I'm so relieved that you like it here."

"Well, dear, I just needed a little kick in the bottom, I suppose." She sipped her coffee and replaced the lid, setting it on the table. "What's that saying? Make lemonade out of lemons? My child, Robert gave me lemons, and I found lemon martinis!" Pippa's chest convulsed with tight little giggles that I'd never seen her produce before.

"You are happy," I noted with a smile.

"I never would have supposed this outcome, but yes, I am." Pippa's cheeks were the color of roses, and she had more life to her face than I'd ever seen at Ashford. She walked over to me and placed a hand on my shoulder. "Enough about me. I want to talk about you for a minute. Let's make some more lemon martinis, shall we?" She sat down next to me on the small sofa opposite her bed.

My face contorted in confusion. "What do you mean?"

"I do hope you aren't still wasting time with Kip. I love him dearly, but he isn't right for you. Have you spoken to Robert?"

"No."

She spread out her fingers in front of her as if admiring a new manicure, then placed them in her lap. "Look, I know that Robert can be… offensive at times. Believe me, I struggle to notice his strengths. But there is something so perfect about him when he's with you that I cannot deny it." She looked directly into my eyes, and I could almost see the young woman she once was. "He needs you. He needs you to make him a good man."

I wanted to say something, but when I tried, there were no words there. I closed my gaping mouth and bit my lip. It was true that I was interested in Robert, but Pippa's observations had shocked me. Was she right? Could we be something more than what we are right now?

"You don't have to appease me, you know. But promise me that you'll consider what I've said and that you'll be open to the possibilities," she said. I nodded, still unable to form a response. "Good girl," she retrieved her coffee and took another sip, winking in my direction.

Chapter Thirty

Even on the third day living with Mom, I didn't feel any more comfortable. I worried that I was crowding her. I was a grown woman. I didn't belong in my mother's house. But despite my original optimism regarding Mrs. Eastwood's interest, it was still the only lead I had for a job. How was I going to move forward with my life?

I had nothing to be proud of—no family of my own, no home that I could call mine, no achievements of any kind. The heat of humiliation burned my skin as a fear like I've never known swept through me. I'd always just flipped a coin, taken handouts as they were divvied. I hadn't taken responsibility for anything. And look at what that had gotten me. I felt the sting of tears, and I squeezed my eyes shut to push them back inside with all of the disappointment that was swimming there.

Mom was at the sink, eating a piece of toast with jelly, and I was at the table crumbling a Pop Tart that I'd found in the pantry. I checked my phone, but all I had were three missed calls from Megan.

I was just about to toss the remainder of the Pop Tart in the trash and head for the bathroom to shower when my phone rang.

Quickly, I grabbed it and peered at the illuminated screen. It was a number that I didn't recognize.

"Hello?"

"May I speak to Allie Richfield, please?"

"This is she." The voice was vaguely familiar.

"This is Tamara Eastwood from Oak Grove Preschool. We met the other day…?"

"Yes, I remember."

"I was wondering if you could come to the school today."

"Sure. Is there anything that I need to bring? References, any documentation?"

"No, we can sort that out if the need arises. I'd like to discuss the position with you."

"Okay. When would you like me to come in?"

"As soon as possible."

"I'll be there in an hour."

"Fantastic. I'll see you then."

After ending the call, I sat very still. Could Mrs. Eastwood be offering me the job? What was this all about? After a moment's contemplation, I quickly got up, chucked the Pop Tart in the trash, threw the plate in the sink, and ran to the bathroom to get ready.

Exactly one hour after ending the call, I arrived at Oak Grove Preschool. That should surely fall in my favor. I walked through the door and my heart nearly stopped. On the wall opposite me, in perfect condition, was The Feet Painting. I blinked over and over as if to clear a distorted view. Certainly, that couldn't really be my painting.

Mrs. Eastwood came from the back office and walked over to me with a grin that spread from ear to ear. "Allie, so nice to see you. Please, take a seat."

I extended my finger toward the painting. "Where did you get that?" I asked in nearly a whisper.

"Well, that's what I wanted to talk to you about. Gosh, I feel like I'm on some kind of game show or something. Here's where I tell you that you've won the grand prize."

"What?" Was this some sort of dream? Was I going to wake up and make sense of all of this? I had absolutely no idea what she was trying to tell me.

"For starters, you're hired." Her smile broadened, making large folds of skin on her cheeks. "And, apparently, this entire school is yours." She must have sensed my confusion because she added, as if to clarify, "It belongs to you."

I wasn't any clearer after the explanation than I was before. "What are you talking about?"

"Let me introduce you to the investor for this preschool." Mrs. Eastwood turned around, and I followed her line of sight. My mouth hung open as Robert stood in the doorway to the office.

His stare was unwavering, a strange sort of smile on his face. "Mrs. Eastwood, do you mind giving us a minute?" he asked, his eyes not leaving mine. She promptly let herself out, jingling the bells with her exit.

A wave of heat burned my face, and I closed my mouth only to notice that my jaw began to tighten. Two minutes ago, I felt like I could do anything. I had landed the best job of my life so far, and I had done it all by myself. But then it was ripped right out from under me. I hadn't done anything. This job had been given to me like some appalling donation for the needy. Suddenly, I felt helpless and small. I tried to breathe as deeply as I could in an attempt to push away the tears that were pricking my eyes, but I couldn't get a breath.

Robert's smile faded to a look of dismay as he took in my disposition. "Allie, what's wrong?" He walked closer to me, and I backed away.

"I said I didn't need any help getting a job." The tears were filling my eyes. I couldn't blink them away fast enough.

"I know."

"I don't need your money. You can't just buy things to make me happy." A tear spilled down my cheek, and I wiped it quickly with my hand.

"I know." He was moving closer. I backed up until I was nearing the door.

"I don't want this job. Not this way. I want my own job that I get on my own merit. Not some ridiculous handout of a job."

"You don't understand."

I pushed open the door. Then I turned away from Robert, striding down the sidewalk as quickly as possible toward my car. The tears were flowing like waterworks now. I tried to wipe them away, but it was useless.

"Allie!" I could hear Robert running after me. "Allie, wait!"

I picked up the pace and hurriedly got to my car. Without looking back, I got in, shut the door, and drove away, sobbing uncontrollably.

By the time Mom got home, I was a puffy-eyed, sniveling lump on the sofa. "Is that my Ben and Jerry's?" she asked, tossing her keys on the table nearest me. "I just bought that."

"I'll get you another one," I said, pulling the spoon through my lips.

"With what, your good looks?"

It was a common reply in our family. I knew she was only teasing, but it hit a nerve, and I started to cry again. Mom noticed. "Allie, what's wrong?"

"It's a very long story, and I can't tell it all, or I'll never pull myself together, but the short version is that Robert Marley tried to give me a job as a preschool teacher."

Mom looked puzzled. "Isn't that what you wanted, honey?"

"Give me. *Give* me. He tried to *give* me a job. I didn't earn it. I didn't get it by my credentials or my work experience. So, I didn't take it."

"Oh, honey…" She dropped her things at the door and sat with me until the tears had come and gone again.

The doorbell rang, and the doorbell never rings, so we both stopped short and looked at each other. Mom answered the door by cracking it and peeking outside. With a gasp, she opened the door wide to reveal two blue delivery-person legs protruding from the largest bouquet of white roses that I'd ever seen in my life. They must have cost a fortune. Instantly, I knew exactly who they were from.

Mom accepted the flowers and shut the door. She set them down with a thud onto the coffee table next to my Ben and Jerry's and plucked the card from the holder at the top of the bouquet. Without opening the envelope, she handed it to me. Reluctantly, I pulled the card from inside and read Robert's message aloud, "My driver will pick you up at seven o'clock. Please let me explain. Love, Robert."

"Girl, this is like Pretty Woman! You'd better get up and get ready. It's six o'clock now!" Mom scooped up my ice cream and spoon and put them in the kitchen. Then she pulled me up by my arms and shoved me down the hallway.

He needs you to make him a good man. Be open to the possibilities… Pippa's words kept rolling around in my head. Robert had screwed up yet again. Was I supposed to go and make him realize the error of his ways? I wanted to see him, but I was so angry with him that I didn't know how to react. I paced around in my bedroom, trying to decide what to do, then I sat down on my bed and rubbed my burning eyes with my fingers. Be open to the possibilities. With a huff, I got ready and waited for seven o'clock to arrive.

The doorbell rang shortly after seven o'clock, and I opened the door to find a strange man in a uniform and a car that I'd never seen before. "Are you Robert's driver?" I asked, closing the front door behind me.

"Yes ma'am. I'm here to take you to see Mr. Marley."

"You didn't work at Ashford, did you?"

"No ma'am. He hires me to take him to the airport sometimes. I don't work for the Marley family outright."

I had been hoping to see a friendly face. I scooted into the backseat as he shut my door. Then I laid my head back on the seat and closed my eyes for the rest of the drive. Where exactly I was going was a complete mystery to me, but I was so exhausted from crying all day that I didn't really care. My eyes ached for relief, so I kept them closed in the darkness of the car and allowed the driver to take me wherever he had been instructed.

When we finally came to a stop, and I opened my eyes, I couldn't believe what I saw. I was in the driveway at Ashford. The house was completely dark except for an outside light illuminating our path to the front door, and the light in the entranceway was on. The driver opened my door and I got out, looking around. Why did he drag me out here to talk? Wasn't I depressed enough without the reminder of *this*?

The front door opened, and Robert was standing there in jeans and a sweater, a cautious look on his face. "Hi," he said, ushering me in with his hand. I looked up at him in silence as I walked through the door.

He led me to the sitting room where a fire was burning in the fireplace. On the floor were a few pillows, a bottle of wine and two glasses, and a smattering of take-out boxes. The items were dwarfed by the emptiness of the room. "There wasn't any furniture, so I brought us something to sit on," he said with a wary look still on his face. I sat down stiffly, waiting for an explanation.

Robert opened the bottle of wine and poured two glasses, handing one to me. I took it hesitantly.

"Allie, please let me explain what happened today. It didn't go at all the way I had hoped, and I wanted to clear some things up for you."

I took a sip of my wine and had to remind myself that I was mad at Robert. He looked so good sitting opposite me, leaning on one hand, his glass of wine in the other. The smell of the fire mixed with the scent of Ashford hurled a pang of sadness through my chest.

"Tamara is a director for one of the top preschools in the area. It's an award-winning preschool. I came to her with a proposition. I told her to hire a teacher for Oak Grove. She was to interview all who applied and make an honest decision as to who would best suit the school. If she chose the one person that I had had in mind— you—then the school would be yours. You will study under her, and when she feels that you're ready, you can take over as director. If she'd chosen anyone else, I'd have allowed her to run it how she liked, and she could eventually buy me out." Robert scooted closer to me, his face only inches from mine. "She loved you. She chose *you*. You impressed her all by yourself."

I set down the glass of wine on the scuffed wood floor. "Is this true? Promise me that it's true, Robert, because I'm tired of everyone helping me. I want to do something for myself and…"

"You did it all by yourself." His finger traced my cheek, sending a chill down my neck.

I looked into his eyes as he took a sip of wine, and I suddenly wanted to kiss him, but I wasn't about to lean over and do it. What if he didn't feel the same for me? What if it was all in my head? Okay, there was wine and a fire. Shouldn't that be a clue? It didn't matter. I couldn't do it.

"There's something else I need to tell you," he said.

"What?"

"Well, the financing for the preschool... I paid for it with coins."

"What do you mean?"

"You told me that collecting coins made no sense because they were worthless unless I cashed them in. So I did. I cashed them in for a preschool."

"You what? Oh, Robert, I didn't mean..."

"No," he cut me off, "you were right. I collected coins because I thought it would honor my mother. The police officers found a coin wrapped up with my name on it in the trunk. It was undisturbed despite the collision, and they delivered it to me three days after my parents were killed. It had been my parents' idea that I collect coins. Not giving it a second thought, I began researching and collecting them. But my parents are gone. I realized that I need to be closer to someone actually alive." He looked down at one of the pillows and toyed with a loose thread on one corner. "So, I traded in the coins for you." Robert looked up at me. "That's why I went back to New York—to sell my coins. And I added a little of my own money to complete the deal. I hope that was okay."

I grinned deviously in response.

Robert scooted closer to me. "I have a difficult time saying what I want. So, I'm working really hard right now." He swallowed. "I want to be with you. What are your thoughts about that?"

"I think you should stop talking so much." I moved a little closer to him.

"Is that so?"

"Yes."

"And what should we do if we aren't talking?" he asked, setting down his glass of wine.

"I can think of a few things."

Robert wrapped his hand around the back of my neck and pulled me gently toward him. His other hand grabbed the small of my back, and he lay me down onto one of the pillows. His lips met mine. I folded my arms around his neck, kissing him back. It was like coming home. I was right where I needed to be—in his arms—and nothing else mattered, not money, not other family members. Being with him was just right. And in that one moment, I couldn't fathom how I'd been able to be near him for so long without allowing myself this feeling.

With his lips still touching mine, he said, "I have to tell you something else."

"Stop talking," I pulled him closer, pressing my lips to his again, but it was difficult to kiss him while he was smiling.

"You may want..." he kissed me. "To hear..." he kissed me again. "This."

"No, I don't."

Robert pulled away and propped himself up on his elbow. I pretended to sulk, and he smiled again, the flames from the fire dancing in his eyes. "I have a gift for you."

I struggled to sit up, light-headed from what had just transpired. "A gift? You don't need to buy me things, Robert. Haven't you learned by now what a disaster that can be?"

"I didn't say I bought it. It's something I already had."

I pursed my lips skeptically. "Okay, I'll bite. What is it?"

"Well," he leaned over and kissed me again, sending my stomach flipping. "I still own Ashford."

I pulled away and looked at him aghast. "What?"

"We'd not agreed on an exact price yet, so I was able to pull it off the market. I told Megan it's not for sale."

I cupped my hand over my mouth and looked around. "You're kidding," I said through my fingers.

Robert shook his head. "And I tried to get Pippa to come home, but she wants to stay at Birkwood. She's happy there."

I had no words, so I just sat in shock with my hands covering my mouth.

"I just hope that your decorating skills are as good as your teaching abilities."

"Me?"

"If I gave you a loose budget, do you think you could decorate it for me?"

"Um…" My head was spinning. "The *whole* house?"

"Yes," he said, his lips on mine again. He pulled away, but his mouth was still close enough to mine to feel his breath. "I know you don't like handouts, but I thought if you don't have anywhere to live…"

"I don't think I could live in this huge house all by myself."

"You wouldn't be alone. The staff would be here with you." His lips found the space just below my ear. "And I would be here."

Despite my inclination to cease all discussion in lieu of other digressions, I pulled back. "What about New York? You hate this house."

"I don't hate it when you're here. I can't keep my thoughts on anything else when you're here. You changed this house for me. It reminds me of you now, and I can't stay away from anything that reminds me of you these days." Robert reached out a hand and rested it on my cheek. "Would you move in with me?"

I bit my lip. "I'd have to think about it."

"You could flip for it," he said.

"Absolutely not," I laughed and leaned in for another kiss.

Epilogue

It has been three Christmases since Pippa passed, but I still leave a place for her at the dinner table on Christmas Eve. Anna brings the food in for us as we all sit down. Kip sits next to Kylie, his Australian girlfriend of four years, Sloane pulls out chairs for Sammy and Paul, and I sit down between Mom and Robert. Megan comes in and takes her usual seat next to Sloane. We're all here. As I look around the original Ashford dining table that Sloane had given Robert and me as a housewarming gift—she'd tagged it before the auction because she couldn't bear to part with it, but in the end, she knew it belonged to Ashford—I see a family in the truest sense.

I think about Pippa all the time. She has missed quite a few firsts for our family: the first time I used my passport with Robert, the first time I watched Sloane, Sammy, and Paul laugh until they nearly cried in our newly-decorated sitting room, the first time Robert said he loved me. I hope that she can see it all as she sits with Henry, filling him in on everything that he's missed.

I still haven't told Robert what Pippa had said in my ear that Christmas. I haven't told anyone. But as I finish my meal, every year, I can still hear her saying the words, "You will be the link that holds this family together. It will be you who heads the Marley table, and you will lead them through generations to come. I'm certain of that."

"So," Mom says, draping her monogrammed napkin in her lap, "have you two chosen a name yet?"

Robert reaches over and gently caresses my protruding belly. "Not yet," he says, the lines of tension erased from his features. "We're leaning toward Carolyn, but we aren't sure." The corner of his mouth turns up in a grin as he looks at me, and I place my hand on his.

Sloane pats her chest. "How sweet. Mom would be so happy."

The rest of the dinner goes by in a flash, as it seems to do every year. Robert helps me out of the chair, and we part briefly with the rest of the family. He wants to show me something new in the nursery. We walk in, and I take in a sharp breath. Hanging over the crib is an exquisite rendition of the brook out back in the springtime. The pinks and oranges and greens blend together like shades of sherbet.

I turn to Robert. "Is this the first happy painting you've ever done?"

"I think so."

"It's beautiful, Robert," I say, reaching up on to my tiptoes to kiss him.

"Shall we head back to the sitting room to be with our family?" he asks. It is our most recent Christmas tradition: we all meet in the sitting room to talk and play games before turning in for the night—it makes Santa's visit a little later, but we don't mind—and, of course, we play "La Vie en Rose," our wedding song, before we all turn in.

A note from Jenny

Thank you so much for reading *Coming Home for Christmas*! I hope that you enjoyed reading Allie and Robert's story as much as I enjoyed writing it.

You can sign up to be notified by e-mail when my next book is out! Just visit my website at www.itsjennyhale.com. I won't share your e-mail with anyone else, and I'll only e-mail you when a new book is released.

If you did enjoy *Coming Home for Christmas*, I'd *love* it if you'd write a review on Amazon or Goodreads. Getting feedback from readers is amazing, and it also helps to persuade other readers to pick up one of my books for the first time!

Merry Christmas!
Jenny

Lightning Source UK Ltd.
Milton Keynes UK
UKOW05f1949061013

218584UK00011B/176/P